LORI HOLMES

The Forbidden

Book One of The Ancestors Saga

Contents

Acknowledgement

A huge thank you to the team at *Writing.co.uk Literary Consultancy*, for all their hard work and endless advice on editing this manuscript and helping me shape this book into what it is today.

Another big thank you goes to the team at *Damonza.com* for their incredible design skills in creating the wonderful book covers for *The Ancestors Saga*.

Dedication

To my husband, Matt, without whom none of this would have been possible.

The Forbidden

Book One of The Ancestors Saga

The unforgettable story of one woman's perilous journey to save, *The Forbidden*.

Rebaa's adopted tribe lies slaughtered behind her. Rebaa's lover, Juran, lays down his life for hers and now she must use all of her cunning and extraordinary powers to survive the inhospitable wilderness alone, ensuring that Juran's sacrifice was not in vain.

But Rebaa's battle for survival has only just begun…

Hunted by savage predators and more terrifying still, the nightmarish Eldrax, a murderous chieftain who will stop at nothing to possess Rebaa's mysterious powers for his own, her very existence becomes a life or death chase in the pursuit and quest to reach the one place that surely offers salvation and a safe haven she can call home.

But what haven could possibly exist for one who bears… *The Forbidden*?

Will Rebaa find her salvation, or will crushing loss, hardship and the burden of carrying *The Forbidden*, first destroy her from the inside out?

The Ancestors Saga

Exciting and compelling, *The Ancestors Saga* takes you on an epic journey 40,000 years into our own dark and forgotten past. As the world teeters on the brink of another glacial winter, homo sapiens are not the only human species to walk the Earth.

When the destiny of the entire human race hangs in the balance, the prize for survivors will be Earth itself.

The Ancestors Saga is a fantasy romance series, combining mythology, folklore, metaphysical elements and adventure, to retell a lost chapter in the evolution of humankind.

1

Massacre

B lood. It defiled the snow. It coated the rock. It dripped from the points of bone-tipped weapons. Rebaa ducked back into the pelt tent she had shared with her mate, blinded by the horror.

She must not scream. If she made any sound, it would be over. It *was* over. The clan was destroyed. It was only a matter of time before the face of an enemy pushed its way through the billowing opening, searching for easy prey.

The Ninkuraa woman flinched as an agonised scream split the air outside, ending in a bubbling gurgle. She tried not to imagine the bone blade to the throat. It was too close. She should not wait here for murder to find her, but as the instinct to flee tore through her, her heart held her fast.

Juran.

Juran had told her to stay. He had told her to wait here until he came back for her. He *would* come back for her once they had vanquished the enemy.

But the enemy had not been vanquished.

Another dying scream rent the air, and Rebaa threw herself

down on her knees. Hands in her hair, she rocked back and forth in desperation. Juran may already lie among the slain, and she was waiting for nothing. *No.* She could not think that. Her heart would tell her if he had fallen. He would come back. She just had to stay quiet and be brave until he did.

Rebaa closed her eyes. Juran should have abandoned this territory on the snowy Northern plains. The choice to flee or fight had been his.

He had chosen wrong.

All of their strongest men had gone into the Mountain forests to draw the enemy out, and the enemy had been drawn. Now they were swarming over the camp, hell-bent on extermination. Juran's clan warriors, for all of their considerable skill, could not stop them.

A monster could not be vanquished by the hand of man.

Rebaa froze. The bitter wind scrabbled at the edges of the tent, but it wasn't enough to cover the sound of heavy breathing and a slow, deliberate tread in the snow outside.

On the other side of the skins, the crunching steps paused.

Go away! She stifled the sound of her own breath. *Please.*

The owner of the footsteps deliberated before the tip of a bloody spear came poking through the parting in the tent, pushing aside the animal hides. Rebaa covered her mouth to hold back her building scream as an enormous head stooped through the gap its weapon had made.

The grotesque face was twice the size of an average man. Reddish hair fell in lank wisps from the point of the elongated skull and the wide-set eyes that regarded her were an alarming shade of blue.

"GO AWAY!" Rebaa scrambled back against the skin of the tent. She spoke in her native tongue, lapsing in her panic. It mattered not. Thick lips peeled back to display double rows of bloodstained teeth, stretching the pale yellowish flesh into a hideous grimace as the giant crouched to push itself further in. Rebaa clawed at the wall of the shelter behind her, trying to break free, but the tough hides would not give. They were too strong. Wild with fear, she pushed her heels harder into the floor, fighting to get away as a thick hand reached forward.

"Nooooo!"

The advancing fingers spasmed in the air as the tip of a second spear came bursting through the monster's throat. The nightmarish face contorted, its mouth gaping wide in a gurgling roar as the head flung back. It clawed at the spearhead protruding from its neck, dripping with its own bright blood.

But the gruesome wound did not stop the beast. Rebaa watched in horror as its maddened eyes refocused on her and its hand extended again; determined to reach her, even as the life drained from its face. Someone unseen cursed, and the spear in the monster's throat twisted viciously to the side, eliciting the distinctive snap of bone. The clutching fingers twitched once, twice, then fell lifeless at her feet.

"Rebaa!" The disembodied voice held the frantic note of one who feared that they were too late and would receive no answer to their call. Rebaa cried in relief and flung herself over the dead creature's body, uncaring in her need to get to Juran.

His dark arms closed about her. Rebaa flinched at the gore and the sickly scent of death that covered his skin. The terrible sounds of the massacre continued to rage on the other side of the thin tent walls. "Juran," she gasped. "Please... Please... " She did not know what she was asking. She was shaking uncontrollably. "Please."

3

Rebaa felt him nod once against the top of her head, understanding her incoherent plea. "It's alright. I will get you out, I will get you both to safety. Come with me now."

He disengaged himself from her and grabbed her hand, his palm hot and slick against her skin. His dark auburn hair was wild, his grey eyes even more so. There was fear there where fear had never existed before, and that scared her more than anything else.

"Can you run?"

Go out there? A shout cut off by a wet gurgle made her baulk violently. *No.* She could not go out there.

Juran held her firm. "Rebaa, you cannot stay here! If you do, you will die, you will *both* die!".

Both. Her free hand went to her rounded belly. The thought of their unborn baby's life gave her the strength she needed to stand upright and give her mate one firm nod. Yes, she could run.

Pride flickered through Juran's grey eyes before his expression hardened with determination. He yanked his spear free from the hulking corpse on the ground, and warm spatters of blood sprayed across Rebaa's face. "Ready?"

Not trusting herself to speak, she simply raised her chin in answer.

Juran threw apart the flaps of the shelter and dragged her into the battle beyond.

The brightness of the snow outside was blinding. The world blurred as she stumbled in Juran's wake. Red. White. Movement. Death. The ferocity of the fighting tore against her senses. As a Ninkuraa, she could *feel* everything. The fear, the anger, the lives as they blinked out of existence.

She fought to close it all out as Juran wove his way through the struggling mass of bodies, only half aware that they were heading towards the steep escarpment on the edge of the camp. The lookouts had used its summit to spy prey and approaching danger. There was a concealed path that wound up into the foothills of the Mountains, half hidden between the rocks.

Rebaa collided with the back of Juran as her mate came to an abrupt halt. A shape rose out of the snow before them, blocking their escape path. Peering out from under a freshly flayed bear's skull adorning its head, the creature beheld them. The milky eyes of the bear still rolled, lidless, in the grisly sockets. The sight was enough to make Rebaa's knees go weak.

Juran thrust her back and out of reach, bringing his spear to bear. The giant figure leered down at them, pleased with its catch. It had been waiting to block deserters such as them. Long stone blades protruding from each massive fist raised in challenge as Juran stepped forward to meet him.

"No!" Rebaa gasped. She cast about, looking for the rest of the clan to rally and support their Chief, but they were gone, dead or dying. Juran stood alone. After everything they had been through, she was about to watch him die.

A guttural roar sounded the attack. The giant made a lunge for Juran, moving faster than Rebaa would have ever thought possible for one so large. Had Juran still occupied the space, the stone blade would have run him straight through. With astounding reflexes, he twisted away from the knife and, in the same fluid motion, he jabbed a blow towards his enemy's midsection. The spearhead made a stinging bite to the pale flesh. The creature snarled and swung with his other knife. Juran danced back, sure-footed as a spear cat. The monster hadn't even got close.

Rebaa felt a flicker of hope. As a warrior, she had never seen

Juran's equal. He lunged and parried, wielding his spear like an extension of himself, a Cro warrior in all his savage glory. Pride filled her heart. Maybe he would survive this.

The beast yowled as Juran's spear cut deep into the muscle of its leg. It fell backwards a step, breaking away from Juran's relentless attack. Its eyes flickered once in Rebaa's direction as Juran came on, closing quarters once more, not allowing the beast to recover. Snarling, the giant struck hastily with its knives. Rebaa thought she heard Juran chuckle as he dodged almost lazily to the side. He swung his spear in challenge, daring the creature to reengage.

It had been a feint.

The clumsy strike had achieved its goal. Juran had left Rebaa exposed. Triumphant, the giant lurched forward on its wounded leg, extending the weapon in its right hand as it bore down on the Ninkuraaja woman. Mesmerised as she had been by the deadly dance, it caught Rebaa unprepared. She stumbled backwards, tripped on a rock, and went down in a heap.

"No!" Juran leaped into the air, spear raising over his head as he prepared to land a killing blow down through his enemy's skull.

The beast's eyes gleamed as it heard Juran's cry of denial. With inhuman speed, it twisted to face the attack. Dropping a knife, it grabbed the haft of Juran's extending spear, yanking him down out of the air and off balance.

The other knife was waiting to sink deep into Juran's belly. "Noooo!"

Juran did not flinch as the blade entered him. Even as his enemy grinned in his face, snapping his spear in two within its mighty grip, Juran was drawing his own bone knife. He let his enemy pull him close before he struck, then buried his weapon into the beast's eye, pushing it on and up through the long, foul head.

The remaining eye rolled back, and the monster fell dead at Juran's feet.

Dropping the now useless remains of his spear, Juran collapsed to his knees in the snow.

"Juran!" Rebaa bounded to her feet and ran to his side. A growing stain of blood was creeping through the furs covering his belly. She sucked in a sharp breath. "Juran..."

"It's nothing." He grabbed her hand again, pulling it away from his violated flesh and heaving himself to his feet. "You need to get out of here. Now."

The escarpment rose before them. Juran's breath came in laboured gasps as he pushed Rebaa towards it. A thin stream of blood was spilling from the corner of his mouth. Her fear for him was almost enough to crush her, but she told herself that they were going to escape. They were going to survive this disaster. Juran would recover, and they and their baby would go on.

She hurried towards the safety of the concealed path, but as she began to climb, she heard a soft thump in the snow behind her. Juran had fallen to his knees and was holding his hand to his bloody midsection.

She ran back. "Juran, please, come on!"

He ignored her, turning his head to face the battle still raging on the plains and the screams of his dying clan.

"There is nothing more you can do for them!" There was no time to waste. He would not survive a second battle if another one of those creatures appeared. She pulled on his furs. "We have to go!"

He shook his head before grasping both her arms in his hands. His beloved grey gaze was awash with regret, but the fear had gone, replaced by a calm resolution. Rebaa's throat tightened.

"Go, now," he said. "Run as fast as you can. Take our baby. Get to safety."

"Not without you! Juran! There is nothing you can do for them! Come with me now. I need you!"

He smiled at her, then down at the hand clutched to his midsection. His fingers were dripping with blood. "You know I cannot. Not now."

Immediately, she reached for his wound.

"Leave it!" He grabbed her wrist. "There is no time."

"Juran, please!" Their baby squirmed inside her, making Rebaa sick with panic. She needed him if she was to face the consequences of what they had done.

Juran did not answer. He let go of her arms, his hands going to his neck and the necklace that hung there. His bloodstained fingers were shaking as he pulled the leather thong over his head. In the same motion, he placed it over Rebaa's neck, letting the carved spearhead dangle next to her heart; the symbol of his position as Chief.

"Take this. Give it to our son when he is strong enough. Whatever he may turn out to be." He drew his thumb over the carving of his clan's totem, marking it with red. "My own blood."

"You can give it to him yourself. Don't leave me!"

"I will never leave you," he promised. *"Remember* that."

Rebaa stared up into his unwavering eyes and felt the strength go out of her limbs. "Do you promise?" she asked in a hushed voice. She already knew the truth in her heart, but

8

she still needed to hear the lie.

"Yes."

Gating a sob between her teeth, she threw her arms around Juran and held him close. "I promise to give this to our son, I promise." He buried his face in her hair as his own arms went around her. She felt him shudder. "Come back to me," she whispered. "I will wait for you."

She could not look at his face again. If she did, she would break. She would never leave him and their baby would die.

Rebaa tore away from his weakening grip and fled up the path. Tears blinded her as she scrambled up and up. She could not keep herself from glancing back once, but Juran had already disappeared. Only a streak of blood marked his passage, leading directly back to the massacre.

2

Escape

Rebaa was scrambling over the last rocks of the escarpment when she felt it, a severing in her heart. The presence her whole life had become bound to was snuffed from existence. The pain of it sent her to her knees as the world blurred before her eyes. She doubled over, clutching at her chest as the aftershocks of the severed bond rolled through her.

Juran, her mate, and the father of her child, was gone.

Denial rushed through her, overriding her pain. Refusing to trust her overwrought senses, Rebaa scrambled up to gaze down over the rocks at the blood bath far below. Her eyes scoured the stained snow, searching for life among the mauled forms strewn about the frosty plain.

The carnage stretched away to the thickly wooded foothills of the mountain range behind. She saw no survivors. Only their savage enemies sauntered about the killing field, huge, grotesque forms spearing the fallen, seemingly for the fun of it. One by one, they disappeared back into their mountain forest lair. Some dragged the bodies of the dead behind them, further tainting the innocence of the snow with streaks of red.

Rebaa turned her face away and grasped at the icy rocks to steady herself, fighting back vomit. He had promised he would not leave her. He had *promised*.

She panted against the crushing grief. Her eyes scanned the way behind, but it was empty. The snow swirled in the void, cold and lifeless. She remembered his grey eyes, filled with determination as he had slipped the carved spearhead necklace from around his dark throat and placed it around hers. *Give this to our son....*

The lie that had got her this far crumbled as the truth closed its merciless jaws around her heart and sank in deep. He was dead. Her senses already told her what she needed to know, but some masochistic part of herself reached out for him all the same.

He promised.

The nothingness that came whipping back to her was crippling. She screamed her loss to the frozen, uncaring sky.

Rebaa did not know how long she crouched there, lost in her grief. The wind howled, whistling through the rocks, tearing at her furs. The loneliness of its wail settled the true extent of her situation around her quaking shoulders.

She was utterly alone; a pregnant Ninkuraaja female abandoned far from her native land with no tribe to protect her. Her breath came faster. She was a dead woman walking.

Why did you make me leave? If she had stayed by his side, at least then the tip of a knife would have granted her a quick death; sparing her the slow, painful demise of starvation.

The last of her will evaporated on the wind and Rebaa collapsed into a ball of despair, unable to move further. What did it matter if she died here or elsewhere in this Fury-bitten landscape? She only wished to be at the side of her beloved when the Great Spirit claimed her, but she did not have the courage to go back to the killing field to find him. This resting place between the rocks would have to do.

Memories of Juran flickered through her mind, each one gouging a wider hole in her chest as they cruelly reminded her he was gone. A fresh wail of agony found its way through her teeth. *Why did you leave?*

The memory of his voice hit her then, as clearly as if he had shouted it in her ear. *Run. Take our baby. Get to safety.*

Fresh tears leaked down her cheeks, stinging in the biting cold. Their baby. He was going to die, too.

That thought was too much to bear, and it fought back fiercely against the crippling emptiness in her heart. Rebaa uncurled and scrubbed the tears from her eyes with the heels of her hands. Her maternal instincts would not let her lie in the snow and allow her baby to die without a fight. She was close to her time. She needed a People, or she and her unborn would die.

She scanned the empty landscape, searching for a direction, any sign of salvation, as the wind whipped her dark hair across her features. The tumbled, frozen rocks of the mountain foothills stretched as far as she could see, lifeless and empty.

A long forgotten desire flitted unbidden through her mind. *Home. Go home. You are free now. Go back to your own People. Go back to the forests.* She shrank away from the thought. That wasn't salvation. She was an outcast now. Tainted. They would drive her away as soon as they saw her. As soon as they saw—

She dropped her head into her hands, closing out the terrifying nothingness that surrounded her as she struggled to clear her mind enough to think. There was nowhere she could take him where he would be safe. The monsters had butchered the only true haven he had had. But as one choice after another crumbled into the dust of impossibility, only that first unthinkable temptation remained.

She wondered if they would kill her if she returned, not even risking the wait for what she carried to be born. Maybe. Not that it would ever come to that. The forests of her birth were many rises and falls of Ninmah away, and she would perish long before the journey was complete. At least it was a direction to follow, a destination to keep her on her feet. She would die in the attempt, but when she met Juran again in the arms of the Great Spirit, she could look him in the eye knowing she had *tried*.

The cold was already seeping into her small body. Her pale red-gold skin prickled; the heavy fur wrappings were not enough to protect her out here, exposed and without shelter. If she gave up now, she would be dead by nightfall. For the sake of her baby and her soul, she must at least *try*.

With one last despairing look at the destruction below, Rebaa heaved herself to her feet. Her mouth set into a grim line. He was not coming back. The life she had known was gone. Turning to the empty wilderness, she walked away.

She was at Ninmah's mercy now.

3

Ninmah's Mercy

The drifting snow was endless. Rebaa stumbled and slipped often on the rock-strewn ground. The forsaken foothills fringing the great Mountains rose all around her in an endless maze. She did not know where she was going and at times she was so consumed by grief that she did not care. Only the powerful compulsion to keep moving in a futile effort to save her baby drew her on.

Rebaa choked. Not for the first time, her knees almost buckled under the enormity of what had happened and the fate that she faced. A terrible anger now overshadowed the grief and longing she felt for Juran. Tremors rolled through her body at the memory of their enemies. He should *not* have provoked them. He had drawn them out of their mountain lairs and brought death upon their heads. In doing so, he had forfeited the life of his own child.

Rebaa cursed the moment she had ever laid eyes on him. He had taken her from her home, entrapped her, made her live a life she hated among enemies and burdened her with his Forbidden child. He had ruined her and all she believed in.

Worst of all, he had made her fall in love with him.

Another sob escaped her throat. She had fought it. She was Ninkuraaja, and he was a Cro. Ninmah Herself forbade such a thing. The greatest of sins. But she had not been able to resist. The attention of a strong mate who provided could not be ignored.

The icy wind blew, whistling through the rocky landscape and the sparse trees. Rebaa wrapped her dirty furs more tightly around her. She marvelled at how what had once seemed so alien was now so natural to her. Her own forest People did not wear furs. When Juran had first made her wear them, her skin had crawled with revulsion. Now her very survival depended on these grisly coverings.

Despite the thick clothing, her feet were numb. After walking all day, Rebaa stumbled more and more often. She had not eaten, and her baby was quiet. She did not know how long she could last without nourishment, but she did not know how she was to find any. Rebaa did not hunt. She had felt the same way about eating meat as she had about wearing furs. It was not the Ninkuraaja way. Her People relied on their sacred forests to feed and clothe them. Fruits, fungi, nuts, roots. That was the extent of the Ninkuraaja diet. The great Ninmah had taught them to live so.

Rebaa looked to the bare, scraggly trees dotting the darkening landscape, the snow piling up about their black roots. Their bounty had long ago perished with the first frosts.

Had she been living with her People, she would have gathered provisions to see her and her tribe through the long Fury. The Cro had no such tradition. How foolish they were. How foolish she had been.

Rebaa passed a hand over her eyes, fighting the weariness

that was seeping into her bones. It begged her to lie down and simply close her eyes. Rebaa shook her head sharply to clear it. She must not succumb. If she did, she would fall into a sleep from which she would never wake. She forced herself to walk on. Only to tumble back into the snow as a hidden rock tripped her trailing foot. Rebaa gated her cry of frustration behind her teeth as she caught sight of something in the snow.

Footprints.

Rebaa pulled herself back to her feet as swiftly as her body would allow. Human footprints. Men had passed this way. From their size and shape, she guessed they were Cro. She might not hunt, but Juran had taught her a few things about tracking. She wasn't as alone as she had thought in these bare hills. The knowledge brought with it an instinctive wave of comfort before better sense kicked in and the hairs rose on the back of her neck. If there were other men out here, then the danger to herself and her baby had just increased. Not all Cro were led by chieftains like Juran.

Rebaa's throat closed. Juran had not been short of enemies. He had captured many a territory from others of his own kind. In these lean times, prime hunting grounds were fiercely contested and feuds between clans could last for generations. If a rival clan found her, they were as likely to kill her as take her in, claiming vengeance for lost lives and land. Even if they did not kill her, they would certainly kill Juran's baby as soon as he was born, and their Chief would then take her as a war trophy and attempt to get his own children on her.

Rebaa backed away from the footprints. She had to get out of the area as quickly as possible. She set off along a different route, heading higher into the hills. The new direction took her further off course from her planned destination, but it might just keep her alive for longer. She kept all of her senses straining for the slightest sound, anything that would alert her of an approach that could spell her doom.

Darkness was creeping over the land before she heard the first warning. A distant snarl from ahead carried back to her on the cutting breeze. The snow muffled all sound, but she knew she hadn't imagined it. Poised in readiness to run, she strained her eyes into the deepening shadows, but could not see much further than her immediate surroundings. Her sight had always been weak compared to Juran's. In the dark, she was blind to attack.

Rebaa quelled the panic before it could rise. She was still Ninkuraaja, and she did not need to rely on sight to perceive her surroundings. Closing her eyes, Rebaa grounded herself, feeling the rock beneath her feet and the wind as it brushed her face. To her, it wasn't lifeless stone, not simply a touch of air. The earth was a great river of energy, flowing through everything it touched, and she only had to reach out to be a part of it. Stretching forth with her higher senses, Rebaa bound herself to the earth's flow, tasting the ripples and eddies that surrounded her, letting them reveal the presences hidden in the shadows ahead.

Not men. Wolves. A pack of fifteen wolves was ahead of her. Their energies burned bright against her awareness. They had made a kill, their minds satiated with the reward of food after an exhausting hunt. Rebaa gasped as other sensations flowed over her. The overwhelming sense of family contentment made her ache with longing, and before she knew what she was doing, she was stumbling forward in the pack's direction.

As she rounded the last of the rocky outcrops, their grey forms loomed against the snow. They had brought down a half grown ox and were lying around the stripped carcass, gnawing on its bones. Ravenous anticipation flared on all sides and Rebaa knew herself to be standing among the scavengers lurking on the outskirts, waiting for the first opportunity to steal a morsel from the apex hunters. Rebaa hesitated before the feeling of warm contentedness washed over her anew and she took another unconscious step towards the family at the centre.

The movement breached the invisible line of tolerance that existed between the predators and the waiting scavengers. The wolves rose to their feet, baring their fangs as warning snarls erupted from their throats.

Too late, Rebaa wrenched her senses back to her own body. Grief and hunger had made her foolish. These were not the forest wolves of her birthplace. They knew not the gentling touch of her people. Their challenge and mounting tension buffeted across her senses. At any moment, the standoff could break and they would attack. Everything depended on her next move. If she ran, they would run her down and kill her, and so she did the only thing she could. Rebaa sank to her knees and submitted. If they were not so well fed, she knew she would have been dead already.

The alpha pair broke rank and approached as the rest of the pack fanned out to pace in a restless circle, cutting off escape. Rebaa breathed deeply, controlling her tension as she lowered her head like a young, lone she-wolf begging acceptance. Their noses snuffled all over her body. Further snarls rumbled in the alpha male's chest as he scented her furs. Wolf furs.

Please, she thought at him, though not in words, words had no place within the realm of the Great Spirit. Tempering her energy, Rebaa filled his mind with images and sensations that he would understand. She was not prey; she needed his acceptance; she needed his protection. For it was true, she would not survive the night alone, and the wolves were better than nothing.

Unused to the outside influence on his mind, the alpha male backed up a step with a startled huff. His mate continued to sniff curiously as Rebaa filled the she-wolf's mind with the same messages. A low whine of confusion came from between the sharp teeth before the she-wolf decided. She pressed her heavy head over Rebaa's neck, letting her feel the weight of her dominance. Rebaa remained still, accepting her authority. The wolf made her point and then a soft lick across her cold, exposed hand told Rebaa that the danger had passed. The she-wolf had accepted her presence.

The alpha pair walked back to the kill, leaving Rebaa to do as she would. She started forward on hands and knees, keeping her head down as the rest of the pack jostled in to take a closer look, heads weaving uncertainly as this strange creature made her way through their midst. Many repeated the she-wolf's actions, bumping her and pressing above her body to mark their authority.

She made her way to the carcass, but a belligerent adolescent looking to make his mark barred her way with a snarl. They might have accepted her, but she was still at the bottom of the pack. Rebaa backed away. There was nothing left but bone and slimy sinew. Hungry as she was, her stomach heaved at the sight of it.

Her almost fatal error had at least paid off in one way. As the wolf pack huddled together for protection against the night's chill, Rebaa found she was allowed to share in their warmth. Among the wolves, she would be safe for this night. Exhausted beyond thought, Rebaa lay down with the pack and let herself drift into a dreamless sleep.

* * *

4

Eldrax

Eldrax marched through the snow on the heels of his Chief. The rest of the clan travelled in close formation behind him. Nobody dared to stray out of line. The totem of the Black Wolf clan marked the landscape here and there in stark warning. If the rival clan's lookouts were to witness their trespass, the price would be blood. Stragglers made for an easy payoff.

Eldrax gripped his spear in his pale hand until bone showed through his knuckles. He, for one, hoped they were spotted. He glanced behind at the two large stags the hunting party had brought down. This territory the Black Wolf clan occupied was bountiful, flowing with prey migrating from the hills to winter pastures.

It was thanks to the Black Wolf that Eldrax's clan were denied such luxury. Pushed to the outskirts as the rival clan expanded their hunting ranges, they had been forced to carve out a living in less than satisfactory conditions. In the ever worsening environment, a lesser clan would have succumbed by now. The indignity still rankled. The totem of Eldrax's clan was the mighty bear. He was the *Red Bear*. And a bear was not intimidated by the wolf.

"You will snap that spear in two if you are not careful, young hunter," a mild voice spoke over his shoulder. Eldrax glanced down to see Rannac had moved up to his side from the rearguard position. The older man's grey eyes regarded him with vexing clarity. Rannac had always possessed the ability to see right through him, and Eldrax hated it. He had done since he was a boy.

"I do not know why *he*," Eldrax jabbed his spear toward their Chief, "will not let me lead an attack on the Black Wolf. We could take this range from them, but he forces us to settle for raiding like jackals. Nothing better than scavengers waiting for the scraps of their betters." Eldrax bared his teeth at his Chief's back. "I am no jackal!"

"No," Rannac said, his lips turning down in the disapproving twist he always seemed to reserve just for Eldrax. "You are a clan warrior, well learned in the ways of the spear. But I never taught you to be a fool, Eldrax. Why do you insist on acting so?"

The jab poked at Eldrax's pride. He rounded on Rannac with a snarl on his lips. He tolerated Rannac's veiled dislike of him, but he would not stand for open insult. Only the high respect he had for the man who had taught him how to fight kept him from striking Rannac to the ground. At sixteen summers, he was a full head taller than the older man now; Rannac no longer intimidated him.

Rannac held up his hands in the face of Eldrax's anger. The gesture highlighted the missing third and fourth fingers on his left paw, a parting gift given to him long ago by his brother. "I was foolish once, and I paid for it. Chief Murzuk is right not to challenge. The seasons have not been kind to our clan of late. It would not be wise to attack the Black Wolf now, well fed and at full strength as they are."

Eldrax snorted. "Their Chief does not frighten me, old man. If it wasn't for them, *we* would be the most powerful clan of the plains and the pick of hunting grounds would be ours. I could lead the clan warriors in an attack and teach the Black Wolf—!"

"Hold your tongue, boy!" Murzuk snapped from the head of the line. "Do you want to bring them down upon us?"

Heat rose in Eldrax's cheeks as the other hunters glanced his way. He chaffed for the day when Murzuk would shame him no longer. Stowing his simmering anger for another time, he took better care to control his voice. "They laugh at us because of his weakness," he hissed to Rannac. "Because of him, they were bold enough to take the greatest prize of all from under our very nose! We hunted that creature for days after we separated her from her cursed shin'ar forest, and the Black Wolf seized her from our grasp. Such an insult should never have gone without punishment." He rubbed agitatedly at his chest.

Rannac remained unmoved. "Murzuk is patient when it comes to the long game. Such a quality is something you must learn if you ever rise to become Chief. The men will never follow an angry boy over a proven man, a Chief who has never failed to keep them alive." With that parting shot, Rannac drifted back to his rear guard position.

"Huh." Eldrax struggled not to show how close Rannac had struck to the heart of the matter. Proving his worth over Murzuk was something Eldrax had striven to achieve since he had been old enough to hold a spear. Rising quickly from a weakling boy into a hard-bitten survivor, he had been fighting for his existence every day since his cowardly mother had abandoned him. Now he was ready. The men respected him, the Red Bear. Nevertheless, Rannac was right; they would not support the Challenge of an untried boy over a man who had led the clan since before Eldrax was born.

That opinion would soon change if he was the one to tear the Black Wolf totem from their hated leader's throat. Defeating the rival clan meant more to Eldrax than gaining a few hunting grounds. Their defeat would at last prove to the clan that he was one worthy of following, gaining him the indisputable right of Challenge. His eyes went to Murzuk's back. He just had to be smart enough to goad him into letting Eldrax lead an attack.

A soft whistle sounded from ahead, breaking him from his brooding. Murzuk raised his fist, bringing the raiding party to a halt. Their scout had signalled an alert. Eldrax gestured sharply to the warriors behind him and watched as they flanked the men carrying the spoils of the raid, flint-tipped spears bristling outward. The Hunting Bear warriors' eyes darted as they clutched at their weapons, and the plumes of mist curling in the frigid air stilled as many of them ceased to breathe. Their tension was palpable, but Eldrax felt only the thrill of anticipation. Perhaps he wouldn't have to manipulate his Chief after all.

He shifted his bulky frame into a ready stance, his mind alive with visions of glory and vengeance. First, he would cut out the Black Wolf leader's heart and cook it on a spit right beside Murzuk's before satisfying himself with the prize the Black Wolf had stolen from them. With the Black Wolf's fallen totem around his neck and their Chief's mate as his own, he would become the undisputed Master of the Plains.

The Hunting Bear scout appeared over a snowy outcrop of rock, running as though the ravens of death were at his heels. The Black Wolf could not be far behind.

Murzuk caught the young boy roughly by the scruff of his neck as he barrelled into them.

"The Black Wolf?" Murzuk demanded. "Did they see you? If you led them to us, I will make sure I pay the debt in your blood, boy!"

The scout gasped, shaking his head as he collapsed at his leader's feet. "No, no, not the Black Wolf. They're gone." The adolescent face was pallid beneath the rich, dark skin, his brown eyes wide and staring. Intrigued, Eldrax shifted closer to hear the terse exchange. The boy's quavering voice dipped in and out of his hearing.

"Wiped out?" Murzuk's voice held a note of disbelief, then one of warning. "Are you sure it was the Black Wolf, boy? I do not take kindly to mistakes."

The youngster swallowed, but gave one firm nod. "I am sure, my Chief."

Eldrax scowled, wishing he'd been able to hear the entire report. The Black Wolf had massacred something or someone, and now he did not know who that was. Perhaps another clan had challenged them and tasted the wrath of the most powerful clan of the plains.

Eldrax's mind worked quickly. If the Black Wolf had just put down a challenging clan, then it was impossible that they themselves would have walked away unscathed. They would have lost men and their remaining warriors would be battle weary. A feral grin spread over Eldrax's face. The Black Wolf were licking their wounds, and his clan was now in the perfect position to strike. The Nine Gods had smiled upon him at last.

"Chief Murzuk," Eldrax pushed forward, cutting off Murzuk's exchange with the scout.

"You dare interrupt me!" Murzuk rounded on the younger man.

There had been a time when Eldrax would have lowered his head and backed away, but that time had passed. He no longer had to his face back to look upon that dark countenance. A fierce thrill rippled through him as he discovered he could look his towering Chief in the eye as no other man could. *I am finally your equal.*

Murzuk saw the realisation glitter in Eldrax's black eyes and aimed his fist at the younger man's jaw. Eldrax set his feet. In the very moment his Chief had bunched his muscles to strike, he sifted through all the ways he could block the strike and kill Murzuk before his fist landed.

Nevertheless, he held still and let the blow connect, same as he had countless times before. Now was not the time to Challenge and cause division in the clan. Now was the time to go after their biggest rivals and prove himself. Once he defeated the Black Wolf, *then* he could take his ultimate revenge.

And so he let the strike land. But Eldrax did not stumble or bow down beneath it; he remained unbent, letting his posture speak. His Chief was still the leader... for now.

He saw Murzuk's blue eyes flicker as he read Eldrax's message before the coarse features arranged themselves into an expression he had rarely seen on his Chief's face: grudging pride.

"You will make a formidable Chief. One day the other clans

will tremble at the sound of your name. But today is not that day, pup." The glow of pride vanished. "Now get back in line where you belong before I gut you and leave your entrails for the crows."

Eldrax gave ground but kept his gaze level. *Soon.*

Murzuk returned his attention to the scout at his feet and gestured for him to lead the way forward.

"No!" The boy grovelled. "Don't make me go back there. It is cursed! The gods have cursed this place! It is against their wish that we should be here."

"The gods abandoned us here a long time ago, boy." Murzuk gave a sneering laugh. "They turned their backs and left our People to perish during the great Winter of Sorrow. If we hadn't turned our own backs on their *wishes*, we would no longer exist, boy. Now take us there, otherwise I will make you beg for a so-called god's curse!"

Whimpering, the scout pushed himself to his feet. Eldrax's lip curled in disdain. The boy was a coward. Once this foray was over, perhaps Eldrax would have some sport with the child before teaching him the penalty for cowardice.

The scout led them on north through the snow. They were drawing nearer to the Mountains of the Nine Gods. Their great peaks pierced the clouded sky above the vast, dark forest that skirted their borders, forbidding and impenetrable. The foothills rose on all sides. Eldrax wondered idly if the gods who had made the Peoples of the world still resided in those rocky towers, their dispassionate gaze looking down on the creation they had abandoned.

The scout's eyes darted continuously to the shadowy trees at the base of the Mountains as they loomed on the horizon, his steps growing ever more reluctant until, at last, he refused to move any further. The boy simply stood, pointing ahead with one trembling finger. No matter how Murzuk threatened retribution, the boy would not take another step towards the Mountains. The Hunting Bear Chief gave up with a snort of disdain.

Eldrax stepped up next to the scout. He did not threaten. In the time it took the boy to draw breath, Eldrax had pulled his flint blade and cut the air short in his throat. The scout's eyes bulged in surprise as his mind caught up with his death. His hands flew to his neck in a futile effort to keep his life's juices within, and with a wet gurgle, the boy collapsed into the snow. Without a second glance, Eldrax stepped over the convulsing body, leading the rest of the men forward over the undulating hillocks behind their Chief.

"You didn't have to do that." Rannac's voice was once again disapproving in his ear. "He was just a boy."

"He was weak. You know as well as I that weakness leads only to death."

"Your mother would not have liked it."

Eldrax's breath caught as his vision hazed to red. "Mention her to me again and I will rip out your tongue with my bare hands! Did Murzuk not order you to hunt her down and do exactly as I have just done to that boy? You know better than anyone the price of weakness, Rannac!"

A trace of old pain crossed Rannac's face, but he held his tongue.

They mounted the last rise and Eldrax saw the land open up into a great flat expanse; leaving the view unbroken until it reached the roots of the brooding forest. Midway between where he stood and the looming tree-line, he spied an extensive camp. The familiar shapes of skin shelters were easy to identify, even at this distance. The jumbles of dark shapes strewn around the dwellings were not so simple. Eldrax's best guess was that they were rocks, though why anyone would set up camp on such rough ground he could not understand.

Eldrax's black eyes flickered over the plain. Aside from the shelters billowing softly against the stiffening breeze, no other movement could be detected. It was unnaturally quiet. Not even the birds were singing. Something… something tasted wrong.

Despite himself, the hairs lifted on the back of Eldrax's neck. The scout's cries echoed in his ears: *It is cursed! The gods have cursed this place!* He shook off the ridiculous notion, but he was too experienced a hunter to ignore such a primal warning. Bringing his spear into a ready position, he signalled to the strongest men to once again fan out in a protective ring around the rest of the raiding party. He did not know what sort of trap the Black Wolf had set, but he was going to be ready for it.

"Keep alert, boy," Murzuk hissed. It surprised Eldrax to see that his Chief's face was pale beneath the rich skin, just as the scout's had been.

"If the Black Wolf are waiting, they will regret setting such a cowardly trap!" Eldrax did not bother to keep his voice down this time. If the Black Wolf knew they were here, then there was no further point in stealth.

"Your arrogance will be your downfall one day," Murzuk warned. "It is not the Black Wolf that makes my blood run cold. The Black Wolf lie before you, boy. Dead men are no threat to the living."

5

Fallen Enemies

A wave of shock rippled through Eldrax's chest. Not rocks. Bodies. The frozen corpses of the Black Wolf clan were lying strewn about the abandoned shelters. *No!* His gut wrenched. It could not be. The first flickering flames began to lick at his plans for the future, threatening to burn everything to ash inside his chest. If the Black Wolf clan lay vanquished before them, then everything he had spent his entire life preparing for had come to nothing.

Bitterness saturated Eldrax's tongue as Murzuk set out across the exposed ground. A few of the men hesitated to approach the killing field, but one glare from Eldrax and a flash of his still bloody knife had them falling obediently into line. They knew his moods well enough to know he would welcome killing something right now.

Eldrax's fury and disappointment mounted with every breath, the flames of destruction within his heart growing greater. At the edge of the camp, Murzuk ordered five of the men, including Rannac, forward. The rest he left to guard their kills on the outskirts, ready to flee if needed. The chosen five bunched closely together with Rannac at their head as they walked among the frozen corpses.

Eldrax could plainly see the totem of the Black Wolf dotted about the camp, leaving no doubt as to the identity of the fallen. The flames in his chest peaked, then burned away, leaving behind a deadened wasteland of disappointment. He kicked savagely at the snow, vowing to find who was responsible and destroy them. He would overturn every rock until he knew the identity of his enemy.

Nothing could have prepared him for the reality of what he saw. The hairs standing on the back of Eldrax's neck quivered again, sending an unaccustomed chill down his spine. From a young age, he had seen men slaughtered, many by his own hand. He had seen their blood flow, their eyes glazing over in the absence of life. He had both seen and caused horrific wounds. But not even he had ever inflicted the sheer brutality he was witnessing now. It wasn't so much bodies he was walking through as body *parts*. He saw torsos cleaved in two, heads absent from shoulders and limbs separated from joints. Gripping his spear, Eldrax crouched down to inspect the nearest headless torso. No butchering blade had parted this head from its body. It had been ripped off by some immense force.

What in—

A shadow fell across the ground, making him start. Murzuk stood above him, and Eldrax growled angrily at his lapse. His Chief's blue eyes were wary. Eldrax could almost smell his fear. *Coward.*

"No other clan did this," Murzuk spoke in a low tone. "It is a bad omen. The scout was right. This is no place for man. We should leave quickly."

31

Eldrax muffled his snort as Rannac gave a soft whistle of alert from the other side of the camp. Eldrax rose away from the disturbing corpse and walked with his Chief to see what the other raider had found. He kept his eyes moving as they waded through the gore, taking in every detail. No one had been spared. Not even the women and children. The bitterness on his tongue swirled again, and he swallowed it down with an effort. Even the spoils of battle had been denied to him.

"What have you found?" Murzuk grumbled as they neared Rannac.

"I thought you would like to see, my chief." The grizzled warrior pointed at the snow before him. His dark face was a mask of conflicting emotions.

A tall man was lying prone in a pool of his own frozen blood. The furs that covered his body were tattered and torn from multiple wounds, though he had escaped the mutilations that had befallen so many of his people. His tortured face was turned to the side, partially revealing his dark features.

Eldrax saw the fear in his chief's eyes transform into a fierce, gloating joy as Murzuk rolled the corpse over with his fur-wrapped foot.

"So, Juran, you finally confronted an enemy that even *you* could not defeat. Perhaps the gods still deliver justice after all."

Eldrax stared down at the dead man. *This* was the feared Cro chief of whom tales were told and rival clans learned to fear? Juran of the Black Wolf, the man Eldrax had spent most of his life hoping to one day face in battle, was lying dead at his feet. A lifetime of preparation and now he would never know who would have walked away alive, who would have been the true alpha wolf of the Cro clans. The desolation spread further through Eldrax's chest.

Rannac crouched down and touched the frozen face. "Farewell... brother," he muttered, bowing his head in a last sign of respect.

Ignoring the older warrior, Eldrax scrutinised the body. The chief had been tall, taller perhaps even than Murzuk, though he was nowhere near as heavily built. Eldrax's lip curled. Juran might have been an agile warrior, but so too was he, and he would have far outmatched the Black Wolf chief in brute strength.

Wrestling with the feeling that he was now without purpose, Eldrax turned away as Murzuk crouched beside his old rival, drawing his sharp flint knife from his fur boot. He did not watch as his chief cut the fingers from Juran's cold, stiff spear-hand as a prize. To the gods with a few fingers. He had been hoping for bigger rewards. A glance at Juran's throat told him that his totem was gone. Claimed by another.

The breeze swirled in the snow and ruffled the abandoned shelters. The clouds overhead lowered as the wind herded them across the sky. Eldrax let his eyes wander over the camp. No totem, not even Juran's prized mate remained for him to prove himself a victor. A victor worthy enough to become a chieftain.

The thought gave Eldrax pause. *Not even the prized mate...* In his mind's eye, he ran through everything he had seen since entering the camp. Nothing but bodies. But maybe it was not what he saw, but what he *didn't* see that should have interested him.

"That witch Juran snatched from you all those seasons ago. He claimed her as his own mate, did he not?"

"Yes." Murzuk's face darkened at the reminder. "Though no stories have been told to say whether he bred successfully with her." The chief's lips twisted as though this gave him some small comfort. "Why?"

"Because she is not here. All the bodies here are Cro." Eldrax did not wait for a further response. He stalked the camp, searching every tent, studying every body part. Some corpses were too mangled to even identify as Cro. It didn't matter, they were all far too large to be the creature that he sought.

She was not here.

With burgeoning hope, Eldrax scanned the snow. Inside the camp and the immediate area, the ground was too churned by the struggle of battle to be read by even his expert eye. Eldrax ranged further out, circling the camp until he found what he was looking for: two sets of human tracks running from the killing field. One set had the size and distinctive shape of a Cro man, but the other prints were half the size, the stride much shorter. A child perhaps, but something told him that was not the case. The shape of the tread did not ring true. A triumphant grin crept over his broad face as he whistled for attention, continuing to track as he did so. Perhaps all was not lost after all...

The prints led away from the dark line of the forest, directly towards a steep escarpment rising into the foothills before being wiped out by another bloody commotion in the snow. A smaller fight had taken place away from the main battle.

On the other side of the churned ground, the two lone tracks continued on towards the seemingly impassible escarpment. The track-makers had survived the fight, but a trail of blood now accompanied their footprints; someone had been seriously wounded in the struggle. Out of the corner of his eye,

Eldrax noted other marks in the snow leading off to his left, but he paid little interest.

Like a wolf on a scent, Eldrax loped along next to his target's tracks until he reached the edge of the rocky cliff. Almost completely concealed, a narrow path led between the rocks. At this point, the smaller set of footprints tracked back and forth as though undecided upon their direction before disappearing completely over the steep rocks. The larger Cro tracks doubled back on a different route towards the camp, still trailed by a thin line of red.

Eldrax's nostrils flared as he made his conclusions and ran back towards his men. Murzuk and the rest had caught up and had gathered around the evidence of the smaller fight.

"He got the witch out," he announced as he approached. "She has perhaps two day's lead, but she is alone. Juran's greatest possession is ours for the taking at last."

"If she is alone, then she's most likely dead already," Murzuk muttered without raising his eyes from the snow.

Eldrax felt a stab of resentment. The rare prize that his clan had coveted for so long was out there somewhere, unprotected, and Murzuk was not even going to bother mounting a hunt? He could not hold his tongue. "Just look at the tra-"

"Silence!" Murzuk hissed. "A rash fool, as ever. Look there and tell me what you see."

Eldrax's hackles rose. Baring his teeth, he gripped his spear threateningly, his anger and disappointment overcoming his better sense. A hand on his arm stopped him. Rannac's gaze held a note of warning. He bit down on his tongue so hard he tasted blood.

His chief jabbed a finger at the strange marks that he had

previously ignored. There was a wide, unbroken scuff making a direct path in the snow back towards the edge of the forest. It appeared as though something very large had been dragged along the ground. Evenly spaced depressions marked the snow upon either side of the drag marks. Disbelief shook Eldrax from his blackening temper. *Not possible.*

"Footprints." Murzuk confirmed.

Footprints. Each one was as long as a man's arm. The stride between each print was twice the length of an ordinary Cro man.

"What in the Nine Gods made tracks such as those?"

"Nothing that I have ever seen," Murzuk said. "And by all the Nine Gods, nothing we ever want to see." The handful of warriors surrounding him shifted, ready to bolt the moment their leader gave the word. "This place is not meant for man. It is cursed. We will leave now." Murzuk turned to lead the scouting band back towards the rest of the hunting party.

Eldrax did not follow. He was staring at the giant footprints leading into the forest. There had been a fight here. That much was certain. He looked at the Cro footprints travelling away from the skirmish and the trail of blood that accompanied them. If Juran had walked away, then he must have killed his adversary. If that was so, where was the body? Eldrax examined the drag mark in the snow with new insight. The other monsters had cleared their fallen away, leaving nothing but footprints to prove they had ever existed.

Eldrax felt a twinge, a flicker of life amongst the ashes of his dreams. He turned in the forest's direction and jogged along beside the tracks. He had lost one opportunity, but perhaps another far greater had just revealed itself. A fever took hold in his heart. He wanted to look them in the eye, this foe who had wiped out the strongest Cro clan in existence.

"Eldrax!" Murzuk's voice sounded dimly behind him.

He ignored his chief and continued towards the dark line of the forest. The trees were dense; black, twisting trunks standing stark against the snow and the grey mountains behind. The thick tangle seemed to frown down, forbidding his presence against entering. There was a quiver, a vibe in the air that danced just beyond his mortal senses. Eldrax's step faltered, and for a moment he truly believed that his chief was right: this land was not meant for the tread of man.

Coward! He admonished himself. *Acting like an old woman cowed by superstitious tales.* It was a forest, just like any other he had hunted in. He plunged on into the depths.

The canopy was so dense that the snow had barely made it through the tangled fingers overhead. Eldrax stood for a few moments, letting his eyes adjust to the dimness. The scent of damp, black mud and leaf mould filled his nostrils. The air was still and stagnant, cloying after the clean sharpness of the snowy plain outside. The ground squashed beneath his fur-wrapped feet.

He could hear the commotion out on the plain as Murzuk raged for his return, and the men fretted over the loss of a brother. Eldrax paid them no mind. Casting his eyes down, he could now make out the over-sized prints in the earth and followed them forward, catching sight of other signs of passage as the ground rose steeply before him. Branches and entire trunks had been snapped and uprooted on either side of the trail. Eldrax studied the halves of one broken tree in the light its absence had permitted through the canopy. The wood was not rotten and yet it had been cracked in two like a twig.

"I'll kill you myself, boy!"

Too late, Eldrax heard the footfalls pounding behind him just as a heavy body tackled him to the ground.

"How dare you disobey me!" Furious, Murzuk pinned his arms. "You insolent fool! I will not have had my efforts on you wasted. You will learn respect!" The older man caught him with a fist. He was holding a hunting knife, and he was not mindful about the blade.

Eldrax felt the skin on his cheek part, and fresh blood spilled forth. The familiar red mist descended over his eyes and something finally snapped inside. With a roar he threw Murzuk off and, with reflexes honed from a lifetime of survival, he leapt to his feet, his spear poised and ready. It was time for Murzuk to die.

Without betraying his motives, he lunged for his chief. He had the satisfaction of seeing the shock on the older man's face as he narrowly parried Eldrax's strike.

"You have no right to Challenge me, boy!" the older man exclaimed. "You are no Chief yet, and the men know it!"

"We'll see about that!" He saw that a handful of the men led by Rannac had been brave enough to follow Murzuk in his pursuit and they were watching with interest. Eldrax knew his actions would divide the clan down the middle, but in that moment of rage, he cared very little. All he wanted was to see Murzuk dead at his feet. The men would accept him as the new Chief or suffer the same fate. He had waited too long to kill the man who had tormented him his entire life.

"You have become an old coward and a fool, Murzuk! You are no longer worthy of following."

"And you are more trouble than you are worth!" Murzuk snarled. "No matter, I have others who will gladly step over your corpse." The old Chief struck back.

Eldrax knocked the blow aside with ease and then he went on the offensive; twisting and striking so fast that Murzuk was hard pressed to defend himself. Still, Eldrax struggled to land the killing blow. Most of his experience came from fighting and hunting on the open plains, and he quickly found that the tightly packed trees hindered his long spear. After missing two killing strikes, he threw it down in frustration. Drawing his hunting knife, he closed the gap, forcing close quarters where his superior strength gave him the advantage.

He watched the uncertainty in Murzuk's eyes turn to fear as he took up his own knife in defence. His Chief had never truly understood how strong Eldrax had become. When their two knives locked together, Eldrax heaved his full strength against his Chief. Murzuk could not match him, and he threw the older man back, smashing him heavily into a fallen log. Stunned, the Chief lay gasping on the ground.

"Red Bear!" the younger warriors chanted. "Red Bear!"

The sound of his warrior name stoked the fire in Eldrax's blood. A triumphant cry tore from his lips as he seized his spear, ready to strike the killing blow. He paused, unable to resist savouring the moment. At the fall of his weapon, he would become the new Chief of his clan and he would have tasted vengeance at last.

Murzuk choked out a laugh as he gazed up at him. "Your mother would be proud, boy. *She* never got this close to killing me, though the gods know she tried. I bet she wishes she could see you now."

Eldrax's spear froze in the air. "She paid her price. You made sure of it!"

Murzuk laughed again. "Yes. Your mother was soft, and I

have spent a great deal of time making sure such weakness had no place in you. It seems I wasted my efforts. You are a fool to hesitate!"

Before Eldrax could formulate a thought, Murzuk kicked the earth and leaves into the air, blinding him for a critical moment. A spear haft smashed into the back of his legs, taking them out from under him. Cries and hoots went up all around from the men at this turn in fortune. Flat on his back, Eldrax barely got the haft of his own spear up in time to block Murzuk's knife as it came for his throat. Eldrax was the stronger, but now the old Chief had the advantage of his full weight bearing down against him as Eldrax fought to keep him at bay. They grimaced into one another's faces, each fighting to gain a fraction.

OOOOOAAAAHHHHGGGG!

The bloodcurdling howl split the air, rising above the treetops and continuing for an inhuman amount of time. Eldrax's breath caught in his throat, paralysed mid-struggle with Murzuk. Never in his life had he heard anything like it.

Nobody moved as the scream played out and shivered into nothingness. Eldrax strained his ears against the breathless silence left in its wake until the ominous sound of trees swaying and snapping broke the stillness.

Something unseen had moved through the forest towards the divided Cro. The scent of dead and rotting flesh assaulted Eldrax's senses, getting steadily stronger.

"We have to go now." Rannac's voice was barely a breath. "Right now."

But Eldrax could not move, and neither, it seemed, could Murzuk. They remained frozen in their battle pose until they saw it. Something pale was shifting through the trees in the near distance. Branches snapped and trunks groaned as they were parted. Then the sound ceased and everything grew still. Somehow the lack of movement was worse. Eldrax searched the trees and spotted the pale silhouette standing motionless just out of his direct line of sight. Only the sound of the Cro warriors' frightened breath could be heard as they waited, too afraid to move in any direction.

Then Eldrax got his wish. A pair of glowing blue eyes snapped open, and he found himself looking up into the very soul of the Black Wolf's death. The eyes were not alone. Another pair and another opened until an entire line of vivid blue was staring down at them from the darkness, high above where an ordinary man's eyes should be. Rotting skulls covered the faces, and severed bones protruded from the shoulders and arms in jutting spikes.

Eldrax gazed up into the row of blank, icy depths and felt the stirrings of an emotion he had vowed to never feel again since the day his mother had died: terror.

"Run!"

Eldrax did not know if the command came from his own lips or from Murzuk's. The inhuman howl sounded again just as Eldrax got his feet into Murzuk's chest and kicked his Chief hard in the direction of the watching eyes. Taking to his feet, he fled just as the shadowed creatures charged. He did not turn to see what they were. The fear he felt was too overwhelming. He concentrated only on escaping this cursed forest. He had made a grave mistake in coming here.

The sound of trees being ripped aside behind him signalled the monsters' pursuit. Deep, primal terror pushed Eldrax's legs ever faster, throbbing to every part of his body as he ducked and dodged through the trees, heedless of the other men flying beside him.

There seemed no escape from the trees, and for a few terrible moments, Eldrax feared he had become disorientated and was heading deeper into the forest. But before he could check himself, the light changed and Eldrax burst out onto open ground. He stumbled as his feet hit the deep snow. He caught himself, then continued to run, fighting for every stride. Survival now depended on who could run the longest. He did not dare look back.

His breath was coming in ragged gasps by the time the camp of the massacred Black Wolf reached out to surround him, the sight of each torn body fuelling the terror of his flight. He screamed at the men still waiting on the outskirts of the camp to abandon their kills. Such a burden would only slow them down. Losing the spoils stoked Eldrax's fury, and it cleared his mind enough to remember the narrow path leading up the escarpment and into the foothills. Their pursuers would be too big to follow them there. He could not hear the sounds of pursuit over the rushing of the wind and blood in his ears, but he could feel the malevolence behind him boring into his back.

"This way!"

Blind in their terror, the men ignored him.

"Follow me if you want to save your miserable skins!"

Without waiting to see if they followed, Eldrax changed direction and ran directly towards the escarpment. His legs burned with the effort of fighting through the deep snow. A few of the men had heeded his instruction and followed. The rest continued to run heedlessly across the open ground, unwilling to follow him into what they believed would be certain death against the rock face.

Uncaring, Eldrax found the narrow path that he remembered. The strongest would survive, the rest would perish and slow the monsters down. Mastering his tiring body, he began the gruelling ascent between the rocks.

Up he climbed, not giving in to exhaustion until he reached the summit. Half of the men had made it to safety with him. Eldrax clutched at the rocks to brace his trembling body. He waited until his heart returned to a steady rhythm before steeling himself to face the plain below.

It was empty. The rest of the raiding party had disappeared, and there was no sign of their pursuers. Chagrined, Eldrax realised the creatures had not followed them out onto the open ground. Terror alone had been enough to drive him and his men to continue their flight and abandon their spoils.

Shame burned through him as he shifted his gaze to the tree line. They were there. Eldrax could just make out their cold blue eyes, staring out from the darkness of their lair. Now that he was away from the strange influence of the trees, the paralysing terror had receded and he bared his teeth in challenge. He would never forget that they had made him run for his life this day.

"W-what in all the gods *are* they?" one man asked as the glowing eyes winked out one by one and disappeared. It was Tanag, a young warrior of his own age.

"Things I am going to *kill* one day." He had made a mistake in entering the forest so rashly, he could admit that, if only to himself. The fate of the Black Wolf should have served as a warning, but he had allowed his bitter disappointment to drive him. He would not be so naïve again. The next time he challenged these monsters, he would be prepared. He would see those blue eyes burn with same the terror that they had inflicted on him.

The cowards surrounding him stared at his face as though questioning his sanity.

"What about the Chief? Do you think he escaped?"

In the confusion, Eldrax had not seen what had happened to Murzuk. A fierce joy burned at the edges of his anger and shame. Murzuk had not made it. The Hunting Bear Chief had not come out of the forest. It disappointed Eldrax that he had not been the one to land the killing blow, but he was certain the monsters would have ensured a more gruesome demise for his hated Chief than he could have dreamed. The thought comforted him. Rannac had also disappeared. Eldrax felt a slight pang at this loss. The older warrior might have been a thorn in his side at times, but he had been a skilled hunter and warrior.

Eldrax was careful to keep his emotions in check as he answered Tanag. "Murzuk fell into the path of those monsters. They will have strewn his body around the forest by now." Entering the forest had not been such a mistake after all. It was time to take the position of power at last. He lifted his chin. "*I* am your Chief."

"But—" Hanak, Tanag's brother, protested.

Quick as a hunting cat, Eldrax backhanded the man across the jaw with enough force to send him crashing to the ground.

"Murzuk is *dead*. *I* will lead you now," he repeated. "Once we return home, I will take my place as Chief. If anyone wants to Challenge for that right, then pick up your spear. I am ready."

The remaining men backed away at the offer and kept their eyes downcast. Eldrax almost purred at their immediate display of submission.

Only Hanak remained resentful as he spat the blood from his mouth, spraying the snow with red. "Then, what are we going to do now, *revered* Chief?" he asked.

Eldrax paused for a moment, scowling into the distance as his mind worked. The raiding party had lost the kills it had risked Black Wolf territory to gain. His gaze travelled back to the site of the massacred Black Wolf.

The knowledge that he would never prove himself the greater warrior against Juran of the Black Wolf still twisted in his gut like a knife. But who was there to say what had actually happened here? There were no other witnesses to spin tales of the massacre that had taken place before the Mountains of the Nine Gods. If he claimed the victory, then when the tales were recounted to small children, it would be the figure of the Red Bear and not the Black Wolf that would have babes cowering closer to the campfire.

He cursed Juran's absent totem. If he had gained that one piece of indisputable proof... Eldrax stared broodingly into the snow.

A predatory smile split across his face as the secrets of the ground leapt out at him, and the missing totem paled into insignificance. Juran had possessed a far greater prize, one that all other clans would not fail to recognise. If Eldrax claimed it, he would control the plains from the Mountains to the southern shin'ar forests.

Yes!

He turned to his waiting men. "It is time we took our rightful place as the power in these lands. No more scratching at the edges." He pointed to the wavering line of diminutive tracks leading away into the foothills. "It's time to go hunting."

THE FORBIDDEN

* * *

6

In The Balance

Rebaa.
    Juran?
    Rebaa...

In her dream, she reached for him. Warmth enveloped her. The scent of furs was strong in her nose. She smiled lazily. She did not wish to leave the cocoon of their bedding yet. Rebaa stretched out her fingers without opening her eyes and searched for Juran's warm skin, preparing to curl into his side as she always did when dawn broke over the horizon. Perhaps she could persuade him that the day could wait just a little longer.

She recoiled in shock as her fingers came up against something wet and icy cold.

The illusion of contentedness shattered as Rebaa woke. Instead of Juran's indulgent face, a great furry head and a pair of amber eyes filled her view. Rebaa cried out and jerked away with a gasp. The wolf that had been sniffing her hair jumped back and stared at her accusingly. Rebaa panted as the harsh reality resettled over her.

47

More noses sniffed at her head, trying to rouse her. Ninmah's golden face had risen over the horizon, and the wolves were ready to move on. They urged their newest member to get to her feet. She had been moving with the pack for an entire day and night, and they were frustrated with her ever slowing pace. Their impatience grated on her nerves, and Rebaa's grief burned swiftly into anger.

"Leave me!" She leaped to her feet and faced the wolves down. Theirs was not the comfort she wanted. She did not want them. "Go! Get away."

The alpha male growled a warning at her. She rounded on him, her energy gathered like a storm cloud, and she could not hold it back. Screaming, she released it, lashing out at his mind with all her bitterness, driving him away.

The alpha yelped as she engulfed his thoughts with her pain. He swiped at his face with his paw, trying to rid himself of the discomfort. Shaking his head, he spun on his hind legs and ran from her, howling as he went. The pack gave Rebaa one last look of reproach before they turned and followed their leader, disappearing over a ridge and melting into the snow. Not one of them looked back.

Rebaa fell to her knees as she buried her face in her hands.

I will never leave you. Juran's voice continued to echo through her mind. *Remember that.*

"Liar!" Rebaa howled to the nothingness. "Liar!"

She pushed his memory aside. She could not face her grief, not if she expected to function and continue in this futile attempt to keep her last promise to him.

She stared at the landscape stretching away before her, the tangle of steep, rocky slopes, gullies and ravines, all the white crags, dead grasses and unforgiving rocks. This was the path she had to travel and survive as long as she could.

For the sake of her baby and *nobody* else, she would continue on until she could travel no more. She had to get out of these desolate foothills and move south across the plains. Only then would she find the ancient forests of her People. The shin'ar forests, as the Cro named them.

Rebaa heaved her ailing body upright. Light-headedness swamped her, and she staggered before the world righted itself. It had been too long since she'd eaten. She stumbled over to the wolves' latest carcass, wrinkling her nose at the mauled bones. Desperate, she pawed through the remains, searching for a bit of flesh, anything that she could eat. As always, the wolves had stripped the bones bare. Rebaa kicked the exposed ribs in frustration.

She ate the snow. The melting frost sated her thirst, and she drank deeply, filling her empty stomach with water in the hopes it would ease her discomfort.

Nothing moved on the stark landscape before her as she drank her fill. The loneliness settled like a weight upon her shoulders. She had been foolish in sending the wolf pack away. They might not have been the comfort she wanted, but at least she hadn't been alone.

Rebaa felt the first stirrings of guilt for how she had treated them. In one flash of temper, she had let her grief and anger get the better of her and she had made a weapon of her Ninmah-given Gift. Such an abuse of power should never be inflicted upon the Children of the Great Spirit. But Rebaa knew deep down that she had done the only thing she could. Even if she hadn't sent them away, she would never have been able to keep up with them for much longer. A pack of mountain wolves would protect its weakest members to the bitter end.

She would have become their doom.

A ray of light stabbed at her tired eyes. Ninmah was rising ahead of her. She was facing east. Struggling to remember the skills Juran had taught, Rebaa knew she needed to head to her right to escape the maze of foothills and eventually come down onto the vast southern plains. The trail of human footprints she had discovered had driven her north of her original path. She did not want to cross their trail again. She must stay clear of other Cro clans. After a moment's deliberation, she continued to follow Ninmah east for a while before turning south.

The wind picked up as she travelled. Icy blasts whistled through the rocks. Rebaa hunched down into her furs and tried to still the chattering of her teeth. Creatures of the Great Spirit scurried away or hunkered down inside their bolt holes in fear as she passed by. It served as a reminder of the harsh world she now existed in: one of kill or be killed. She whimpered in longing for the peaceful forest home of her childhood. Rebaa kept her higher senses thrown out as she picked her way over the often treacherous paths through the hills, alert to signs of ambush, but could detect nothing greater than a hare's quivering energy.

The dark crags and rock faces surrounding her rose higher on all sides. Different paths twisted and turned through the rocks in every direction. Rebaa turned her face to the sky to determine Ninmah's position only to find Her guiding face had also abandoned her, obscured behind thick, threatening clouds. Rebaa fought down a wave of fresh panic as she realised she no longer knew which direction to walk in. The wind seemed to come from all directions. She could stumble around in these hills for days and get no closer to her destination.

When darkness fell, Rebaa wept out loud when she came upon a set of footprints she knew to be her own. They were too small for any Cro, and no Cro would be foolish enough to walk these desolate places alone. She had wandered in circles. An entire day of travel and strength she could not spare, wasted.

Rebaa stopped walking and leaned against a rock for support. The skin on her face was burned raw by the wind. Heavy flakes of snow started to fall from the laden sky, masking the darkening landscape in a haze of white. There was no point in continuing her journey in the darkness; to struggle on into the night would only waste further energy. She had to find shelter from the building elements or she would not live to see the dawn. There was no longer a wolf pack to watch over her and keep her warm this night. Pushing away from the cold rock, Rebaa forced her body to move, flitting between crags, doing her best to stay directly out of the wind.

Her numb feet were about to give out from under her when a cave rose out of the darkness. Its jagged, black mouth split a low rock face almost in two. Yawning wide in the swirling snow, it offered salvation. Despite her numerous sins, Ninmah must still be watching over her.

Or so it seemed. Shivering, Rebaa hesitated on the threshold; survival instinct holding her in place. She could not see very far into the shadowy depths, and the falling snow had obscured any footprints that might betray a current occupant. There was a strong probability that something else had already made this place home. Something just as hungry as she was who wouldn't mind a snack wandering so willingly into its den in the dead of winter.

Gathering her remaining energy, Rebaa reached out, trying to sense what the darkness might hide from her eyes. She did not wish to walk unwittingly into the lair of another predator, as she had with the wolves. This time, she might not be so lucky.

There was nothing. No vibration of life shivered against her questing touch. The cave was empty. Relieved beyond words, Rebaa stumbled at last into its sheltering embrace. It was narrow, craggy, and wound a long way back into the rock face. The scent of the cold, damp stone was unwelcoming, but the tang of animal habitation was absent.

Bolstered, she ventured farther inside, feeling the temperature rise as she went. It was warmer out of the cruelty of the wind and the blanketing snow. It would be enough. Unable to stand on her feet any longer, Rebaa sank to the rocky floor, leaning her back into an alcove where the wall was smoother. When Ninmah was unmasked, she would try to re-find her way, but for now she would rest until the snow storm passed.

Despite her exhaustion, sleep did not come immediately. After a day of listening to the constant crunch of her own footsteps and the howl of the wind through the hills, the silence of the cave was oppressive, unnerving. Rebaa strained her ears. Somewhere deeper inside, water was dripping from the damp ceiling into an unseen pool below. The sound echoed back and forth dimly from the surrounding rocks. Besides the faint whistling of the wind outside and the beating of her own heart, there was no other sound.

Sitting in the empty darkness, Rebaa had the irrational wish that she could have carried on trudging throughout the night just for the company of her own footsteps. The concentration needed to keep putting one foot in front of the other had been a distraction. Now, in the silence of this cave, the sense of isolation threatened to crush her beneath its weight. The night stretched on, the wind howled, the water dripped, and Rebaa remained alone.

Alone.

The emotions that she had been so carefully holding at bay broke loose from her control. Clutching at the carved spearhead that dangled over her heart, she dropped her head upon her knees and cried herself to sleep.

When she awoke, it was still dark. The clouds had moved on, and she could see the glimmering pinpricks of silver sky spirits peeping through the cave opening. The wind had died, having blown the storm out, and there was a hushed stillness in the air.

She ought to be relieved by the reprieve from the incessant whining, but she wasn't. Instead, a chill crept along Rebaa's spine. Something had awoken her. Something more than just a lull in the wind. Instinctively, she froze in place, staring hard towards the empty mouth of the cave. She could hear nothing in the silence, only the continued drip, drip of the water somewhere in the darkness behind her. But something was wrong. Her skin was prickling, every instinct on alert. Rebaa recognised the dreaded sensation in an instant.

The feeling every prey animal knew and dreaded.

The sensation of being hunted.

Rebaa stopped breathing. She did not know what stalked her. The presence danced just beyond her senses. *The Cro?* The thought had barely crossed her mind when a greater terror caused her heart to leap against her ribs. The monsters of the Mountains.

Perhaps they had pursued her after all, their blood lust driving them to catch her, the last survivor of her clan, and finish what they had started.

She bit her lip hard to keep from whimpering in panic as ghostly, blood-stained hands reached for her out of the darkness of her mind. Her muscles thrilled with the need to flee, to get out of this trap before it was too late. Almost she bolted for the entrance, but on the exposed land, there was nowhere for her to go. She could not hope to outrun her pursuers. She was not fast enough, but perhaps if she laid low, her adversary might miss the cave in the darkness. The heavy snowfall would have covered the tracks she had been careless enough to leave behind.

The nebulous presence solidified against her hypersensitive awareness, and she knew the time for choosing was over. It was close. Rebaa concentrated harder, and her heart skipped a beat. The approaching consciousness bore the chilling focus of a ravening hunter.

Crunch. Crunch. Crunch. The muffled tread of heavy footsteps sounded, getting steadily louder until a massive shadow fell across the mouth of the cave, blocking the twinkling spirits of the night sky. Blocking her escape. Rebaa flinched back as an unseen nose sniffed the air, searching for the prey it had been tracking. She felt it deliberate.

The skitter of stones across rocky ground announced the creature's entrance. It tested the air again and gave a hungry growl. Rebaa shrank into her alcove as all hope of remaining hidden evaporated. She had made the wrong choice.

The presence was vast, but not that of the monsters she most feared. The thoughts brushing against hers were slow, deliberate, and implacable. Rebaa knew them instantly to be those of a bear. She fought to control her breathing and remain silent. The scent of her fear would draw him to her like a vulture to a carcass.

The snuffling drew closer. The bear's energy throbbed with excitement. It could certainly smell her, but it could not see her. Yet. Rebaa gritted her teeth. The passage was narrow. There was no way this hunter would miss her in the blackness. If she moved so much as a finger, she would be lost. Tears trickled down her cheeks. Two days alone, and she had already failed Juran.

Her baby kicked, snapping Rebaa out of her despair. It was not just her life hanging in the balance. She pushed her panic down. She had to think. Concentrating hard on the surrounding rocks, she shifted her energy to match her environment; slowing her heart rate as she cooled her body. Hiding her presence was a skill that had always come easily to her. As a child, she had driven her tribe to distraction. But that was when she had been strong. She was not strong now. She was hungry, traumatised and exhausted. She almost didn't have the power. Weak. Too weak.

The bear was so close now in the narrow passageway of the cave that she could feel its body heat. Rebaa held her breath, fighting to keep her concentration. The massive bulk swayed into view before her. Rebaa closed her eyes as the shaggy head swung around. Hot, damp breath saturated her face. The bear sniffed again and Rebaa tightened her fists, the cold sweat in her palms moist against her fingers. *Go away!* She thought at the creature. *There is nothing here!*

He did not move on. His great muzzle was a mere hand's breadth from her flesh. He sniffed again. A confused rumble sounded in his chest.

This was no good. She could hide her presence all she liked. She could not hide her scent. The bear growled, sniffing harder. His lips peeled back from his thick teeth.

The illusion had failed. The only choice remaining was to run for her life. She needed a head start. Using what energy she had left, she drew on the power of the Great Spirit and touched the bear's thoughts. Rebaa gave him the overwhelming sense of another presence deeper inside the cave. The only presence that would distract the beast now. The threat of another bear.

The creature's angry bellow reverberated through Rebaa's body. The massive head swung away as he reared up to challenge his imagined adversary. Released from the bear's focus, Rebaa dropped her illusions and bolted. The rocks cut at her feet through their damp wrappings as she fled. She hardly felt the pain in her need to get away.

The cave shuddered as the bear dropped back to the stones with a heavy thud. Confusion aggravated its thoughts. There was a pause before another furious bellow rent the air as it spotted its prey escaping from beneath its very nose.

Rebaa burst from the cave as the beast gave chase. Her eyes darted. Ninsiku's evil, silver eye was almost fully open in the night sky, staring down as he revealed her maliciously to her enemy. She searched for a bolt hole, anything to save herself. She tried to run faster, stumbling and falling and dragging herself back upright. She dared not look back. She didn't have to turn to know the bear was gaining on her with every mighty stride. The ground vibrated beneath her feet, signalling its proximity.

Rebaa reached again for the animal's mind, but her influence slipped away like water. He was not like the wolves. A loner, he had no regard for protecting family. And he was *hungry*. Rebaa's People could influence the Great Spirit, but the Power of the Earth, once set, was beyond any of them. She could not sway this creature. She was as good as dead.

She felt the bear gathering himself to lunge and dodged quickly. Heavy jaws snapped shut around the empty air where her arm had just been. A tree rose from the shadows before her. Acting on pure instinct, Rebaa scrambled into its branches. The feel of rough bark beneath her fingers was a distant relief.

Roaring, the bear swiped upwards. Rebaa screamed as she felt the razor claws rake her right leg, ripping through the furs and deep into her flesh. The pain was blinding. She almost lost her grip.

No, no, she chanted to herself, dragging herself higher even as she felt hot blood sliding down the torn skin and muscle of her calf.

She pushed herself to climb as high as she could go, then clung there, staring down at her death. Rebaa's blood and tears dripped down on to the bear's upturned face. His beady eyes were furious, filled with frustration. She was only just out of reach. The tree was thin, a twig compared to the bear's monstrous strength. He could snap it like firewood if he so chose. She watched helplessly as the bear came to that same dreadful conclusion.

He reared up on his hind legs and slammed into the tree, hurling his weight against it again and again. The trunk creaked and splintered before the vicious onslaught.

Rebaa closed her eyes and cast one last prayer to Ninmah, pleading for forgiveness as she prepared her soul to join with the Great One. *I'm sorry, Juran. I failed.*

The spear came out of nowhere.

7

Unexpected

Rebaa had barely finished her prayer to Ninmah when a challenging cry answered the angry snarls of the bear. She watched, feeling strangely disembodied as something streaked like lightning through the darkness, and struck the bear full in the side, burying itself between his ribs to bite at his heart. The creature threw back his head, jaws gaping wide as he roared his pain and surprise to the sky.

Staggering on his hind paws, the bear toppled over backwards. Rebaa watched in detached horror as he thrashed in the snow, turning everything around him a dark shade of red. A trickle of blood streamed from his mouth as the struggles became more and more feeble. Then with a dying gurgle, the bear finally lay still.

Rebaa could not move. Her fingers were frozen in shock around the branches she had clung to for her very life. She stared down at the now lifeless form of her foe as her mind struggled to catch up. A violent trembling started all over her body, and she knew it was not a good idea to remain in the branches. As much as height offered protection, she would have to take her chances on the ground.

Stiff and feeling strangely outside of herself, Rebaa climbed back to the rocks below. Her injured leg immediately gave way beneath her, and she collapsed to the ground.

Ninmah, preserve me!

She was crippled. The furs that covered her calf were soaked crimson. Her shaking grew worse. Too much, it was too much. Falling forward onto her hands, she vomited into the snow beside the dead beast. Her empty stomach had nothing to surrender, and she dry heaved until her body ached.

When at last the retching stopped, she rolled onto her side and rested her hot cheek in the snow. It was nice. Her thoughts spiralled idly as Rebaa let her eyes wander over the bear's carcass. He should have long ago disappeared into hibernation. She frowned, finding even that small motion an effort. She saw now that beneath the thick fur coat; the beast was emaciated. He had been in no condition for a long sleep. The Furies were getting longer, colder, and it was not just Man that was suffering.

Her vision darkened around the edges. Rebaa blinked, fighting to keep focused. She had to get up or she would perish in the snow, but she could not find it within herself to even raise an arm. Her eyes continued to rove over the bear's body and lighted on the object that must have killed it. A long, thick pole was protruding from its side.

The sight flashed a warning through Rebaa's fading consciousness. Such an object could only mean one thing. Cro. Struggling to get her boneless arms beneath her, Rebaa fought to rise.

"Shalanaki?" A throaty voice cut the air.

Too late. The owner of the spear had already arrived. With

a despairing moan, Rebaa dragged herself forward in one last effort to escape. Her leg trailed behind her, leaving a streak of blood. She could not run, she could not even get up.

A pair of thickly booted feet stumped into view before Rebaa's face, blocking her path as her vision began to fade. The owner of the feet crouched down. Rebaa just had time to take in a broad face and a pair of black eyes staring impassively before the world turned dark and she knew no more.

A pale, red-headed giant was reaching for her, Juran's blood encrusting its fingers. She tried to run, but she could not. "Juran!" she cried. But he was not coming. He was dead. Helplessness washed over her as she faced death alone. Alone. The bloody fingers brushed her face—

Noooooo.

Behind the darkness of her eyelids, Rebaa's mind awoke from the nightmare, only to find waking was not an improvement. She hurt *everywhere.* Her muscles ached, her fingers and toes were searing, but the most prominent agony of all came from her right leg. Her wounds felt as though they were on *fire.* She tried to pull away, but a powerful grip closed around her knee and held her firm. Her eyes shot open.

The inside of a cave greeted her focusing vision, but it was not the cold, damp crag from which she had just escaped. The smooth walls glowed hot with the light of a fire, and the air smelled of furs and burning wood. That was all she could take in before the pain in her leg intensified, accompanied by the sound of a sizzling hiss. Rebaa shrieked, eyes watering as she scrabbled at the stony ground with her fingers, fighting to escape. Somebody was burning her. The sickly sweet scent of her own scorched flesh filled the space. Her empty stomach roiled, and she retched in agony and disgust.

"*Runuk,*" a deep voice barked as the unseen grip tightened further. Rebaa sobbed, fighting all the harder to get away from her captor. They were cooking her *alive.*

There came an impatient sigh, and the grip on her searing leg loosened. Rebaa kicked backwards and heard a satisfying grunt as her foot contacted with what she guessed to be her captor's hand. She could feel a large presence behind her, but she did not turn to look. She was loose and she would not make the mistake of hesitating a second time. Boosted on adrenaline, Rebaa scrambled away towards the mouth of the cave. She might not get far, but she sure as Ninmah would not give up without a fight. She tried to get her protesting legs under her to run.

"Stop."

Rebaa froze, shocked to hear a vocalisation she understood.

"Go. You die."

The words were not Ninkuraaja but thickly accented versions of those used by the Cro clans. Rebaa rolled over slowly and looked back. The light of a small fire burning in the centre of the cave seared her eyes. Rebaa blinked and a large silhouette sitting alone before the flames came into focus, thickset and powerful in appearance. Her vision adjusted further and a mass of vivid red hair was the first feature Rebaa noticed. It framed the head in a flaming halo and flowed in a tangled mass down the thick shoulders.

Rebaa recoiled, the memory of her mate's murderers filling her mind as her eyes darted to the face. Milky-pale skin stretched over coarse features and broad cheekbones. But the eyes were not the vivid blue she so dreaded. It was a black gaze that glittered from beneath a short but prominent brow.

The being was large but nowhere near as big as the giant, red-headed figures that haunted her nightmares. Despite the brutishness, the face was distinctly female. The stranger watched Rebaa carefully as a pair of gnarled hands folded away beneath the heavy, reddish-brown furs she wore.

Rebaa glanced down at her own grey-clad right leg. Her furs had been ripped away and the long claw marks that had slashed her smooth, red-gold skin were now sealed with ugly red and black burns. The pain of the searing continued to keep her teeth clenched, but she was no longer bleeding.

The shaggy head inclined towards the wounded limb. "Stop bad blood," was the halting explanation.

Rebaa remained poised, ready to flee at the slightest provocation. She had been healed, in a fashion which pointed to the fact that her captor must not intend to kill her.

Not yet.

Go. You die. She was unsure if that had been meant as a threat or a statement of fact. Rebaa reached out with her higher senses, probing the stranger's mind for signs of danger. She detected only curiosity over-shadowed by a great sadness. Rebaa shied away from that sadness. It was like a dark chasm inside the stranger's soul.

Rebaa's eyes flickered over the pale, brutish face again. Her voice croaked as she asked: "You're a Thal?"

The stranger frowned in confusion; the contraction of skin pronouncing an ugly burn mark that marred her brow just below the vivid hairline. She obviously knew some of the Cro language, but not much. Rebaa drew a steadying breath. The Cro opinion of these People had been one of brutish savages, quick to attack. If that was so, a misunderstanding here could mean her life. This creature was many times her strength and weight. To show she meant no offence, Rebaa gave the stranger a sense of the meaning straight into her mind.

The stranger blinked, her confusion clearing. "Yes. Thal. From-" she pointed upwards.

Unthinkingly, Rebaa followed her direction, frowning up at the stone ceiling until the Thal's actual meaning dawned on her.

"The north?" Rebaa guessed. From her scant knowledge of Thals, she knew they could survive in the harshest of lands inside the northern wastes where no other people could remain, hunting the giant beasts of the ice. Rebaa eyed the shaggy, long-haired furs of her unexpected companion. They bore no resemblance to the comparatively short-haired, grey wolf furs she wore. She had never seen such garments. "You're a long way from home," Rebaa commented, cocking her head as she conveyed her message both verbally and mentally.

The Thal woman shrugged. "Cold times get worse. People move south or die."

Rebaa shuddered. She couldn't deny the truth of that. "And where are your People?" She glanced around. This particular Thal may be more curious than murderous right now, but the same might not be said for the rest of her tribe.

The deep-set eyes grew shadowed. "No no. Lost."

"You're alone?"

The shaggy head inclined. "Like you."

Rebaa found herself unable to meet that sad and somehow all too knowing gaze. "Yes," she admitted. There was little point in lying. The Thal already knew she was without protection.

The silence stretched as each of them sank into their own separate thoughts. Rebaa re-assessed her chances of making it out alive if, like the bear, this Thal also decided she might

63

make a decent meal in these lean times. She remembered with mounting apprehension that some Peoples were not averse to the taste of human flesh. There were even some Cro clans who observed such rituals.

This woman had killed the bear single-handed. She was dangerous, and Rebaa could not guess at her purpose for carrying her all the way back to her lair other than as a potential food source. Perhaps she was still alive because Thal tradition dictated that sacrifices only be made when Ninsiku was at his zenith or some other such nonsense.

"Come." The Thal woman beckoned, breaking the mounting tension. "Fire. Warm."

The Thal gestured to the ground beside her next to the glowing beast. The dark gaze was hopeful. Rebaa tensed. The stranger was inviting her to come within arm's reach. *Does she take me for a fool?*

"Shalanaki!" Her companion held up her rough and empty hands. "You freezing in snow. Need warm."

She wasn't wrong. Rebaa could not feel her hands or her feet even inside their thick wrappings. The fire drew her like a moth. The promise of warmth almost overpowered her caution. But unlike the moth, she would not be burned by desire. Instead of moving towards the comfort, Rebaa edged towards the cave mouth. She stopped and cried out when the skin on her burned leg pulled and seared with the motion. Eyes watering, she twisted and clutched at her calf in agony.

Clucking her tongue, the red-headed woman rose to her feet. Rebaa cowered down as she passed by. Feeling around behind her, Rebaa found a loose rock and gripped it in her hand, readying herself to fight if needed. The Thal's every motion was slow and measured. It appeared she was trying not to

64

cause alarm with any sudden movements. She went straight to the cave entrance, and Rebaa's heart sank. The Thal was going to block her exit. But the stranger only reached outside and then returned with a great handful of snow. Keeping her eyes upon Rebaa's, conveying she meant no harm, she dumped the icy handful straight on to Rebaa's tortured flesh. Rebaa gasped in shock, then her breath rushed out in a great sigh of relief as her pain eased, numbed by the treatment.

"Thank you," she whispered in helpless gratitude, though she did not let go of her rock.

"I go." The Thal backed up again. She eyed the rock in Rebaa's fist. "You no trust. Wise."

Rebaa made no reply, lost once again whether the Thal meant she was wise to be cautious or wise not to trust her.

The other woman sighed in the face of her scrutiny. "I go out. You no rest with me here. Need fire more."

Nonplussed, Rebaa watched as the Thal turned and exited the cave in two long strides, leaving her alone. Rebaa's thoughts buzzed. She was more than a little bewildered by this turn of events. Careful of her wounded leg, Rebaa crawled to the cave entrance. The Thal's presence was disappearing into the night. Now might be her only chance to escape.

The shock of the night air took her breath. The cold ravaged her face, stealing the warmth from her skin as she peered out. Rebaa scuttled back into the embrace of the cave.

Go... You die....

She groaned. She was trapped here by injury and the inhospitable night as surely as if the Thal was still holding her leg in her mighty grip.

At least she was still alive. Her hand went to her round belly. They both were. It was more than she could have hoped for when the bear had held her tree bound. She would see to it that they remained that way for as long as she could.

Rebaa crawled back to the fireside, careful to keep part of her mind connected to the ebb and flow of the world outside, alert to an approach. A spear leaning against the nearest wall drew her eye. It was a less refined weapon than those Rebaa had become accustomed to seeing, but still deadly in appearance. It towered over her, and her fingers barely fit around the haft. She had never used a spear in her life, but she grabbed it all the same, feeling instantly more secure.

Thick furs were spread all around the burning tongues of the fire. Rebaa groaned again as she sank down upon them, this time in relief as her tense muscles melted; knowing comfort for the first time in days. The heat from the fire washed over her and her icy fingers and toes seared as one extreme met another. She endured it with a fierce pleasure.

There had been a time when fire had frightened her. It was a skill her own People did not possess. Out in these cold wastes, however, it was a blessing, a life giver. She stretched out her hands, only wanting to be nearer. Her hunger gnawed and her baby squirmed in protest. Rebaa quieted both. She would find a way to feed them somehow. At least now they were warm and may yet live long enough to see the dawn.

Lying down with her back to the fire, she faced the dark cave mouth, clutching the spear to her. There were markings carved into the stained haft. Rebaa occupied herself by studying their unfamiliar design, determined not to sleep. She must not let her guard down, even for an instant. But as the warmth spread through her body and the familiar sounds of a crackling fire comforted her mind, Rebaa's eyes drifted closed.

UNEXPECTED

* * *

8

Cold Trails

Eldrax's mind was ill at ease as he and his men laboured through the thick snow. The initial elation he had felt at Murzuk's death had waned in the time since they had left the summit of the escarpment. At first it had mattered little that he had not landed the killing blow himself. He had been rid of his Chief and gained control of the young warriors accompanying him with ease. But he was not fool enough to miss the traces of uncertainty on their downcast faces, and the glances shared between them when they thought he was not watching.

Being the strongest and most skilled fighter counted a lot towards the struggle for leadership, but it was not everything. By tradition, the position of chief could only be achieved in one of two ways. The first was when a worthy Challenger, supported by a united clan, defeated the previous leader in combat, the other was by gaining a dying Chief's blessing as his chosen successor. Eldrax was acutely aware that he had now failed to accomplish either of these.

If neither a successful Challenge nor blessing had been

achieved before the previous Chief's death, then the elders of the clan chose among the most worthy males and Eldrax knew it was not always the strongest who would achieve the honour.

If he was to hold on to power unchallenged, Eldrax must now prove himself indisputably greater than Murzuk had ever been. Gripping his spear, he lengthened his stride.

There was a faint grumble as the men protested at the increased momentum; Eldrax had already set a merciless pace in his desire to capture the witch. They had travelled light to poach the Black Wolf territory, and already their meagre rations were running low. There was very little to hunt in these hills, most of the herds had moved south for winter grazing. A couple of hares would not replenish their supplies for long.

Their growing doubt in his leadership only galvanised Eldrax's will. Claiming an enemy's mate symbolised ultimate victory in the eyes of all Cro. And Juran's was a prize above reckoning, a prize that Murzuk had always failed to gain for his own. Eldrax would not fail.

The rocky foothills closed in all around them as they travelled on the heels of their prey. It was easy to get lost in such a place, but Juran's mate had proven herself a fool. She had not even tried to conceal the tracks she had left in her wake; a dangerous mistake for one travelling alone. It made hunting her as easy as tracking a witless beast. Nevertheless, Eldrax knew what made life easy for him would also make it easy for others. His skin crawled with the need to catch her and make her his own before another did. Greater still was the risk that, alone and exposed, she would perish long before he could get to her.

They had travelled for less than a day when Eldrax's worst fears were realised and large lupine paw prints crossed those of his quarry.

Open mutterings of discontent broke out as his men read the tracks for themselves. They were all skilled hunters; it did not take them long to draw their own conclusions.

"The wolves got her." Eldrax heard Hanak echo his thoughts. "Murzuk was right. There was no way she would've survived this long alone. We've wasted our energy."

Eldrax roared out in his frustration and kicked viciously at the snow. No totem and no mate. The pathetic creature had not known how to take care of herself. Her stupidity had made him look foolish and sealed his defeat. He glared at Hanak, daring him to say more. He would fight all of them if he had to. To the gods with tradition.

"Chief Eldrax?" There was not an outward hint of mockery as the title slipped from Tanag's tongue, but it rankled all the same, blackening Eldrax's mood further. "I do not understand these tracks. What do you make of it?"

"What can't you understand?" Eldrax sneered as he stepped up to Hanak's brother.

The other man pointed. Eldrax followed his direction and saw the paw prints leading off into the snow. At first he could not figure out what was so complex about the trail. Then he saw a set of very familiar footprints intermingled with those of the wolves. His heart leaped. *So... not so pathetic after all.*

"Is she tracking the wolves?" Tanag asked incredulously. "Why would she do that?"

"No, fool, she's travelling *with* them."

"But-"

Eldrax did not have time to explain to this idiot. "Prepare

70

for a fight. The wolf pack has what we desire."

"But that pack is at least twice our number!" Hanak protested.

"And what of it? I never thought of you as a coward, Hanak." Eldrax's tone was mild, but Hanak would not mistake the dangerous undercurrent.

"My Chief," Tanag ventured. The other warrior's throat flashed when Eldrax turned his dark glare upon him, but forged on nevertheless. "Is one weakling woman worth such a risk?"

"Weakling woman?" Spinning on his heel, Eldrax grabbed Tanag by the scruff of his neck. With his other hand, he ripped aside the furs on his chest, exposing the scarred, mangled flesh to the other man. "Look well, boy! I should be dead, and yet here I stand as your Chief. To possess such a one, I would risk ten times your number! I *will* have that witch and when I do, no one will question that *we* were responsible for the Black Wolf's demise. We will be respected and feared from the Mountains of the Nine Gods to the shin'ar witch forests of the south!" He released Tanag with a rough shove. "Until we find her or her corpse, we will continue to hunt and if you dare question me again, Tanag, you will not live to see another dawn."

Fear and resentment settled over Tanag's face, but he fell silently back into line next to his brother. Retaking point, Eldrax led his men on in the wake of the wolves. This little trick with one of the most formidable predators in the land only proved her worth and his longing to possess her found new depths.

If she had thought a pack of wolves could protect her from him, she was mistaken, for he was more dangerous than they.

In fact, taking her from the heart of a pack would provide a refreshing diversion. The encounter with the monsters in the mountain forests had shaken his confidence more than he liked to admit. Winning a fight and taking the spoils that would come with it would go some way towards restoring his faith in his own power.

His buoyant mood carried him on for the latter half of the day, but he should have known better than to think that wolves would be the only challenge put before him. Eldrax cursed as the wind changed direction and took on a threatening chill. He knew what such signs foreshadowed, and it wasn't long before the clouds gathered in force overhead. As the hunting party struggled to find sufficient shelter for the night, the lowering sky released its load of snow upon the lands.

By the time Eldrax and his men awoke the next morning, a thick, blank covering had concealed the details of the landscape in a secretive layer for as far as the eye could see. The witch's trail was no more.

Incandescent, Eldrax lashed out with his spear, swinging it in an arc. His men took a nervous step back, but he ignored them. He had lost. There were pathways upon pathways leading in all directions through the hills and gullies and, without a trail, there was no way of knowing which direction his prey had taken. He could search for her until the seasons turned and still find no sign. Juran's mate had eluded him.

"My Chief." Eldrax snarled, furious that one coward had dared to draw his attention. It was Tanag who once again shifted under Eldrax's dark gaze. "What does it matter if we have lost the trail? If she survived the storm, then we already know where she will be headed."

"Do we now?" Eldrax lifted his spear and pressed the tip

against Tanag's chest. "This had better be good, Tanag."

The young warrior considered his words. "She is alone. She has no one to turn to. She knows what will happen if another Cro clan happens upon her. Worse if the Thals catch her. The only place she will ever be safe is with her own People. She's trying to reach her old forests. That means she'll go south. We only need to head her off before she reaches the safety of the trees."

Eldrax's eyes widened as the truth of Tanag's words hit him. The other warrior had weighed his prey's behaviour and gauged the next step like any expert hunter should. It frustrated Eldrax that he had not done so sooner. He was letting his desire cloud his judgement. Mulishly, he dropped the spear from Tanag's chest and heard the relief sigh pass from the other man's lips.

Turning the new insight over in his mind, he looked to the south. It would take her days to reach the southern forests and it would be a blessing from the cursed gods themselves if she made it there alive or without being captured. Time was running out, and they were heading in the wrong direction.

"We make for the southern plains," he commanded. "And no man is to rest until we get there."

* * *

9

Nen

When Rebaa awoke, she was warm. Too warm. Beads of sweat were rolling from her brow, and her damp hair clung to her hot neck. She groaned, trying to roll over and put some distance between herself and the fire. She had come too close to the flames in her sleep.

Dizziness swamped her as she moved, and Rebaa struggled to open her eyelids. She wished she hadn't. They scraped against her eyes, making them sting and water as the cave turned nauseatingly in her vision. She struggled to focus on the fire that was scalding her, but it was no longer lit, only the charred remains of the wood smouldered in the cool air. Yet still she burned. She rolled her eyes shut again, coughing dryly.

She was sick. Turning her senses inward, she could feel the fire radiating from her leg. The Thal's crude treatment had not been enough to purify her wounds. The bear's claws had cursed her blood. Rebaa whimpered as another wave of heat rolled through her body, and the ground lurched beneath her. She needed a healer. She needed her brother.

She felt rather than saw the shadow fall across her. Rebaa flinched and tried to move away, but her body would not obey her commands.

"Nagathe!" The word sounded like an expletive. Firm hands wound around her leg, and Rebaa struggled against the grip. "Runuk!"

Rebaa blinked. Red hair and brown furs blended together in her watering vision. She could make out a smudge of white which must have been the Thal woman's face. It was shaking back and forth.

"Bad blood." Rebaa heard her sigh.

Rebaa's head was pounding. She could not keep her eyes open, and the heat of her body was becoming unbearable. She started pulling at her furs, attempting to remove them from her flaming skin.

"Ahna!" Large rough hands grabbed at her own, halting their feeble quest to rid herself of the claustrophobic furs.

"Leave me!" Rebaa tried to bat the hands away. She had to heal herself.

"Ahna! Leave fur. Heat make better."

Rebaa ignored her. She tried to call on the energy of her body, but her control slipped away like water. She could not heal herself alone. Her vision faded in and out.

Cold water poured over her cracked lips. Rebaa sucked it greedily into her parched throat. She couldn't get enough; her thirst was insatiable. She drifted again.

She lost track of the passing of time as the fever took its toll. She existed in a half waking, half dreaming world. At times, she did not know where she really was and couldn't bring herself to care.

Sometimes she thought she heard a low voice chanting from

close by and saw what looked like the Thal woman crouched over her legs while waving a bunch of smouldering dead leaves. It mattered little. This dreaming world was preferable to reality. She didn't have the strength to fight any more. She was dying, and that knowledge came as a relief. She had done her best to fulfil her promise to Juran. Now it was time for peace. When the blackness washed over her again, she went with it willingly…

Rebaa shot upright, disoriented. The flickering stone walls of the Thal's cave were gone. Instead, the familiar hide-walls of home surrounded her. She was no longer in any pain, not even the pain of hunger plagued her stomach. She was warm and comfortable. Thick fur blankets tangled around her naked body. She blinked, and then—

"Rebaa?" Juran sat up beside her.

He was there. His grey eyes regarded her in mild concern as his long mane of dark auburn hair tumbled over his strong dark shoulders. She could feel the living warmth radiating from his skin.

"Oh!" Rebaa threw herself into his arms, burying her face in his bare chest. "I h-had a terrible dream." Her voice hitched. "There was a battle. You were dead. Everybody was dead. I was dying. Dying and I was completely alone."

"Shh," her mate soothed. "I'm here. You're safe."

Rebaa shook her head and pulled back to give him an accusing stare. "You left me. You went back to die and left me alone to save our child. But I couldn't…" The words tumbled out. "I couldn't do it! I can't survive without you. How could you leave me? How *could* you?" Furious, she beat her fists on his chest as the tears poured down her face.

Juran caught her wrists, halting her attack with little effort. "Rebaa. Rebaa." He repeated her name until she stopped struggling and looked him in the face. "*You*, who have lived through what none other of your People ever has, should know yourself better than that. Never once have you given up on anything in your life. You can and you *will* survive. Whether or not the gods wish it, you will save our child. I trust you to always keep him safe. You *always* find a way."

She shook her head vehemently, but Juran only pulled her back into his arms, kissing her forehead. "You need never be afraid, for I will never leave you."

Liar. She wanted so badly to believe him. *Liar.* "Please let me stay. I-I don't want to be alone anymore, there is so much pain. Please... I want to be with you." She rested her heavy head against his chest and let her eyes drift closed. She was finally at peace. All she had to do was let go...

"No," came the firm answer, startling her. "You must go back. Live and save our son. You promised me."

Tears spilled over her cheeks. "I can't."

"Yes, you can. *Survive* this, Rebaa."

"No." Stubborn, she tried to pull him closer...

"Survive!"

Her fingers came up against cold hard rock. Juran evaporated from between her arms as the fur-lined walls of her old home morphed back into the unforgiving rock of the cave. Rebaa screamed out loud as the full force of her loss washed over her anew. She pounded the empty ground with her fist. "NO! I can't. No. Liar!"

Gasping, Rebaa pressed her face into the furs beneath her body. Breathing deeply of their musty scent, she fought to regain the tenuous control she had struggled to maintain since losing Juran. Once she was sure she had pushed her emotions down far enough, she tried to get herself upright. Her arms shook even with that minor effort, and her head swam. Her throat felt parched; she needed water.

The cave was dim with pre-dawn light. Ninmah had not yet risen, and she was alone. There was no sign of the red-headed Thal. Rebaa remembered flashes of Red standing over her as she had battled the curse of the bear's claws. She couldn't decide now if she had imagined the whole thing in her weakness and delirium. It made no sense for a Thal to help her.

She swallowed, then gave a wracking cough as the motion irritated her dry throat. Water. Rebaa pushed herself to her feet. She swayed slightly as she fought to gain her equilibrium. Her wounded leg shook, but held under the barest weight as she stumbled to the cave entrance. In her hazing mind, she knew only one thing; she had to keep moving.

The outside world was still and silent. She was in the midranges of the foothills at the centre of a wide gully that swept down from the higher hills above. The cave in which she had resided was set into a hillock covered in dead grass and tumbled rocks. The landscape before her feet fell away into the vast southern plains far below. The cold pinched at her exposed flesh.

Rebaa grabbed a handful of snow and stuffed it in her mouth to quench her fierce thirst as her sluggish mind attempted to separate dreaming from reality. She needed to hurry; she needed to get out of these foothills and set out across the plains. Once she reached her home, she would be safe. Once she reached her home, the only threat would come from her own People.

Rebaa pushed away from the cave, struggling off through the snow toward the plains. She fought to keep focused. A thick yellowish haze that she couldn't be free of distorted everything. She kept her head low as she travelled, her higher senses focused on the surrounding landscape. Unlike her eyes, they were clear in their vision. But using her skills like this was getting harder the weaker she became. A hare vibrated in its nest, but no other signs of life could be detected. Her leg screamed in protest and she had to rest often, her body shaking from the punishment of moving.

The wind cut like a knife. It seemed to Rebaa that the icy gusts wanted to punish her for escaping from their deadly kiss, but they had blown the storm on towards the north and Ninmah's golden light spilled uninterrupted over the distant hills. Ninmah was no less forgiving than the wind and She stabbed mercilessly at Rebaa's flinching eyes. Despite the discomfort, the knowledge that she had lived to see the Golden Mother's spirit rise one more time gave Rebaa hope.

Keeping Ninmah's rising face on her left, Rebaa picked the easiest route through the slippery and twisting rocks. She searched for the barest sign of anything edible but saw only rocks, snow and bare, isolated trees. Rebaa swallowed down her growing fear. She would not last much longer without nourishment. She *would* find something. She had to believe it.

Juran's voice floated unbidden through her mind. *You will always find a way...* She blocked it out. She could not let herself think of him. She had to forget her hunger and what might be. All she could focus on was putting one foot in front of the other.

Ninmah was clear of the hills and riding at her zenith when Rebaa came to a halt. The winding path she had been following fell away before her in a dangerously steep slope. Her wounded right leg burned, threatening to give out with every step. She did not have the energy to spare to heal it; the act of standing alone was taking everything she had.

She limped one way and then another, searching for another path that would lead her on her way. She did not want to tackle the slippery slope in her current condition. She had to minimise the risk of further injury as much as she could.

Her search proved fruitless. Unless she gambled travelling further off course, hoping to find another way down, the treacherous slope was her only option. She was weakening. The slope was risky but to go off course looking for other ways was more so; time was not in her favour.

Gathering herself, Rebaa started down the path, leaning back to keep balanced. Beneath the snow, the ground shifted and rolled under her weight. A scree slope. She tested the ground with her toes before placing each foot, hanging on to fixed rocks and dead tree roots with her hands. She slipped and slid often, occasionally sliding a whole gut-wrenching body-length before she found purchase once more. Her breath came in quick gasps from the effort. Her palms were cut and stinging from holding on.

Reaching a tree root, Rebaa paused. The next handhold was out of range. Her good leg was braced beneath her. The only way to move was to trust herself to her wounded limb. Gingerly, she shifted her weight forward, stretching out for the tree branch that lay just out of reach.

Her leg gave way, crumpling beneath the strain as her weight shifted onto it. She could not re-balance herself. With a soft cry, Rebaa lunged for the branch but caught only air. She tumbled away, rolling over and over.

Curling in on herself to protect her baby, the dislodged stones pounded against her body as she fell. She hit the bottom in a heap, feeling the air whoosh out of her lungs on impact. Fighting for breath, she kept herself locked in a protective ball, closing her eyes tight as the shifting rocks and snow continued to slide down the slope, cascaded over her, hissing on all sides until it snuffed out the light.

Rebaa did not know how long it took for the landslide to stop, but when eventually the low rumble ceased, she was in total darkness. She shifted against the weight of the rocks and snow above and found to her relief that they moved easily; she wasn't trapped.

Having ascertained that she could escape the rocky blanket, she turned her senses to her unborn. Rebaa prayed thanks to Ninmah that he was unharmed. She tested her body, wincing as she felt the new bruises, but found nothing broken.

The rocks clattered away as Rebaa pushed herself into a sitting position. She felt a trickle start down her face and reached up. Her fingers came away bloody. A sharp stone had gashed her forehead, but a quick probe told her the wound wasn't deep. It could have been so much worse.

Rebaa heaved herself to her feet, only to collapse back to the rocks when she tried to take a step, her wounded leg giving way beneath her again. The strain of the descent had been too much to ask of the limb.

Ninmah, preserve me!

She just needed to rest, she told herself, sitting back amongst the rubble and resting her aching head against her knees; just a while. She tried to deny the knowledge that she was too weak, too wounded. The bear had sealed her doom. *Just a few moments...*

81

Shifting her head to the side, she stared into the near distance. Her roving eyes paused as she spied a pile of objects sitting on the snow beneath a tree. They held her attention because they were out of place in the mainly white and black landscape. A pile of nuts. Rebaa blinked, sure her hazing sight was playing tricks on her, but no matter how she tried to clear her vision, the nuts remained. *Could it be...?*

Rebaa crawled forward until she came close to the miracle. There appeared to be enough forage here for her to eat her fill and still take some with her for later. A gift from Ninmah Herself!

She halted a short distance away from the inviting shells. Though the nuts were plain before her, her spiralling thoughts could not comprehend how they had come to be there. Then her stomach snarled, and she decided she did not care. Throwing caution to the wind, Rebaa hauled herself upright and threw herself forward over the remaining distance, intent on swallowing the nuts down as fast as she could.

A sharp snap was her only warning. Something unseen tightened around her good ankle as she stepped forward and she was yanked off her feet. Her leg wrenched as she was pulled swiftly towards the sky. Between one thought and the next, Rebaa found herself dangling upside down, hanging from a branch in the tree.

The world spun as she swung around and around, and for a moment Rebaa was stunned. Blood dripped from the wound at her forehead and splashed onto the snow beneath her dangling hands. The weight of her pregnant belly pressed down on her chest. Fighting to draw breath, she twisted as best she could to see what grasped her ankle. A rope made of twisted skins snared her leg. Rebaa went cold.

No! Rebaa kicked as hard as she could at the rope that bound her. Her head felt as though it would explode. She struck at the knot, aiming for what she judged to be weak points, but the rope held.

Something nagged at the edges of her mind, but she ignored it, struggling to figure out the best way to escape. Spots danced behind her eyes, and she had to halt her exertions. She could not get a full breath. Her mind nagged again and, in her current stillness, she finally understood it for the warning that it was. Something was approaching, whispering across her awareness. It was a signature she knew well. Cro.

Abandoning all thought or caution, Rebaa twisted wildly. She would rather be dead than in their hands. *Ninmah, save me!*

The plea had no sooner crossed her mind when she was falling. One moment she was thrashing in an attempt to escape, the next she was on the ground with a soft bump. Rebaa didn't wait to question what had happened. She kicked the slackened rope from around her ankle and clawed away from the trap, dragging her wounded leg behind her.

She could hear the voices of the hunters now. The breeze swirled the sound in the air, making it impossible to tell which direction they were coming from. Throwing herself once more on Ninmah's grace, Rebaa turned south.

Powerful arms seized her from behind and dragged her back. A rough hand clamped over her mouth, blocking her scream before it could emerge.

"*Runuk!*" a familiar voice hissed in her ear.

In her shock, Rebaa stopped struggling. *Not a hallucination.* The Thal took advantage of her lack of resistance and dragged her backwards. One arm released her as they passed the tree, and a pale hand reached up to snap a thick branch from the boughs with little effort. The show of strength was frightening, but the Thal's hold, while denying any hope of escape, did not hurt her in the slightest.

With her free arm, Rebaa's captor brushed at the snow with the branch, eliminating their footprints as she continued to draw Rebaa swiftly backwards. They went no more than six paces before the Thal threw the branch away and ducked down beside an outcropping of rocks. There was a small opening at the bottom and the other woman shoved Rebaa into the tiny hole before squeezing down into the space beneath the jumble of stones beside her.

Her mouth released, Rebaa gulped at the air. While feeding her starved lungs, she stared wide-eyed at the red-haired being beside her. Black eyes stared back reproachfully. Rebaa opened her mouth to speak, but Red shook her fiery head and put her thick fingers to her own lips, indicating that Rebaa should be quiet.

The voices sounded again outside, much closer now. Rebaa dared to peer out of the small hole next to her rescuer and watched as the furred figures materialised out of the snow. Six tall Cro hunters, each bearing weapons. She could not recognise their totem from this distance, but she could see feathers dangling from their weapons and what looked like the mark of an eagle or a hawk. As they drew nearer, Rebaa felt the large body next to hers tense.

Intense bitterness that was not her own washed over Rebaa's senses as the Cro reached the tree. They had been hoping for a meal and returned only to find an empty, ruined trap.

Red's large, pale fingers twitched. "Evil men. Takers and killers!"

A shout went up from the hunters. A scuffle had broken out as each of the men tried to blame the other for the trap's failure. Rebaa was sure the fight would have continued, but a shouted order from an older man with grizzled grey hair stopped the antagonists short. The leader searched around, studying the area for a few brief moments, though it felt like an eternity to Rebaa. In the end, he gave another terse order and led his men back the way they had come with a frustrated gesture. Their dark forms and voices soon disappeared into the distance.

It was a few moments before Rebaa realised she had been holding her breath, and she released it in one long sigh. Muttering a few grumbled words that Rebaa did not understand, the Thal woman shrugged out from beneath their rocky shelter. Rebaa hesitated. There was no other way out of this bolt hole. It left her with no choice but to follow. As she hobbled to her feet, swaying on one leg, Rebaa waited in a daze to see what Red would do next. Running away was out of the question. She was at the other woman's mercy.

The vivid hair billowed in the stiff wind as the Thal returned to the tree and picked up the severed rope. She stared at it in disgust for a few moments before holding it out to Rebaa, pointing at it and shaking her head.

"What?" Rebaa had the sense that she was being scolded like an errant child for her foolishness. "H-how was I to know?"

"Cro trap. More careful." The rough voice was bitter as Red threw the offending rope out of sight. "Come."

Rebaa leaned away as the other woman approached with an outstretched hand. The coarse features fell in the face of her continued mistrust. Red raised both of her hands as she had on the night they had met.

85

"I no hurt. You foolish to leave cave. Sick all night. I look after. Come."

The scattered memories of the Thal sitting over her during the brief waking moments of her illness flashed through Rebaa's mind. It seemed they hadn't been hallucinations either. She paused, struggling to think, the haze in her mind only seeming to get heavier.

Taking advantage of her hesitation, Red took her elbow and Rebaa gave in. She took one step and her leg buckled from under her. With a reproachful cluck of her tongue, Red reached down and lifted Rebaa into her arms. She strode off, and Rebaa could not find it in herself to protest.

The Thal knew the range well; treading hidden paths and winding tunnels that Rebaa would never have found or dared to navigate on her own. They arrived back at the cave in half the time it had taken Rebaa to reach the Cro trap. The mouth opened up in the gathering shadows before them and then they were inside; the dimness pressing down on Rebaa's eyes once more. Red laid her back down upon the furs surrounding the fire pit at the centre of the cave.

Rebaa lay where she had been placed, too exhausted to do anything more. She lifted her heavy head to regard the stranger sitting across from her. Her irritated throat tickled, mouthfuls of snow had done nothing to quench her thirst.

Without a word, Red moved to her side and slipped one arm behind Rebaa's shoulders, supporting her as she pressed a skin to her parched lips. Cool water flowed over her tongue and soothed her painful throat. Rebaa drank greedily until the skin ran dry.

"Thank you." She wiped her wet lips and forced herself to remain still as a large, pale hand reached out to cover her brow.

The Thal woman nodded, satisfied.

"Curse pass. But still weak. Rest." Red moved away and began fussing about the fire, rebuilding the fuel from piles of wood stacked against the edges of the cave. She rekindled it using a couple of pieces of flint.

As she watched the Thal's activities, Rebaa could feel herself sliding back towards unconsciousness. She drowsed as Red moved about the cave, sometimes leaving, only to return moments later. The rebuilt fire crackled and spit as it devoured new wood. Warmth washed over her…

"Hungry?"

Rebaa jolted awake to the smell of cooking meat and spied the hunk of browned flesh spitted over the fire. Her mouth watered as her empty stomach growled. *Food.* Tears welled as she looked across the flames with desperate eyes, forgetting her suspicion in her need.

Red understood. She pulled the stick of sizzling meat from the fire. Using pieces of worn hide, she took hold of the flesh and tore a piece from it, handing the bounty to Rebaa. Rebaa snatched it from her fingers before the Thal could change her mind. She did not wait for it to cool; she sank her teeth into the scorched flesh, hardly feeling the pain when it burned her mouth.

Her protesting stomach eased with the first scalding swallow, but the single helping wasn't enough to slake her hunger. Her baby kicked. He was becoming more aware, his thoughts and feelings hazing against her own. It was nearly time for him to greet the world. Apprehension shot through her. She would need all her strength for that fast approaching ordeal. Meeting the black gaze across the fire, she held out her hands, pleading for more. The Thal gave it readily.

She was on her third ration and feeling much stronger when her strange companion gave a throaty laugh, coarse features alight with amusement. "He tried to eat you, now you eat him!"

Rebaa almost brought the contents of her stomach back up as the meaning of the Thal's words hit home. She was eating the *bear*. Juran had always known better than to draw attention to what went into her stomach. "Please, don't," she warned.

It surprised Rebaa when Red's expression lightened with understanding before becoming apologetic. "You Dryad? Wood sprite?"

Rebaa frowned. She had heard her people called many names since she had left her forest home. These were new.

"Ninkuraaja," she corrected.

"Nink—Ninku—" Her companion gave up. "Hard. You Dryads live in woods. Down." She pointed.

"South? Yes."

"Eat plants." She pointed at herself and then at her ear. *I hear*, Rebaa read the meaning. "Talk animals?"

Rebaa nodded. "In a way."

"You should not alone." The voice became reproachful. "You no know danger. Foolish to go near men."

"Then what were you doing there?" Rebaa demanded, irritation spiking in the face of her failure to do as Juran had asked. She did not need her short comings pointing out. She was Ninkuraaja, she was not meant for these Ninmah-forsaken places.

The Thal's expression closed and she shrugged evasively, rubbing at her scarred forehead with one hand.

Rebaa sighed, struggling to regain her temper. She had

been through so much, lost so much, but this woman had undeniably saved her life twice now. She did not deserve harsh words. "Thank you," she murmured across the fire. "If it wasn't for you, I would be dead."

Rebaa just wished she could figure out the reason for it. As the Furies got longer and harsher, the Peoples of the land had enough of a challenge looking after their own. Strangers could not be tolerated, and the weak were a burden that must perish in order for the strong to survive. She undoubtedly fell into both descriptions. "Thank you for saving my life."

Red's face brightened at her words, and she inclined her head in acceptance of the thanks. Rebaa dropped her gaze and stared down into the furs, brooding. She did not know how she was ever going to fulfil her promise to Juran.

"You wear clothes of Cro, not Dryad. They catch you? How escape?"

Rebaa grimaced. "It's a long story." She was not ready to relive her ordeal, and certainly not with a stranger. Her eyes were heavy again, fighting against her efforts to keep them open. She couldn't seem to shake this bone weary tiredness, but her stomach was full at last and she was so warm...

"Baby." Red patted her own belly. "Soon."

The words ripped the exhaustion aside. Instantly alert, Rebaa struggled to keep her face impassive as her heart thudded against her ribs. This Thal might have saved her life, but if she ever guessed at the baby's Forbidden heritage, then Rebaa was as good as dead. "Yes," she hedged. She hoped her companion would simply assume the father was Ninkuraaja and not pry further.

"Should not be alone." Red repeated.

No, she should not. Rebaa pressed her lips together to

suppress her longing for the one she would never see again. Her anger burned anew. It was his fault. He should have fled with her. She might have been able to heal him. A tear slipped down her cheek. She brushed it away angrily. He had made his choice. He had abandoned her and burdened her with an impossible promise to save their Forbidden child.

A Forbidden child.

Rebaa shivered. She did not know what that could mean and her panic rose in the face of the unknown; this terrible consequence of the love between herself and Juran.

It took an effort to calm her breathing. There was nothing she could do about it now. The sin had been committed.

"Not alone now," Red comforted. "You safe here."

Safe? Rebaa blinked at the words. The concept had become alien to her. But now that she was no longer trying to escape, she found the Thal's energy to be strangely... comforting. Perhaps it was because Red was the only human companion of any sort she had known since her adopted family had been ripped from her. The aching weariness washed over her anew. "Why are you helping me?" she gathered the will to ask.

"I alone, too," came the melancholy reply. "Long time."

It surprised Rebaa when her heart went out to the lonely creature opposite her. She stared into the dark eyes peering across the flickering flames, searching for any sign of deception, an ulterior motive. She could sense nothing more than a heartfelt sincerity and a deep, desperate desire for companionship, however brief. The last of Rebaa's misgivings crumbled. She lay down upon the soft furs lining the fire, accepting the offered comforts at last. Her foolish attempt to continue her journey in her current state had failed miserably. She needed to regain her health and allow her wounds the chance to heal. She decided to trust her new companion. For now.

"What's your name?" Rebaa asked as she slid back towards the unconsciousness her body so craved. If she was going to remain, she could hardly keep thinking of the Thal woman as *Red*.

"Nen."

Rebaa smiled. "Rebaa."

10

Need

Rebaa woke to the thick, smoky scent of a dying fire. She had slept fitfully, her dreams filled with monsters and death. She remembered waking often with a cry on her lips, clutching her chest against the raw, aching loss. Each time she had found Nen sitting close by, watching her with that sad, knowing expression. She had been singing. The songs she sang were strange to Rebaa but had possessed a soothing power that had returned her to sleep each time, wrapping her in a cocoon of comfort.

Rebaa sat up and saw that light was streaming in through the cave entrance. Ninmah had already risen. She glanced around and found that she was alone. Her twice saviour was nowhere to be seen. Cautiously, she got to her feet. Although her sleep had been far from peaceful, she felt more rested and stronger than she had done in days. Her mind was clear at last; blackness no longer threatened on the edge of her vision, begging to drag her to its depths. A full belly had worked its magic.

Rebaa realised it was the first time she had seen the cave

with the light of Ninmah shining in from outside, and she moved to study this unexpected haven. The cave walls were cold and grey now that the fire had burned low, but the space had the feel of having been lived in for a long time. The ground had been cleared of loose rocks, all of which were piled neatly against the curving walls along with the stored firewood. Her attention was drawn upwards where dozens of reliefs had been scratched into the grey stone.

Putting as much weight on her healing leg as she dared, Rebaa moved to take a closer look. There were many pictures of animals, of birds, bears, lions, horses, all crudely drawn, but still very distinct. There were yet more creatures that she did not even recognise. Giant beasts with great curving tusks sprouting from under a long snake-like limb, located where most ordinary animals' noses would be. The most numerous of the creations, however, were the images of people. Rebaa ran her fingers over the rocks, feeling the nuances beneath her skin.

Each picture was telling its own story. Here was a scratching of a settlement. All the people appeared happy and at peace. There, Rebaa could make out a hunting scene. The people had brought down one of the tusked beasts. She moved along the wall, trailing her fingertips, fascinated. Some images were not so happy. One illustrated a battle between Peoples. Many were dead. Rebaa shied away from that image. The memories it conjured were far too fresh and horrific for her to face. She did not need any more nightmares.

The next picture was that of a woman holding a baby. Rebaa lingered over that one, her hands unconsciously moving to her belly where her own baby dozed beneath her heart. Somehow the image was sad. Rebaa turned around and saw another picture where a figure appeared to be fleeing from others who were hurling stones. She only caught a glimpse, however, before a throaty voice called from behind her.

"Wake?"

Rebaa flinched and spun to face the cave entrance. Nen had appeared and was observing her. Rebaa couldn't help but notice that her large hands were covered in red gore. Rebaa shuddered, but nodded in answer.

"Come, help," Nen beckoned with her bloody fingers. The Thal turned and disappeared back into the white landscape beyond without waiting for an answer. Rebaa paused for a moment before deciding to follow. Her leg still hurt; the skin over the burns was stiff and pulled with every motion. She gritted her teeth, promising herself that she would get some more snow on it.

The sky overhead was clear and as Rebaa stepped out of the dim cave, the gleaming light bouncing off the endless white blinded her. Rebaa blinked rapidly until her eyes adjusted. The cold, fresh air and the scent of snow were sharp in her nostrils, contrasting against the warm mustiness of the cave.

A flash like flame against the snow caught her attention. Nen was walking away down the slope to her right, her bright hair billowing in the breeze as she moved steady and surefooted over the rocks. Rebaa started after her but quickly found it wasn't as easy as the Thal woman made it look with two good legs. The rocks were treacherous underfoot and progress was slow. Rebaa tested every step. When she finally reached their destination, she took one look and had to brace herself against a wave of nausea.

Nen was standing beside the body of the massive cave bear. She had skinned it and carved sizeable chunks of meat from its bones. The scent of blood and raw flesh overpowered all else. With a sharpened flint knife, Nen began carving out another huge hunk of flesh from the grisly carcass. She glanced up at Rebaa in grim satisfaction.

"Good kill." She indicated the stacks of meat cuts and the great, shaggy pelt piled behind her. "Buried body in snow till chance to cut. Some scavengers found but still plenty food." Nen swiped at a wayward strand of hair, unconsciously smearing more blood across her coarse face.

Rebaa forced a smile, trying her best to appear pleased when all she really wanted to do was turn away. Nen hefted the heavy pelt.

"Help?" she asked again.

Suppressing a shudder, Rebaa moved down to help drag the hideous thing back up the hill to the cave. It was still dripping with sinew and fat and was a dead weight, slimy beneath her fingers. It smelled awful; of sickly sweet death. It was all Rebaa could do to bring herself to even touch it. The only thought that kept her there was the need to repay Nen for coming to her aid and providing her with warmth and safety while she recovered from her wounds. It was the least she could do.

Even so, she did not feel she was of that much help as they tugged and heaved the bloody hide over the rocks. Nen was a full head and shoulders taller than Rebaa and massively strong.

Rebaa was winded when they finally reached the mouth of the cave. She collapsed to the hard floor; her legs refusing to hold her any longer. Her wounds burned. She reached outside and doused them with another handful of snow.

Nen's face was alight with amusement. "Dryad not strong."

Rebaa chuckled ruefully; the sound was strange to her ears.

"I guess Dryads don't need to be, Nen." She tapped her temple. "We have different means."

Nen frowned then. "Not good for you." She patted her stomach. "Rest. I carry." She stooped to pick up a smooth stone that fitted comfortably into her large hand. One curving edge was knapped into a sharp blade. "You strip." Nen pointed to the fur.

She wanted her to prepare and clean the skin. Rebaa wrinkled her nose. As Juran's mate, she had avoided such mundane chores as much as was allowed. When first adopted into the Black Wolf clan, she had only partaken enough to prevent the other women of the tribe from resenting her more than they already did.

Rebaa had soon proven her worth in other ways. Her skills as a Ninkuraaja healer were average when compared to her brother's, but to the Cro, they were miraculous. After saving a few infants from illness and hunters from gorings, the other women had cheerfully taken up her workload, finally accepting this outsider in the coveted position as Juran's chief mate.

She would be allowed no such favours now. Rebaa clenched her teeth together and braced herself for an unpleasant morning.

By the time Nen had finished bringing the rest of the bear meat up the hill, Rebaa was covered to her aching elbows in greasy fat, stray hair, and stinking bits of flesh. The pelt was finally clean and ready for further preparation, however.

Nen spied the revulsion that must have been showing on her face, for a smile touched her wide lips. She was shoving most of the meat supply into a snowbank outside to keep it fresh. Nen had stripped the hunks of what little fat had been on the bear, keeping only the lean meat, further lengthening its life. Once she had finished, Nen picked up the cleaned bear-skin and beckoned to Rebaa with one gnarled hand. Her lips were still twitching with suppressed mirth at Rebaa's disgruntled expression as she walked back out into the snow without a word.

Rebaa guessed she was supposed to follow. Keeping her stinking arms as far away from her furs as possible, she limped after her companion, wondering what other unpleasantness could lie in wait.

Nen had set out in the opposite direction from the bear, slinging its skin across her broad shoulders as she trudged through the snow across the wide, shallow gully. The pelt was much lighter now that Rebaa had stripped it of its wet, excess flesh, and Nen managed the load on her own.

Following along, Rebaa glanced into the crisp blue sky above. The spirit of Ninmah was now at Her zenith. Not that Rebaa would know that from the bitterness of the air. Ninmah's golden face shone down, but Her touch held little warmth. Rebaa frowned. Ninmah's power of late had waned, letting Her evil mate's cold times increase.

Long ago when she was but a child, Rebaa's People had started to whisper, whisper that Ninsiku was finally winning the battle for dominance in the heavens. Rebaa shuddered. From the beginning of time, her forefathers had passed down the teaching that if Ninsiku ever grew more powerful than Ninmah, it would signal the end of the world. The end of the Ninkuraaja and their way of life.

Feeling the weakness of Ninmah's light now, Rebaa hoped her ancestors' teachings were wrong. It wouldn't have been the first thing her People had been wrong about, after all. She tried to ignore the plume of her breath freezing in the midday air. She already had enough to worry about.

Climbing up the steep slope that marked the edge of the gully in which Nen's cave resided, the sound of running water pulled Rebaa from her thoughts. Nen paused and pointed ahead over the top of an outcropping of rocks. The sound was coming from there. Rebaa joined her new companion and looked down into the adjoining valley. A sparkling mountain stream was rushing before her on its way to the southern plain below. Nen motioned to her, mimicking washing her arms.

"Ah," Rebaa said, understanding. "Thank you." She picked her way over the icy rocks down to the tumbling water. She shuddered at the thought of bathing in the freezing flow, but anything was better than putting up with the mess she was in right now. Sinking to her knees, Rebaa dipped her arms into the stream, almost crying out at the shock of it. She washed as quickly as she could, scrubbing away the greasy fat and hairs sticking to her skin.

Once her hands were clean, Rebaa splashed her face and neck, slicking away the stiff, sweaty traces of her fever. Catching sight of her rippling reflection in the stream's silky surface, she paused. It had been a while since she had seen her own face, and she flinched now at the sight of it. It was not the reflection she remembered. Hunger had sharpened the smooth roundness of her cheeks, and her eyes... her eyes were nothing more than sunken pits, hollowed out by grief and despair. Their deep indigo colouring stood stark against her pale red-gold skin.

Rebaa found she could not maintain her own gaze. She searched for some familiarity, some sign that she was still herself. Her fingers went to her forehead, where a deep purple marking curled delicately between her brows. A short vertical line stood at the centre of two tapering coils, which branched off in opposite directions, finishing over her eyebrows. It was the symbol of Ninmah, bestowed upon her at birth, claiming her as part of the Ninkuraaja People.

She paused, taking comfort from this familiar sign of self, before her fingers travelled upwards to brush against other markings standing just below her dark hairline. These marks were red, a dotted pattern proclaiming her as a Cro Chief's mate. Her fingers lingered. She remembered as if it were yesterday the pain she had felt as the old ashipu medicine woman of the clan had pierced her skin with the ritual dyes, a pain overshadowed by the glowing pride she had seen on Juran's face as she took her place by his side.

Tears pricked at her eyes and she dropped her hand, striking out at the water to shatter the image.

Busy as she had been with her own ministrations, Nen did not seem to notice that Rebaa's violent shivering was not all to do with the cold. Catching hold of her, Nen rubbed Rebaa's arms to restore warmth. The physical contact surprised Rebaa, but found she could not protest. Nen's hands were rough but pleasantly warm, unaffected by the harsh temperature of the water.

"What now?" Rebaa asked, eyeing the bear pelt Nen had brought along.

"Cold water," Nen pointed to the stream. "Make last." Rebaa nodded her understanding. The skin needed to be preserved before it festered. Nen soaked the hide in the running water, then pulled it out, and between them they wrang it dry. They repeated the process again and again, and the shadows were lengthening before Nen decided she was satisfied.

Rebaa let Nen lead her back to the cave as Ninmah set below the horizon. Her very bones ached from the exertions of the day's work, still recovering as she was from the effects of her fever. She welcomed the numbing exhaustion the physical work had brought. Perhaps tonight she would be spared from dreaming.

Back inside the cave, she sank onto the furs by the fire and watched distantly as Nen spread the half prepared skin flat on the cold ground before turning to build the flames back up.

Weary as she was, Rebaa knew she must force her mind to sort through her situation. This respite could not last. Nen had been a blessing she had not foreseen, but who knew how long the Thal woman would tolerate the burden of another mouth to feed. As soon as her strength returned, she would have to face the journey she had set for herself again.

"What think?" Nen asked.

Rebaa opened her half-closed eyes. Her concern must have shown on her face. "I'm thinking about how I'm going to get back to my People."

A flicker of disappointment clouded Nen's features. "You should not be alone," she admonished. "Why not stay here until cold time over? After baby born. Then find People. Too danger to travel now."

Rebaa blinked in surprise. Her preconceptions about Thals were taking a dramatic shift. She glanced around. The thought of spending the rest of the Fury inside this cosy cave was a serious temptation. And she liked this Thal woman, she decided. Nen had a good spirit. The pending birth of her son, however, made such an agreement impossible. Nen could not see her baby. *That* was something she knew the Thal woman would not tolerate. She would need to be long gone before then.

"I'm sorry, Nen," she said. "I must leave. I have to get back."

"Father waiting?" Nen guessed.

No, Rebaa thought, *father dead.* Instead, she nodded, glad that Nen had jumped to that mistaken conclusion. "Yes, father waiting," she lied. "I must get back to him."

Nen accepted her words sadly. "Stay just bit longer? Until recover? Still tire easily and leg hurt." Her eyes were hopeful; the longing in them tugged at Rebaa's heart.

Rebaa plucked at the soft fur upon which she sat, undecided. Her leg was stronger than Nen could guess. Now that she was better nourished, Rebaa had been directing what extra energy she had at her wounds over the course of the day; encouraging the flesh to knit and become whole.

She flexed it, wincing against the dull ache. It still wasn't fully healed, and she knew she would always walk with a limp from now on. The bear had done more than tear skin; he had damaged muscle. She reasoned that in its current half-healed state, the leg would most likely give out again under serious strain.

That was what she told herself. But deep down, Rebaa knew she was clutching at any excuse to put off the impossible danger she faced for a short while more. She scolded herself for such weakness, but found she could not resist the temptation of just a few more warm nights.

"That would be nice." She gave in to Nen's offer with a soft smile, then cocked her head. Nen seemed so desperate for company, desperate enough to want to share her scarce food supply with a complete stranger who had little to offer in return. Rebaa could not understand why such a compassionate being was living in isolation. "Why are you not with your own People, Nen?" she asked. "Why are you alone?"

Rebaa watched the glittering light in the deep-set eyes grow dim. The open soul she had been becoming accustomed to closed with a snap. "Not talk." Nen shook her large head evasively.

Rebaa guessed her meaning from the reluctance she could feel in the Thal woman's heart. "You don't want to talk about it?"

Nen shook her head again, avoiding her gaze. Tears formed in the gentle eyes and Rebaa realised with a sharp pang that she had dug into old wounds. The depth of the guilt she felt was surprising. She had only just met Nen and yet somehow she had already come to care for her; she couldn't help it. Rebaa hesitated for a moment, then moved to Nen's side and took her hand, wanting to offer what comfort she could. She wasn't the only one battling painful memories, it seemed.

Nen blinked in surprise at the contact, then stifled a sob and leaned against her. As they drew comfort from one another, Rebaa made her decision. She could not fix whatever Nen had suffered anymore than she could fix her own past, but she could do this one thing for the woman who had saved her life.

"Don't worry, Nen. I will stay for a little while longer." She smiled. "I cannot refuse the offer of a friend." As the word left her mouth, a sense of *rightness* flooded her.

Nen's eyes lit up, her pain forgotten. "Friend?"

Rebaa smiled sadly back at her. "Yes, Nen. Friend."

* * *

11

Power

The southern plains stretched away before Eldrax's feet. His heart sang in response to the open wilderness ahead of him, the lands of his birth. It had taken a day of travel, but they had finally shaken off the rocky foothills of the Mountains.

The wind was stronger over the open ground. He drew it through his nose as if to scent his prey on the icy breeze. Out here, the witch would have nowhere to hide. If he drove his men hard, they would catch her the next time Utu rose above the horizon. Juran's mate might have had a few days head start on them, but she was small and physically inferior. Eldrax's men were neither.

With a brusque order, he set off at a ground-covering lope. This was a hunt he was impatient to bring to conclusion. The fear that another clan might claim his prize before he could catch up to her was now a constant gnaw in his gut.

His men kept pace with him easily. Their moods had lifted now that they were free of the hills. As they travelled, Eldrax kept a sharp eye on the landscape, searching for any clue of his quarry's passing, but the fresh snowfall from two nights past had obscured all tracks as thoroughly on the plains as it had in the hills. Eldrax tightened his wide lips. The new, soft snow cover also gave the added hindrance of dragging at their feet, making the going hard. But Eldrax surmised that anything that slowed them would also slow the witch.

The day had dawned clear. Utu rose overhead, warming the air as she climbed. Sweat dripped from Eldrax's pale brow, but he did not slacken the pace he had set. Despite the improved visibility, he could not yet see to the horizon as the plain undulated gently, reducing his view to the next approaching rise.

Eldrax ran his men until Utu was high in the sky. He kept his breathing deep and even; he wasn't winded yet, but he was growing hungry. Their rations had run out two days ago. He did not wish to stop, but Eldrax knew they would soon weaken if he did not feed his men soon. If another clan had taken his desire, then he needed his men at full strength. He glanced back at the now distant foothills behind, pleased with the ground he had covered, and decided it was time to divert the hunt to a different target.

"Tanag." Since his insightful suggestion of the witch's direction, Eldrax had made him his unspoken second. "Go on ahead and find something suitable to eat."

Tanag obeyed without question, peeling away from the group. Eldrax prayed to the gods that the search would not take long. His patience with this delay was thin at best.

The gods must have been listening, because Utu had not risen much higher when Tanag returned. "There is a herd of gazelle to the east, my Chief."

My Chief. A shiver of pleasure rolled down Eldrax's spine.

The uplift in his men's mood seemed to have eased their doubt in him remaining as leader. "Good." Gazelle might not be his favourite meat, but he would suffer it this time. He lifted his hand to the wind, assessing its direction. West. The elements were with them.

The beasts were in a shallow valley, digging in the snow, searching for the meagre grazing beneath. Low rocky rises surrounded them on all sides. Eldrax snorted from where he lay hidden downwind. In their need for food, the senseless beasts had made themselves ridiculously easy targets. He assessed the situation and then gave his orders, making the sign for his men to fan out. As Murzuk's second, he had led many hunts, and he knew what to do to catch swift prey such as this. They would surround the small herd on the ridges, blocking escape and ensuring a greater chance of one of their spears striking true.

As the last of the hunters moved into position, the lead buck caught their scent on the breeze. Too late. Eldrax had enacted his plan to perfection, trapping the herd. In a panic, they ran. A smile curled over Eldrax's lips as he watched their desperate attempt to escape him, waiting for just the right moment...

"Now!"

As one, his men rose from their positions and let their spears fly at the fleeing herd. Two fell to the attack. The rest of the beasts did not look back as they bolted away into the snow, interested only in saving their own hides. Eldrax let them go; he did not have time for sport, and two beasts were more than enough to feed his men. A joyous crow went up around him in celebration of the successful hunt.

Eldrax savoured the jubilation in his effective leadership for a couple of moments before snapping: "Silence! Take what we need and do it quickly."

In the open, the scent of blood would carry on the breeze. Wolves or worse, would home in on their position before long. Much as he enjoyed a fight, Eldrax was conscious of Utu's warmth slipping over his skin and how, with each passing moment, the witch that he sought was getting further away from him, perhaps even now running into the arms of another. Wrestling with other predators was not a luxury he could permit.

"Hurry!" He barked when he felt his men were not working fast enough in butchering their kills. He did not permit time for a fire and so they ate the fresh meat raw. The men obeyed willingly enough, so he feigned ignorance to the fresh resentment on their tired faces. They had been hoping for a respite long enough at least to have a cooked meal.

It still took too long. By the time Eldrax had cleaned his bloody fingers and mouth in the snow, the light was already waning; the winter days were frustratingly short. Eldrax shrugged off the inconvenience. They would travel through the night. He wanted Juran's witch in his clutches by dawn.

On they ran, through the shadows, cursing often in the blackness as their reckless speed caused them to trip on hidden rocks and stumble over pitfalls. Dawn broke to find them weary with frustrations simmering to the breaking point, and there was still no sign of their quarry. As the light of a new day spilled over the snowy ground, empty-handed, Eldrax was forced to rest his failing men.

The faintest tug of desperation took a hold in his heart. His men dared not look him in the eye for fear of rousing his temper. He knew he was losing their respect again, but he would not show weakness and give up. He *would* succeed, even if he had to chase her all the way to her accursed forests. Driving his men harder than even he thought he could, Eldrax led them in pursuit of Juran's mate for another day and night. He even risked thinning their forces by sending out scouts to extend their ground coverage.

Eldrax mounted a low rise as dawn broke over their third day of pursuit over the plains and peered into the distance, sure that this time she had to be within his sight.

Nothing.

No small vulnerable form struggling through the snow in a last desperate bid to get home. Eldrax paced back and forth as his rage and frustration crawled beneath his skin, fighting for release. He was not used to being thwarted by his prey. There was no way in the Nine Gods that she could have travelled this fast. His mind worked furiously. If she had not come this way, then where could the witch have gone? Juran had no friends among the other Cro clans. Tanag had been right. She had nowhere to go other than back to her own People.

"You have failed, Eldrax."

Cold shock rocked through Eldrax as he faced Hanak. The other warrior stood before him without deference. The remaining men whom he had not sent forth to scout were gathering behind Hanak in support.

"We have chased this witch on your command for four days and nights since finding the Black Wolf, and we are no closer to catching her now than we were when the pursuit began. It is madness! A *true* Chief would see that."

"I *am* your true Chief!" Eldrax raised his spear. The men behind Hanak shifted apprehensively, but their faces were determined as they gripped their own weapons.

"Eldrax!"

Haleb, the youngest of the group, came running over the snow from the scouting mission Eldrax had sent him on. The boy's blue eyes were bright with excitement. "There is another camp to the west. I did not approach for the risk of being caught, but I believe it to be the Eagle Clan."

Eldrax's heart leaped. He turned away from Hanak and his rebellious supporters to face the direction Haleb had indicated. The barest movement on the horizon caught Eldrax's roving gaze, curling and insubstantial. His lips peeled back from his teeth.

The telltale column of smoke grew in his vision until it was all he could see. *There* was the answer to the mystery of the missing witch. He ground his jaws together. Attacking would mean starting a blood feud with a clan that had never been a threat, but Eldrax did not have to think twice about his next move.

The Eagle clan was not powerful. They had numbered a little over fifteen on their spy's last count; nothing more than a troublesome gnat to the Hunting Bear clan. The elderly Chief Rikal had made a grave mistake meddling in Eldrax's affairs. Eldrax would slaughter every man, woman, and child in that camp until he possessed what was rightfully his.

He paced before his men, searching each of their features in turn. "The Eagle clan has taken freely what you have shed your sweat for!" He jabbed at the horizon with his spear and their faces turned towards the distant column of smoke. The bitterness that they had directed at him just moments ago now flickered toward the rival clan.

"Murzuk might have allowed others to take what was ours, but *I* will not! I am your Chief now and I will ensure that no one will take what is ours again!"

Murmurs of agreement went up from the gathered men as they raised their spears in support.

"The name of the Hunting Bear Clan will be feared from the Mountains of the Nine Gods to the Witch Forests of the south! Distinguish yourselves as warriors and I will grace you with the spoils of battle!"

"Red Bear!" His men crowed. "The Red Bear!" Their hands tightened upon their weapons, faces bathed in fierce determination, all qualms regarding Eldrax's right to lead forgotten with the promise of blood and glory.

"Follow me, brothers!" He could almost feel them vibrate at his back, and his lips twisted in pleasure. The possibility that any of them might be dead by nightfall had not crossed their bloodthirsty minds. They were young, powerful, invulnerable. Eldrax relished their eagerness; these were exactly the men he needed to fulfil his vision of a ruling clan.

If, by the end of battle, a corpse littering the ground did belong to one of the Hunting Bear Clan, he hoped it was Hunak's.

A sentry from the Eagle clan was the first hapless creature they came upon. The boy was inexperienced, and Eldrax was on him before he could raise an alert. Clamping his hard hand over the boy's mouth, he snapped his neck in one sharp motion and let the body fall boneless to the ground, the sound of the snow muffling the impact. The enemy's camp was now only a short distance away, on the other side of a low rise.

Eldrax felt his blood sing with the promise of battle. Motioning his men to keep low, he inched forward on his belly until he could look down on his unsuspecting victims. Their own scout's last report had been accurate. The Eagle clan was small. They had erected five hide shelters around a large campfire where a haunch of ox was roasting, tended to by the women and a handful of excited children. Eldrax felt his mouth water at the scent of cooking meat. He was hungry. This raid would provide more than one spoil.

He could not see the witch, but that meant little. She was most likely hidden away inside Rikal's own shelter. Two warriors stood guarding the largest construction, confirming his suspicions. No Chief he knew would waste time before Claiming such a gift. Rikal was probably at her right now, hoping for half-witch spawn of his own. Eldrax's jealously spiked, and he laid his plans. The Eagle men were at ease. They did not suspect what was to come.

"Slaughter all of their warriors first and take what women you desire," he hissed to his followers. "But if anyone harms the witch, I will hang your guts out for the scavengers."

He gave no more instruction before he bellowed the attack, throwing himself from concealment and charging over the hill.

"The Red Bear!" The terror on the faces of his adversaries as they screeched his warrior name was the sweetest of thrills. "The Red Bear!"

Eldrax pounded towards his enemies, the rest of his men moving to flank him. Two young Eagle warriors rushed forward to meet him in a brash move, but their fear and inexperience betrayed them; their hands trembled upon their weapons.

Eldrax's hands were steady as his spear swept theirs aside. He twisted, driving the sharpened tip between the ribs of one defender before the adolescent could recover his balance, digging in just far enough to kill. In the same motion, he brought the butt up to block the desperate swipe the other made at his back.

Pulling the flint tip from the body of the dying warrior, Eldrax pivoted so fast that the second defender did not have time to get his spear back in position. Eldrax's weapon found the soft flesh of his throat. He laughed as his victim's blood decorated him in the colours of battle.

"The Red Bear!" This time the cry went up from his own men as they revelled in the strength of their leader.

The rest of the Eagle warriors were not so rash. They had formed into a defensive formation against Eldrax's raiders. Tanag was leading the Hunting Bear warriors in making quick strikes, testing the capabilities of the rival clan, trying to taunt them into breaking rank.

Eldrax's eyes flickered to the largest tent again. He did not have time to play these games. The taste of blood burned on his tongue and his muscles quivered until he could no longer contain the killer instinct clawing to be free. Roaring like an enraged bear, he charged the line of Eagle warriors, aiming right for the centre.

He was only one man, but the Eagle men quailed at the sight of his twisting face, unnerved by the savage magic that drove him. He crashed headlong into their lines. The fools tried to put up a miserable defence. Howling, Eldrax parried their blows and threw himself bodily at them. The force of his blow sent several warriors to the ground. Eldrax barely felt the impact. Laughing and bellowing, he fought off all their attempts to bring him down.

A few Eagle men landed glancing blows, but the stings only fuelled Eldrax's blood rage. He had killed three men before the rest of the Hunting Bear warriors came to his support, swarming through the chaos he had created. It was too easy!

Yanking his spear free of yet another kill, Eldrax twisted, searching for another, but found only bodies littering the ground. Panting and dripping in blood, he turned this way and that, muscles twitching with the need for further release. His own men kept to a safe distance.

"What are your orders, mighty Red Bear?" Tanag's voice cut through the pounding in his ears. It took Eldrax a few moments to comprehend the words. *The witch!* His blood rage drained away, and Eldrax lowered his spear. All the Eagle warriors lay dead or dying in the snow at his feet. Only one of his own men had fallen. Unfortunately, it was not Hanak. Hanak crouched by the fallen man's side, muttering a blessing as he closed the staring eyes before spearing a moaning Eagle warrior in vengeance, hastening his demise.

There was one face Eldrax did not see, however.

"Find me their Chief."

Tanag bounded away at once with another of the men.

Beyond the scene of the battle, the women of the Eagle clan were cowering on the ground, wailing in their grief and begging for mercy. Eldrax turned away disdainfully.

"We have him!" Tanag called only moments later as he dragged the Eagle Chief before Eldrax. "We found him trying to escape, he was near his shelter."

Rikal's tawny eyes were wild with fear and rage. "Why have you done this? We were no threat to you! You had no right to attack us!"

Eldrax flicked his spear, bringing the dripping tip up under the defeated Chief's jaw. "I have come for what is mine. Hand her over to me now and nobody else need die."

Rikal spat in his face. The Hunting Bear men gasped, but Eldrax only wiped at the spittle mixing with the blood staining his face. He gave a laugh, then plunged the tip of his spear into the meat of the other Chief's leg, watching him fall to the ground at his feet. It was a mere flesh wound. He did not want the other Chief dead; not yet. He needed Rikal to understand who was the power here before he finished him.

"Search the shelters!" He ordered his men. "Once she is turned over to me, your reward is these." He gestured to the grovelling women. His men dived into the shelters. More shrieks of terror rose as they uncovered those who had attempted to hide from the initial wave of slaughter.

"No!" Rikal cried as two of Eldrax's men entered his tent. One warrior emerged with a sandy-haired Thal woman. Eldrax narrowed his eyes at the sight of her. He *despised* Thal women. The second warrior reappeared carrying an infant boy whose hair matched the Thal's perfectly. The boy struggled and kicked against his captor.

"He's a strong one!" Tanag gasped as the boy's heel connected sharply with his midsection.

Witnessing the capture of his mate and son, Rikal diminished, his shoulders sagging in defeat. "What do you want?" he asked, as the rest of Eldrax's men completed their search of the Eagle camp.

Empty-handed, Hanak approached, uncharacteristically nervous. "We can find no sign of the witch," he muttered close to Eldrax's ear. "She is not here."

Ice slipped through Eldrax's gut. He could feel the eyes of his men weighing heavily upon him.

No! He would not accept failure. Rikal had that witch and he was going to take her from him no matter whose blood he had to spill.

"Where *is* she?" Spittle flew into Rikal's proud face. "The witch from the shin'ar forests. Where have you hidden her?"

"I do not know what you mean! Have you lost your mind? You know as well as I that no witch other than the one belonging to the Black Wolf has ever survived beyond the forests."

Eldrax's mouth twisted as he lifted his chin. "The Black Wolf are no more, Rikal, *I* slaughtered every man, woman and child in their camp!" Eldrax had the satisfaction of seeing firsthand the shock that rippled over the other Chief's face at this news. "Juran's witch eluded me, but by our lore, she rightfully belongs to me now. She would have passed this way attempting to rejoin her People, so stop *lying* and tell me what you know!"

"I-I can't! I have seen no witch!"

"Bring her." Eldrax jabbed a finger at the Thal woman his men had dragged from Rikal's tent and parted the furs at his waist. To take another Chief's mate before him was the ultimate insult. "Hold her down for me."

The Thal woman screamed and lashed out, fighting her captors.

"Wait!" a high voice shouted over the noise of Rikal's fighting mate, but Eldrax did not heed it. His focus was now completely on the woman. It took three of his men to subdue her. Despite his aversion to Thal women, Eldrax felt his arousal peak. He would enjoy dominating such a creature. Perhaps he would keep her alive long enough to bear children for him.

"*Wait!*" the voice cried again. Irked, Eldrax's eyes flickered over to a young man. The scant whiskers on his chin and the cracking of his voice suggested he was just leaving boyhood. He had survived the assault by cowering with the women. He stood now despite the best efforts of the woman who must be his mother to drag him back down. "Two days ago I went with the hunters to set traps in the foothills of the Mountains."

Ah! This sounded more like what he wanted to hear. Eldrax turned his focus from the woman his men were holding for him and gave the boy his full attention. He did not back away from Rikal's mate, however, keeping his threat present. "And?"

"One trap, it was sprung, but the rope was cut clean through. Whatever that trap caught... it was no animal."

"Another clan stole your kill, maybe?" Eldrax drawled.

Rikal shook his head and broke in. "We are the only clan within days of here. My hunters also spoke of strange tracks, small tracks, like those of a child wandering alone. They left the area quickly because no child could be alone so far from a tribe. They suspected unlucky spirits. But," his voice became pleading, "if what you say about the Black Wolf is true, it's possible the trap was sprung by the quarry you seek. That is all I know, I swear on all the gods—"

Eldrax's men shifted unhappily, rebellion rekindling in their eyes. If Rikal's scout was correct, the witch was still in the foothills of the Mountains and they had been led on a blind hunt. Tanag drifted completely out of Eldrax's line of sight.

Feeling like a cornered animal, Eldrax snarled and, before anyone could draw breath, he had the tip of his flint knife pressing into the other Chief's neck. "The gods abandoned us long ago, Rikal!" he spat. "What I say *is* true. The Black Wolf are dead by my hand. *I* am the power in these lands now. All that you see belongs to—"

Eldrax's threat was cut short as a spear seared past his ear. It passed so close that the tip sliced his cheek. Crying out, he whirled, ready to gut the man who had dared to strike him.

"You make one more move and you are dead, *boy*."

The blood drained from Eldrax's face as he froze, knife in hand. The figure of a man was standing before him, his familiar blue eyes glinting like shards of ice.

"*Murzuk?*" It was Eldrax's turn to believe in unlucky spirits. He took an involuntary step back, shaking his head in an attempt to clear the terrible vision, but the old leader of the Hunting Bear clan remained, a mere ten paces away, with three other men at his back. Rannac was among them. The older warrior still had his spear arm extended, an expression of disgust on his face as he surveyed the bloody destruction around him.

For a moment, nobody moved as Eldrax struggled to comprehend this turn of events. Then the wind bit at the fresh wound on his cheek, the pain convincing him of the reality of what he saw. Rannac had thrown the weapon that had wounded him; Eldrax knew of no other who possessed such precision. His fingers twitched upon his own spear.

"Chief Eldrax!" One of his men, who had not witnessed the unexpected arrival, bounded up. He stopped short, paling when he saw Murzuk, risen from the dead.

"*Chief* Eldrax, eh?" Murzuk's living breath curled in the air before him. "The gods, boy, you have been busy."

"I thought you dead," Eldrax growled between his teeth.

"Obviously not. I am sorry to disappoint you, boy. Despite your best efforts, I still live. It was not easy to escape those beasts, I'll admit, but the gods were watching over me when you so kindly threw me into their path. In the confusion, I eluded them, and I have been trailing you ever since. You are not safe to be left alone yet." His blue eyes scanned the decimated camp.

116

"You made a grave mistake in returning, Murzuk." Eldrax set his feet. This time there would be no mistakes. Power had suited him, and he was not about to give it up. Murzuk only had three men at his back. Ten warriors had followed Eldrax across the plains, and nine remained. He outnumbered his old Chief three to one. Lifting his chin, he looked to the men flanking him, then pointed with his spear, motioning for them to move against Murzuk and his inferior band. "Kill them."

The men did not move. They stood, exchanging glances, looking between Murzuk and Eldrax. Hanak went so far as to drop his spear and fold his arms.

Murzuk barked a laugh and swaggered towards Eldrax. "They will not obey you, *boy*! I thought I'd taught you the lore better than that. They may support a Challenger only if they think me no longer fit to lead them, and I have never yet given reason to doubt. *You*, on the other hand, have driven your men half to death on some futile chase across the plains. I doubt very much they'll fight to put you in my position now, do you, young *pup*?" He closed the remaining distance and backhanded Eldrax to the ground.

Eldrax tasted blood in his mouth as the iciness of the snow shocked his exposed skin. He fought to rise, only to find himself on the business end of three spears pointing directly at his heart. He halted. No matter what Murzuk claimed, Eldrax was no fool. He tempered the murderous anger thrilling through his veins and forced himself to lie still.

He locked eyes with Murzuk as he spat the blood from his mouth, assessing his next move. There was no mercy in the blue gaze of the old Hunting Bear Chief. Eldrax was under no illusion that Murzuk would order his men to drive their spears down through his heart if he so much as twitched a finger the wrong way. His coup had failed and his life hung in the balance.

The only way to survive and live to fight another day was to submit. More than that, he had to give Murzuk a good reason to let him live. And quickly.

He lowered his eyes with an effort. The words almost stuck in his throat. "Forgive my foolish Challenge and spare me, my Chief. I... beg you, take this defeat of a rival clan and their spoils in exchange for my life. I claim it in your honour."

Murzuk snorted, unimpressed.

"A pitiful offering for such a transgression," Eldrax acknowledged swiftly as the spear tips pressed closer, "which is why, as a further gift, I have also found for you the location of Juran's mate. She lives still, in the foothills of the Mountains." He pointed to the trembling teenager still clutching at the hand of his half-Thal mother. "Rikal's scout knows her last position. I intended to find her and claim her for our clan, then none can dispute that it was *we* who destroyed Juran and the Black Wolf."

Murzuk blinked as he divined the meaning behind Eldrax's words, and a slow smile spread over his dark face. "You always were a cunning one, I'll give you that." He gestured to his warriors. "Let him up." The spears withdrew, but as Eldrax rose to his knees, Murzuk flicked his own weapon up under Eldrax's chin, pressing it to his jugular. "Just know, if you ever cross me again, boy, I will not hesitate. This time I was simply repaying the favour." His gaze roved over the remains of the Eagle clan. "Now, what to do with this mess."

"Chief Murzuk." Rannac's voice cut in. "We should keep this boy." He indicated Rikal's sandy-haired infant son. "I like the look of him. He will make a powerful hunter and warrior."

The boy's Thal mother screamed her protest from the ground but was silenced by the men still holding her. Murzuk nodded his ascent to his loyal favourite and, dropping his spear from Eldrax's neck, moved to stand before Rikal.

Eldrax rubbed at his throat. Now that Murzuk had released him from his scrutiny, he let his submissive demeanour dissolve and his face twisted into a mask of hatred as he glared at the older man's back.

"I will let you keep your life, Rikal, but your infant will grow to be Hunting Bear." Murzuk spoke. "I also claim the boy who can lead me to the witch. If he serves me well, I will give him a place in my clan. If he attempts to deceive me, he will die painfully by my hand." With that ruling, he turned, gesturing to Rannac and five of the strongest men from the remaining Hunting Bear warriors. Eldrax was quick to notice that he was not among their number. It was the first time he had not been chosen for a hunt since he had learned to wield a spear.

"Take all the rations that you can carry and return with me to the Mountains." Murzuk ordered his selected few. "I will claim Juran's mate for myself. The Hunting Bear are now the rulers of this land."

"*I* am coming with you!" Eldrax protested. "I am the one—"

Murzuk's spear was under his jaw again. "You will go home, boy. I want to seek the witch, not have to be constantly watching my back for your knife. Go back to the clan and stay there until I return."

Eldrax bared his teeth, but with the sharpened tip of Murzuk's spear biting into his skin, he swallowed back his protest. He *would* live to fight another day. Murzuk's men began stripping the Eagle camp of anything of value. Furs, weapons, the carcass roasting over the fire was butchered bare, leaving nothing of use. The Eagle women still cowering on the ground whimpered, clutching their hungry children close.

"What shall I do with these?" Eldrax indicated Rikal and the snivelling women.

"Keep the boy for Rannac and any women the men deem of worth. The gods know they should get something for their efforts. Leave the rest to the plain's mercy."

Eldrax watched as Murzuk then grabbed the Eagle scout by the scruff of the neck and dragged him away.

"No, Yatal!" Another of the women grabbed the mother as she tried to keep hold of her son.

The wind whistled mournfully through the silent camp as Murzuk and his followers disappeared into the distance. A violent trembling began at Eldrax's fingertips, spreading to the rest of his body. Only Murzuk's presence and the threat of death had kept his fury in check. Now it unleashed, and he flew into a fit of rage.

The gods must truly be against him to have allowed Murzuk to live. Howling like a wounded animal, he rounded on Rikal; he who had witnessed his humiliation and cut his throat. As the life drained from the Eagle Chief's eyes, Eldrax savagely took his mate before him. They would *all* see his power. They would *see.*

As the woman's screams and sobs heightened his pleasure, he vowed to regain everything he had just lost. Soon he would take all that Murzuk had, just as he was now taking all Rikal had. Next time, there would be no mistake. Eldrax savoured the thought and, as his pleasure peaked, he imagined the entire time that it was Juran's mate he was Claiming for his own.

POWER

***

12

Stories

"You need to learn hunt."

The hunk of bear meat stilled half way to Rebaa's mouth as her appetite evaporated. She looked up at Nen, askance.

Nen pressed her lips together in a firm line. She reached out and grabbed her spear from where it leaned against the cave wall. "If you going to leave, then you learn how to survive alone. I teach you."

"But... I can't," Rebaa protested, forgetting her breakfast altogether. "I'm Ninkuraa. We do not harm the Children of the Great Spirit. I *can't*."

"Then you die. Baby die. What more important?"

The words cut off the protest building in Rebaa's throat.

"Come." Nen strode out of the cave without giving her a further chance to think. Rebaa swallowed her last mouthful and hurried out after her friend. Nen was already testing the air in the morning light when she caught up, checking the direction of the wind. She appraised Rebaa for a moment. "Start small. We go down."

Rebaa's stomach churned as she followed in Nen's wake. Her thoughts tangled as their exchange echoed through her mind.

I can't.

Then you die. Baby die. What more important?

Nen had struck where she was most vulnerable, leaving her reeling. In a decision between her baby's life and the tenets of her People, could there be a choice? She had already sacrificed so much of what it meant to be Ninkuraaja; her baby's very existence broke the most sacred of all lores. Although that scared her more than anything, what did she have left but him? If she ever lost him...

As the initial shock of what Nen was proposing wore off, Rebaa's resolve hardened. *Survive...* Juran's voice echoed in her mind. Nen was right. If she did not do this, then she would not survive on her journey and she would lose her only reason to keep on fighting. She had to do what she must.

Reaching a relatively flat surface, Nen singled out a particular tree. Rebaa got the impression it was a frequent destination for her friend. Deep scars pitted the trunk.

Nen moved to a distance of twenty long paces. Raising the spear, she twisted around and let it fly at the tree. It embedded itself unerringly in the centre of the trunk with a dull thud. Rebaa flinched at the sound, imagining the weapon striking into the heart of a Child of the Great Spirit, and her newly found resolve trembled.

Nevertheless, she could not help but be impressed by Nen's prowess. After all, this was the talent that had saved her life. She gave a low whistle of admiration. "You are very skilled."

Nen beamed and held the spear out to Rebaa. "Try."

Rebaa gritted her teeth and took hold of the offered haft. She doubted she would have the strength to throw it, much less hit the tree. Her predictions proved embarrassingly accurate. Rebaa drew back her arm as far as it could go while supporting the heavy weapon, then launched it forward with all of her might. The spear clattered to the ground just one pace from her own toes.

A wheezing sound started up behind her. Rebaa turned to see Nen vibrating with the effort of trying to keep her laughter in.

"Yes, very funny," Rebaa said.

Nen did not respond. Giving up on her effort to hold her amusement in check, she sat down with a thump on a rock, barking laughter coughing from her throat as she wiped at her streaming eyes.

"Stop laughing at me!"

This only made Nen laugh harder, and Rebaa found she couldn't hold on to her annoyance as her own lips started twitching in response. "I suppose that was rather pathetic."

Regaining a modicum of control, Nen heaved herself to her feet. As the last fits of laughter hitched from her chest, she patted Rebaa on the shoulder and stooped to pick up the spear.

"Like this." Nen demonstrated the proper posture, displayed how her fingers curled around the haft just so, and then let the weapon fly. The tip thudded unerringly into the tree once more.

Rebaa again murmured her appreciation of the skilful display. "I doubt even a Cro warrior could be more accurate."

Any lingering mirth melted from Nen's face. She ducked her head to hide her eyes and handed the spear back to Rebaa. "Try gain."

Rebaa did so, attempting to emulate Nen's skill, but after

several tries, her throws still came up woefully short. It wasn't a question of skill. She simply lacked both the strength and the stature. When her arm grew tired from trying, she threw the spear down in frustration and buried her face in her hands.

"I can't do it!" She could try all she liked. She was not built to survive out here! In that moment of defeat, all she wanted was to be home and out of this world of savagery.

A gentle hand squeezed her shoulder. Nen picked up the spear. "Spear not for you," she said. "Show you another way."

Huh. Rebaa wallowed in her self-pity. She was sure that whatever Nen came up with, the result would be the same. Failure. She would not bother arguing, however, her friend would see that her efforts were useless soon enough.

They returned to the cave and while Rebaa watched mulishly, Nen sliced several long, narrow strips of hide from the bearskin, scraping the fur away as she did so. She showed Rebaa how to twist them together to make two thin, strong ropes, one slightly longer than the other. Next, she selected a stick from her wood pile and snapped it in two.

Rebaa's heart still felt like a stone in her chest, but she watched as Nen took a piece of flint and carefully carved the two halves, notching one and cutting the end of the other so that it hooked snugly into the notch of its partner. Last of all, Nen whittled the tip of the notched stick into a sharp point. Rebaa couldn't help but envy her competence in everything she did.

Satisfied with her work, Nen slung the ropes over her shoulder and headed back out into the open. Despite wanting nothing more than to curl into a ball of misery, Rebaa followed once more. They travelled east for most of the morning. Nen was surveying the ground as they went, scanning for tracks

125

among the sparse trees, then moving away with a look of disgust when her search came up empty. She asked nothing of Rebaa, and Rebaa was happy to keep to her morose melancholy as she followed behind.

Ninmah was high above as they walked along a path hemmed in by prominent ridges. Rebaa had become so lost in her own self-pity that she had ceased to notice her surroundings and failed to follow her companion when Nen suddenly changed direction, taking a lower fork in the path. She was startled from the mire of her thoughts when Nen grabbed her elbow.

"No go that way!"

Shocked by Nen's unusually harsh tone, Rebaa looked ahead at the trail she had started to wander along. It branched left, winding on until it reached a cliff face and continued, clinging inoffensively to the sides of the steep slope. She frowned, failing to see the danger.

"Stop using that path. Look." Her friend pointed towards the top of the cliff, looming high above the trail. Rebaa could see that ice and snow had cracked the crown. "Last storm weakened. Could slide any time. Sweep everything away." Nen made a swiping motion with her hand and then pointed to where the slope disappeared below the path. Rebaa shuddered. She could not see the bottom.

"Always remember when get to this point: take lower path."

Shaken by her own carelessness, Rebaa followed Nen with more care until they came to a small copse of trees and went inside. Ducking through the low branches, the Thal woman studied the snow covered ground. This time she appeared satisfied by what she found. "To make trap work, put where animals go most." Nen pointed to a trail of rabbit footprints crisscrossing through the trees; well-worn routes in the snow.

Taking the notched stick, Nen drove the sharpened end deep into the ground close to the roots of a young tree before tying one end of the shortest rope around its hooked partner. "Hold." She passed the ropes to Rebaa. Reaching up, Nen caught the tip of the tall sapling and bent it down towards the ground. She motioned to Rebaa, pointing at the free end of the short rope. Rebaa handed it to her, and she tied it securely around the top of the stooping tree.

"Make sure knot strong," Nen instructed. She untied the knot and did it a second time, but more slowly, so Rebaa could take in how she did it. Keeping the tension on the straining tree, Nen hooked the stick tied to the other end of the short rope into its notched partner driven into the ground. Carefully, she let go. The locked sticks held the tree down. Nen nodded in approval.

"Now make noose to catch animal."

Rebaa swallowed as Nen took the other rope from her reluctant hands. Deft as ever, she quickly made a loop out of the twisted length.

"See?" Nen demonstrated how her knot allowed the noose to draw tight.

Rebaa nodded once as Nen tied her noose to the hooked stick attached to the tree. It was exactly the same trap that she herself had fallen victim to only a few days before. Only this one was much smaller.

"Thal no make traps like this," Nen explained. "Small game no satisfy Thal. But this Cro trick do for you."

"What now?" Rebaa asked.

"Wait." And she moved off, sinking down into the snow out of sight from the trap. Rebaa followed Nen to her concealed

127

spot and sat down next to her, getting as comfortable as possible as the moments slipped away. By and by she realised Nen was eyeing her speculatively.

"What is it?" She asked.

Nen motioned she should keep her voice down, then asked on a breath, "Know where animals are?"

Rebaa did know. At the back of her mind, she could feel the birds roosting in the branches above, the sleepy presence of the trees below their clutching claws, she sensed the rabbit family sheltering underground, blissfully unaware of the trap that awaited them on their daily route. She cringed. "Yes," she said. "Yes, I know where they are."

Nen picked up on her reluctance. "Still no happy hunting."

Rebaa shook her head. To survive with Juran she had had no choice in taking the flesh of animals to sustain herself, but it had been a blessing to her that it was not a Cro woman's place to join the men on the hunt. Not seeing the act of killing had allowed her to close out what she was having to do to survive. Now Juran, his hunters and even the other women were gone and she could not be afforded the same luxury.

"How?" Nen's whisper drew Rebaa from her spiralling thoughts. Her friend's face was eager now.

Rebaa frowned, confused. "How...?"

"How you know where animals? How talk them?"

Rebaa's brows rose. This was going to be difficult to explain, but it didn't appear that they would be going anywhere for a while, and so she gathered her thoughts. "When the blessed Ninmah came from the skies to create our People, She made us with the essence of KI, the Great Spirit himself, and Gifted us with a sacred awareness of him."

"Great Spirit?"

Rebaa's voice grew more hushed. "KI is the very life force of the earth. He exists in every plant, every creature, a great and powerful energy that guides all life. Ninmah's Gift means that my People can influence and use the energy. Ninmah made us a part of the Great Spirit. I can hear him in the wind, in the water, in the murmurings of the animals. They are his Children, the vassals of his wisdom, and it is they who preserve his balance. Ninmah tasked my People to learn from them all."

Rebaa realised she had got rather carried away in her passion, and she wasn't sure how much her companion had followed. She marvelled at the strangeness of her current situation, telling of her People's origins while sitting with a creature whom those very People would consider an abomination.

Nen frowned as she processed Rebaa's words. "Then... why not talk bear? Tell not hunt?"

"I tried." Rebaa rubbed tiredly at her face. "Sometimes the will of the Great One is just too powerful. The bear is a Child tasked by the Great Spirit to weed out the sick and the weak. It is his purpose as a hunter and it is not my place to interfere with that."

Nen frowned, but accepted slowly. Rebaa was sure she did not fully understand. It mattered little. It was impossible to explain Seeing to someone who was Blind.

"*Your* task now." Nen's eyes brightened. "*You* become hunter of Great Spirit."

She broke off when a snapping noise and a shriek of distress broke the stillness. Rebaa flinched as the animal's panic washed over her senses. Nen was out of hiding in a flash, running towards their trapped quarry as Rebaa followed.

A rabbit was dangling by its leg from the top of the tree, which had sprung back into place the moment the rabbit had disturbed the noose. A sick feeling filled the pit of Rebaa's stomach as she watched the hapless creature kick and fight for its life.

A soft rasp told her that Nen had drawn a flint knife as she moved towards the trapped rabbit, intent on slicing its throat. Rebaa knew that was a scene she could not bear to witness.

"No!" She grabbed Nen's arm. "Let me."

Nen appeared confused at Rebaa's sudden eagerness to finish the rabbit herself, but held the knife out willingly. "Yes, need to learn quick. You do."

Grimacing, Rebaa pushed the knife away and stepped towards the squealing rabbit. Its terror filled her heart. Tears slid down her face as she reached up and gently took hold of its soft neck.

Rebaa gasped as the sensations doubled in strength upon contact, and her own right leg throbbed as though it too was broken. Struggling not to lose herself in the rabbit's emotions, Rebaa stretched out with her own.

The rabbit's body became a mere extension of hers. She tuned her awareness to the rush of his blood, the sharp zings of pain and panic firing through his muscles, the pounding of his heart against his ribs. Using her latent healing abilities, she numbed the creature's pain, soothing the stinging messages rushing through his fragile body. Within moments, the rabbit grew still under her hand; its wide, liquid eyes fixing upon her.

Shhh, sleep now. While holding his pain at bay, Rebaa filled his mind with an irresistible sense of calm. The eyes drifted closed. Slumbering, he did not even feel it when she stopped

130

his heart. The vibration of life fell silent under Rebaa's fingers and the body fell limp.

"I'm sorry," she murmured. "Go now with the Spirit, little one."

Rebaa dashed away her tears and loosed the dead rabbit from its cruel bonds. Nen stepped aside in amazement and not a small amount of fear as Rebaa walked past her, cradling the creature she had killed with a single touch.

Without a word, Nen gathered the trap, and they set off for home. All the way back to the cave, Rebaa fought against the revulsion at what she had just done. *Survival, survival,* she chanted to herself. She pressed her lips together to hold back the sadness and regret.

She wondered just how Ninkuraaja she really was anymore. She had violated too many things that were sacred to her People in the name of survival. Taking the life of a Child of the Great Spirit had been the last bond to break. She hoped with all her heart that Ninmah could forgive her and understand. Her baby chose that moment to kick inside her, and another tear escaped her control.

There were some things she was certain would never be forgiven or understood.

It was dark by the time they reached the cover of their cave. Nen stoked the fire back to life, giving Rebaa space as she laid the rabbit on the ground and stared numbly at it. A bag of fur, muscle, and bone. That was all it was. No life remained. Fur. Muscle. Bone. Rebaa kept this firmly in her mind as she grabbed one of Nen's flint knives and cleaned the carcass. She could not let herself dwell on what she had done.

By the time she had finished, the fire had grown hot enough to cook the meat. Nen spitted the rabbit and held it over the flames until it browned and blistered. They ate quietly. Rebaa still did not feel like speaking, and Nen seemed to understand her need to work through the thoughts in her head.

Only when they had finished their meal did the Thal woman rise and squeeze Rebaa's shoulder. "Know hard to go against teaching of People but you learn well. Keep you and baby alive."

One corner of Rebaa's mouth lifted in response, but she let it drop again as soon as Nen left the cave. Rebaa's son rolled over inside her, elbowing for room, causing her to wince and her anxiety to spike. If only Nen knew just how far she had gone against the gods' teachings. If she did, she was sure her friend would not be so sanguine. Bearing a Forbidden child of two Peoples was punishable by death; a curse not to be suffered lest it evoke the wrath of the gods. Rebaa dug the heels of her hands into her eyes. Couldn't she have at least been permitted to preserve one small part of her soul? She stared listlessly at the bones of the rabbit. It seemed the answer was no.

Her eyes grew heavy, but she did not want to sleep. The horrors of her nightmares, which melted into the dark corners of the cave each morning at Ninmah's first light, were there lurking in the shadows, awaiting the first sign of weakness. Rebaa felt suddenly cold, despite the glowing of the fire.

The sound of singing floated in from outside and tugged at her. Keeping the heavy fur blanket wrapped around her shoulders, Rebaa got up and crept out into the night. Nen was sitting on a jumble of rocks, her face upturned towards the dark sky as she sang. This nightly habit seemed to be a custom of Nen's. Rebaa usually allowed Nen her privacy, preferring to remain in the cave's warmth, but she could no longer bear the solitude. Choosing a rock, she sat close beside her friend, taking comfort from her steady presence. Nen fell silent.

"No sleep?" she asked in a hushed voice, her deep eyes shadowed in the darkness.

"No." Rebaa shivered. It was so cold out here, beyond the protection of the cave. The smell of frost was strong on the crisp air. "I don't want to dream."

"Talk?" Nen offered.

Rebaa shook her head in one quick motion. She did not want to put words to the horror she had witnessed or the loss she had experienced. If she tried to speak, the thin walls she had built around her emotions since she had lost Juran would crumble. She had to keep them at bay. And she certainly could not confide in Nen about the desperate fears she carried for her baby.

"*Shalanaki*," Nen murmured.

Rebaa cocked her head. She had noticed Nen use the word several times since they had met. It was the first word she had ever heard her speak. "What does *shalanaki* mean?" she asked.

Nen shrugged her shoulders. "Thal use as greeting and parting. Means close like 'peace.'"

Rebaa smiled. "That's nice." The silence of the night pressed in on her. She wanted to ask more questions to keep Nen talking. Her friend's voice kept her many sorrows and fears in check. "What were you singing about?"

Nen blinked. "I sing praise to Eron. Ask him to forgive and watch over."

"Eron?"

"Great being," said Nen. "Like your Ninmah, came down from sky and made the Thal People." She tilted her face towards the blackness with its many burning spirits. She waved her hand against the endless purplish line that glowed

133

through the middle. "Came here following sacred Sky Path. Gave People life."

Rebaa followed Nen's gaze into the vastness above. "Yes," she whispered. "Our most holy came from the skies at the beginning of time to create the Ninkuraaja People and teach us how to be one with the Great Spirit and his Children."

Nen's face brightened. "Maybe Ninmah one of Eron sisters from the sky?"

Rebaa smiled. "Maybe. Does Eron guide your People still?"

Nen shook her head. "Left us. Our spirit men say Eron took to sky when we fail his teaching and went to live alone in forbidden Mountain. We not see him. Do not know where to find. He ignore us. We anger him. Your People anger Ninmah?"

Rebaa folded her arms against her chest. *I have*, she wanted to say, but to do so would raise too many questions. "No, I don't think so, but she had to leave us, too. Our teachings say that her mate, Ninsiku, grew jealous of my People and sought to destroy us out of spite. He brought about the Great Fury that nearly killed us all. Ninmah fought him and she was forced to leave us lest their battle destroy the world. She dragged Ninsiku with her and imprisoned him in the sky. She remains there also, guarding against his return as she watches over us, continuing to give us life. She is the great Golden Mother of the Day Sky."

Rebaa shuddered and pointed to the silver eye staring balefully from the far horizon. "The night is Ninsiku's, his spirit trapped forever in that great eye. He watches us in the darkness, ready to expose the unwary. He and Ninmah are doomed to chase each other through the heavens until the end of time, holding each other in balance. Heat and cold. Day and night. It is said if Ninmah ever falters, if she ever falls to her mate, the cold times that come will last longer than even the Great Fury and our People will cease to be. Only Ninmah's power protects our way of life and keeps us safe from our enemies."

Watching the bitter landscape rolling out before her, the fear of the previous days crept back into Rebaa's heart. "I am afraid, Nen. Afraid that that time is already upon us. The Furies grow longer and our enemies, the children of Ninsiku, grow bolder. My People are weakening. Our forests are dying." She stared helplessly up at the sky. "Maybe our time has come."

Nen reached out and engulfed Rebaa's hand in her own. "My People grow weak, too. Cro get stronger. Eron not protect us. I sing for his return along the Sky Path. Save People." She smiled sadly. "He not answer yet. Maybe our time come, too."

Grimly, Rebaa returned her friend's grip and for a while they both stared up into the endless night, Thal and Ninkuraa together. It was easy to imagine they were the last of their kind, sitting there alone in the vastness. Nothing more than dust motes caught up in some vast plan. The world was changing, and Rebaa wondered if her People were even meant to be a part of it. It was a saddening thought.

"Sleep now?" Nen offered at last, bringing Rebaa back to earth. "I watch. You need rest."

Rebaa squeezed Nen's fingers. "No," she whispered. "I don't want to go back to sleep." Only death awaited her there. "I'll watch tonight and keep the fire going."

Nen's eyes searched hers for a moment before nodding her consent. She rose and went back inside the cave, settling down on the furs next to the fire. Rebaa remained outside for a while longer, but she could not stand the loneliness for long. She felt in danger of floating away, like the dust mote she was, and becoming lost in the vastness above, to be swallowed up and forever forgotten. Ninsiku's silver eye stared on unforgivingly.

Rebaa rose and hurried back into the embrace of the cave. This solid, immovable rock was a far cry from the living, whispering canopies that had protected her through childhood, but at least it blocked out the unnatural, terrifying openness. She added more fuel to the fire and sat down beside Nen, wrapping the heavy covers more tightly around her slight shoulders.

Rebaa stared into the flames, letting the warmth and light banish the gnawing fears of the dark. It could not do so fully. Her nightmares sat in the nooks and crevasses where the light of the fire could not pry and waited. Reaching out, she took hold of Nen's hand once more. It remained firmly in hers throughout the long night.

13

Threat

The next day dawned with the promise of snow in the air. During the night, the clouds had rolled over, and the skies were a flat, endless grey, stretching from one horizon to the other. Ninmah's sacred face was entirely masked.

"Lot of snow coming." Nen commented as she reached out of the cave to bring in more meat to thaw by the fire for later.

Rebaa's heart sank. This was bad news. She could not afford to be trapped here before the baby was born. She reminded herself again that Nen's acceptance would end as soon as her friend witnessed what she bore. Nen would be compelled to enforce the sentence laid down by her precious Eron. But if Rebaa went back on her promise to Nen and left the shelter of the cave now, she would get caught in the coming blizzards and she would surely die.

She should never have given in to temptation and remained here. Her weakness had once again trapped her between two impossibilities. She stared up at the ominously silent skies. Ninmah was indeed punishing her for her heresy.

Nen was busy scrutinising Rebaa's clothes. "Not enough," she spoke. "You journey. Need better." She moved over to the giant bear skin that was ready for tanning. "Bear skin good. Great tough. Warm. Better chance."

It seemed that Nen had decided to spend Rebaa's remaining time in the cave preparing her fully for the journey ahead, making sure she had the best chance of survival. Rebaa's heart swelled with fondness and gratitude. She wished she could do more for her friend than offer a few scant days of companionship.

"Why are you being so good to me?" she murmured.

Nen frowned. "Want to make sure you find People. You baby survive. Most important thing."

Rebaa grew conscious of the heavy swell of her belly beneath her wolf furs. Yes, he had to survive. It was important. More important than anything else. Somehow, that knowledge transcended even her own maternal instincts. Whatever he turned out to be, no matter her fears, she had to make sure this baby survived. He was the only reason she had made it this far. She looked at the remains of the rabbit carcass. There was nothing she wouldn't do for him. She smiled up at Nen. "You are a blessing from Ninmah herself. Maybe she isn't abandoning me after all."

Nen blushed as she handed Rebaa crushed bits of bark and leaves. They rubbed these into the dried skin until it was stained dark with the essence of the trees.

"Tell me about your People, Nen," she asked to distract herself from her worries. "You seem to know a little of mine, but I know nothing of yours."

Nen raised an eyebrow. "No?"

"No, my People take little interest in anything beyond our

forests."

Nen was silent for a long while. Rebaa guessed she was gathering her mastery of the words. She wondered distantly how Nen knew part of the Cro tongue and their hunting techniques. She got the impression Nen knew quite a lot of the world. It was hard to guess at her companion's age. The few threads of grey standing above the blistered scar upon her forehead and the faint lines on her face suggested she was older than Rebaa, though both could be the marks of hardship rather than the passing of seasons.

Nen handed her the tools needed and instructed her on what was necessary to make new garments. The snow fell outside, and the world took on the peculiar silence that came with the blanketing. Nen used her sharp flint knife to cut up the bear pelt into the needed sizes. Rebaa tried not to wrinkle her nose when the Thal woman started chewing on the edges of one piece, softening it up to prepare it for stitching.

"People live where Eron lead us long ago." Nen said at last, softly spitting bits of stray hair from her tongue. "Vast places further up. Dangerous. Life hard. Eron want us to be tough, tougher than any other People. We live in caves like this or in bone and skin shelters. Eron showed us how to make flame, how to make tools. Hunt the Great Ones."

"Great ones?"

Nen pointed to her etchings on the cave walls, and Rebaa saw again the image of a massive tusked beast with a snake for a nose.

"Mighty spirits," Nen murmured. "If young man kill one, revered by People. He become worthy warrior. May choose any woman he want."

"I see."

Nen's hands faltered in their work. "M-my Alok killed Great One. He was going to choose me. Make strong children."

Rebaa was quick to catch the shift in Nen's energy as she spoke. The great sadness that she had felt when they first met yawned open like a bottomless chasm. "What happened?" she dared to venture, though she was not sure she wanted to hear.

Nen opened her mouth to respond but was cut off when a sharp howl split the muffled air outside. Rebaa flinched as Nen's head snapped around towards the cave mouth, her ordinarily gentle face twisting into a terrifying mask of hatred. Rebaa shrank away as her friend leaped to her feet, grabbing her spear from the cave wall. She threw the flint knife in Rebaa's direction. "Weapon. Need."

"What's wrong?" Rebaa asked, frightened by Nen's reaction and the coldness of her expression.

"Men." Nen replied. "Not animal." She crept out of their shelter. Her hand was firm on her spear, though Rebaa could not miss how the flint tip trembled upon the air.

"Nen!" Rebaa whispered, alarmed. "Don't go out."

"Just look. No see me. Make sure leave. You *stay*." She gave the last command with a level stare.

Rebaa opened her mouth to protest, but stopped when she tasted Nen's energy. Beneath her friend's fear and anger, Rebaa thought she could detect a faint sense of... longing, of a desperate hope. Before she could be certain, however, Nen had disappeared into the falling snow.

Rebaa hissed in frustration. She waited in the dimness, tense and alert. She should do as Nen asked and stay in the cave. She remembered keenly what had happened the last time she had come near a Cro hunting party. But as the moments crawled by, her imagination ran away with her, conjuring the worst.

The strangers might get around Nen and catch her here. That thought alone had her on her feet. She snatched up the flint knife Nen had thrown to her, clutching it awkwardly. The silence stretched.

Why was Nen putting them both at risk like this? It was madness.

In the end, Rebaa could bear it no longer. Nen had told her to stay, but she would *not* wait around to be trapped. She had made that mistake one too many times to her detriment. Cautiously, she crept to the cave mouth and looked around. All she could see was white land, grey sky, and the falling snow in between.

She turned her attention to the ground. Nen's tracks were leading off towards the bear kill. Rebaa cast her higher awareness outward, feeling the energies of the land. A large herd of oxen was picking its way through the rocks somewhere further up the slope, stragglers on their way down to winter grazing on the southern plains. Their huge individual energies burned hot in Rebaa's mind as they rooted through the snow. Further down, Nen was not far away.

Rebaa let out a breath she hadn't realised she had been holding, only to suck it back again when she sensed the strangers. There were five or six of them, she guessed. Mouth dry, she stole out after Nen, determined to bring her back to the cave. It terrified her that her friend may be seen and killed... or worse.

She knew the path well by now, and it did not take her long to catch up. She found Nen crouching stealthily behind an outcropping of rocks. The snow had fallen on her reddish furs, blending her into the landscape. Rebaa crouched beside her. Nen glanced at her once in irritation, then turned back to stare down the slope. Her black eyes raked over the scene with a strange hunger, and Rebaa felt again that inexplicable taste of longing amidst the anger. Baffled, she followed her friend's gaze.

Approaching the bear kill from down the slope was the group of Cro. They were still too far away for her to pick out details, but she instantly recognised their tall forms, long legs and lean bodies made for running. Their minds possessed the fierce intelligence she had come to know; agile, adaptable... merciless. Rebaa's heart thudded uncomfortably at the sight of them. There were four. She thought she had detected more, but fear could have muddled her senses. Then they drew close enough for Rebaa to make out their totem, and she felt the blood drain from her face. It was the totem of a rampaging bear.

It was *them.* Her beloved Juran's bitterest rivals. Worse than wolves, worse than bears. She shrank back against the rocks; the terror pulsing through her veins pounded in her ears.

The Cro picked over the stripped carcass of the bear. Travel worn and weary, they had obviously been hoping for an easy meal. One of the brutes threw his spear in temper when he found that there was nothing left worth scavenging. It shivered in the nearest tree.

A shout went up, and the hunter twisted around to stare in the opposite direction. Two more men appeared out of the snow. Rebaa's initial instinct had not been wrong as to their numbers. The first newcomer was comparatively short compared to his hulking companion. With his left hand, he gestured sharply at the hunter who had lost his temper. Two fingers were missing. The second new arrival was as tall as any man Rebaa had ever seen, too tall to be pure Cro, but she could not guess at the rest of his heritage. Tangled black hair wreathed his face, billowing in the wind. His eyes were cold and pitiless. She recognised him instantly. *This* was the man who had separated her from her home and mercilessly hunted her until Juran's clan had intervened. *This* was the man who had forever changed her peaceful life from what it would have been and set her upon this cursed path of fear and death.

Murzuk.

Rebaa's nails bit into her palms. The savage leader of the Hunting Bear was only thirty paces from where she cowered. He would know her on sight, and Juran was no longer here to keep her from falling into his clutches.

As paralysing tremors rolled through her body, Rebaa heard Nen draw a sharp breath as she too laid eyes on the Hunting Bear leader. The outrage at this invasion of her territory flamed into outright hatred. To Rebaa's horror, she started to rise from concealment, staring down at Murzuk with murder in her eyes. Her grip was white on her spear as a low growl built in her throat.

"Nen! What are you *doing*? Get down!"

She didn't think Nen even heard her, but pulling with all her might, Rebaa kept the Thal woman in place.

The half-handed man continued to gesture at the hunter who had thrown his weapon. The brute obviously did not like being scolded and struck out at the smaller man in challenge. But what the half-hand lacked in height, he made up for in skill. In two swift moves, he had his adversary on the ground, his spear pressed to his throat in warning. There was something familiar about the way he moved that made Rebaa's breath catch in her throat.

143

Murzuk's booming laugh carried on the wind. He laid a hand on the half-hand's arm and pulled him back. He motioned to the fallen hunter, ordering him to rise.

Murzuk gestured again, and the men studied the area. Rebaa knew what they were looking for. Nen had stripped the bear of its skin and meat. It would be obvious that the work had not been carried out by tooth and claw. As she watched, they examined the ground, assessing the strength of the other clan who must have made the kill.

"Nen, we have to go," Rebaa whispered in an urgent breath. "They'll wonder who took all that meat. They can see our tracks. Only two tracks. They outnumber us."

Nen snarled, gripping her spear as if she would very much like to plant it between Murzuk's shoulder blades. Her white skin was paler than usual.

"Nen!" Rebaa urged. "Please! We need to hide our footprints!" She crept away, pulling Nen behind her. She remembered what Nen had done when the last hunting party of Cro had passed through and grabbed a loose branch from the base of one of the bare trees. She started sweeping the snow behind them to blot out their footprints. She hoped it would be enough to throw off these apex hunters.

She was not careful enough. Focused as she was on smothering their tracks, Rebaa had not paid attention to the ground beneath her feet as she edged backwards. A loose rock dislodged under her weight and with a soft cry, she tumbled onto her backside. Before she could stop it, the rock skittered away, bouncing loudly down the slope, echoing all around the surrounding foothills.

Nen and Rebaa froze.

There was a moment of absolute silence before the hunting

cries split the air.

"That way! They're up there!" The tread of muffled feet followed the shouts, running in their direction. Rebaa shared one terrified glance with Nen before they threw caution to the wind and ran for their lives.

It was a futile effort. As with the bear before, Rebaa could feel their enemies gaining on them. The Cro were made for running long distances. The best hunters. Nen was built for tireless strength. Rebaa for climbing. She was also pregnant, and her damaged leg slowed her even further. This was not a race they could win.

Howls of triumph sounded behind as the Hunting Bear warriors caught sight of them fleeing ahead. Rebaa gasped, hobbling now, and tried to run faster. She was almost spent when Nen grabbed her and yanked her back into the shelter of their cave.

Doubling over, Rebaa fought to catch her breath. She clutched at a pain in her side. It was hopeless. This cave was no protection. It was a trap with no way out. Nen disappeared into the depths of her home, but Rebaa stood in the entranceway and waited as the baying of their pursuers grew steadily louder. There was little point in hiding. She would face her fate as Juran would have wanted.

A clatter of stone told Rebaa that Nen was gathering rocks. Her friend was deathly pale, but her eyes were fierce. "They not take me," she swore over and over as she worked. Rebaa latched on to her determination, letting it give her strength. They would not go down without a fight. She grabbed a rock of her own and stood firm, waiting.

Nevertheless, Rebaa's heart quailed as the dark figures materialised out of the snow. They drew to a halt and paced restlessly at a distance of about fifty paces. They stared up the slope at the lone Ninkuraaja woman waiting for them in the cave mouth.

They were cautious. Rebaa's apparent confidence unnerved them. They had no way to tell for certain that she was alone. The Hunting Bear raiding party was not strong in number, and Murzuk was no fool. He would not take the risk of starting a fight he could not win. It was the reason he had never challenged Juran for her possession.

But it would not take his men long to figure out the truth. When that happened, they would move to either capture or kill. Rebaa locked her teeth together to stop them chattering.

Murzuk pushed his way to the front of his men. He locked eyes with Rebaa. His face registered shock, then the slow, dreaded smile of recognition curled across his face. The expression turned Rebaa's innards to ice. She gripped her stone until the rough surface bit into her skin.

"At last!" His voice rasped over the snow. "You were right after all, boy," he said to a trembling adolescent flanked by two fully grown raiders. "If you continue to behave, you will have a place of honour in my clan."

The Hunting Bear Chief returned his attention to Rebaa, baring all of his teeth as he grinned up the slope. "I thought you lost when I found the Black Wolf clan slaughtered beside the Mountains. I never dreamed a witch could survive without protection. You are full of surprises, girl. I found *his* corpse, though. Or what they left of it." Murzuk brandished his spear before him. What looked like fingers dangled from black cords below the tip as trophies.

The ground pitched beneath Rebaa's feet and she had to catch herself on the stone wall of the cave before her knees could buckle. She turned her head against the grisly sight. She could not let herself imagine. Those were not Juran's fingers. They were not. She could not close out the hated voice, however.

The cool blue eyes travelled over her appreciatively until they came to rest on her belly and widened in shock.

"No..." Murzuk breathed. "So it *is* possible." The Cro Chief's lips peeled back even further from his teeth. "You are mine now, witch. Once you are rid of that spawn, you will provide me with my own! There is no one to keep you from me now. I will have what no other clan can possess!"

Rage and horror blazed inside Rebaa at the same instant she heard a terrible hissing sound from beside her.

"I am *not* yours, Murzuk," she warned with as much courage as she could muster. "And I never will be!"

Murzuk only laughed and advanced up the hill. It was then that Nen twisted out from behind the wall of the cave and planted herself defiantly in front of Rebaa.

The Hunting Bear leader stopped dead in his tracks, the predatory smile faltering into an expression of utmost shock. "You?" His eyes darted, and then he turned angrily to the half-handed man standing beside him. "*You*—!"

Nen did not give him a chance to speak further. With a fierce cry, she hurled her heavy rock. The half-handed warrior grabbed his Chief and yanked him out of the way. The stone flew through the space where Murzuk's head had been. Had it made contact, it would have killed him outright.

The Cro leader's face was pale under his dark skin as he returned his attention to the woman who had come close to crushing his skull. He blinked and then the grin fixed itself back into position, his eyes glittering with an unpleasant promise. "Such *spirit*. Maybe I'm glad you're not dead after all. You, like her, will be mine again." Raising his spear in the air, he roared his challenge and charged, bringing the rest of his men with him.

Shrieking her defiance, Nen hurled rock after rock at the approaching Cro. Some of her missiles found their targets. Two of the men crumpled to the ground, bones shattered by the force of the impacts. The others did not slow their charge, driven as they were by a raging passion and blood lust. Rebaa hurled a few of her own stones, but they fell pathetically short and rolled harmlessly past their enemies. Still, they came on.

It was no use.

Nen seemed to come to this realisation at the same time Rebaa did. Spitting a low oath, she grabbed Rebaa's hand. "Run! Run!"

The next thing Rebaa knew, she was being dragged along in Nen's wake. It was a last desperate bid for escape. Rebaa's breath rasped loud in her ears, but it was not enough to drown out the pounding of footsteps in the snow right behind her.

A rough hand clamped around her arm and pulled her backwards, ripping her from Nen's unprepared grip. Rebaa screamed in fright as the Cro man subdued her, bringing an arm around her body to hold her securely against him. She could feel his hot, excited breath next to her ear.

"I've never had a witch before," he panted as he slid his fingers along her neck and dipped them down inside her furs. "Perhaps Murzuk will share."

A roar of fury was the Cro warrior's only warning. Nen's fist came out of nowhere and smashed into the head above Rebaa's. The Cro's grip slackened and Rebaa twisted away in time to see him fall back into the snow, blood streaming from his broken nose, eyes unfocused.

He had barely hit the ground when another Cro joined the fight, this time attacking Nen head on. Faster than Rebaa thought possible for such a bulky frame, Nen twisted away from the charge. She grabbed the extending spear as it scythed through the space she had just occupied. Holding tight to the haft, Nen continued her twisting motion, shouldering the Cro in a circle until he was yanked from his feet and thrown into the air. He came down hard upon the snow-covered rocks and rolled away down the gully.

Hollering in maddened triumph, Nen snapped the Cro's spear in two and spat in the direction of her fallen opponent.

Dazed by fear, Rebaa did not sense the approaching danger, and her cry of warning came too late as Murzuk himself leaped into the fray out of a swirl of snow. He barrelled into Nen with the force of a charging ox, knocking her to the ground and striking her forehead against a hidden rock.

"No!" Rebaa cried. "Nen!"

Nen blinked rapidly, struggling to regain her senses as Murzuk descended upon her. She got her large hands up just in time to grab at his thick wrists. Murzuk was powerfully built, but Nen's Thal strength was a match for his as she held him at bay by a hand's breadth. Striking out with her legs, she tried to knock Murzuk's feet out from under him. But the Cro Chief was too cunning a fighter and he was careful to keep his knees just out of reach. He began to twist his wrists from Nen's grip—

Rebaa snatched a rock from the ground and dashed forward. All that consumed her vision was the back of Murzuk's unprotected head. Carried forward by the intent of smashing it into pulp, Rebaa swung her arm back.

"No, you don't!" A hand caught her wrist as another Cro seized her from behind. The fingers squeezed until her bones creaked and with a cry of pain, Rebaa dropped the rock. Twisting madly, she attempted to kick and bite her opponent, but her struggle against him was woefully inadequate.

Nen was about to lose her fight. Freeing one wrist from her desperate grip, Murzuk landed a solid blow across the point where the rock had already stuck against Nen's skull. Horrified, Rebaa could only watch as Nen's grip on Murzuk's remaining wrist slackened, releasing the monster. All the remaining Cro were converging on their leader's position.

Murzuk's triumphant laugh boomed out. Standing over Nen as she tried to rise, he ripped his clothing apart, exposing the whole of his powerful body in a show of primal dominance and threat.

Rebaa knew what was going to happen next, and her struggles became more frenzied. The arm that restrained her was crushing her ribs. She could feel her heart labouring against the constricted cage.

She could also feel… his heart. It pounded against her senses in a thumping rhythm. Rebaa gasped as her mind cleared for one shining instant. She was Ninkuraaja! It was time to fight like one.

Struggling to get enough air into her lungs, Rebaa fought to master her fear and focus her mind, concentrating on the pulses of life racing against her own. Closing her eyes against the scenes unfolding before her, she focused with all her might on the Cro's body.

Stopping the rabbit's heart had been one thing, manipulating the heart of a creature whose body lacked all connection to KI was another. Feeling like her head would explode, Rebaa

150

drew on the Great Spirit and threw all of her power against the pulsing organ, closing the passageways. The Cro gasped as his heart stuttered, but it resisted her effort and struggled on.

No! Sagging from the effort, Rebaa dragged all of her energy forth, calling upon everything within reach from the surrounding land, but still it was not enough. The Cro's body resisted all her attempts to sabotage its functions. Dark spots were dancing before Rebaa's eyes. *I can't do this alone!*

Then it happened. A wave of power burst to life from somewhere within. It burned through Rebaa, crackling invisibly along her skin like the static from a thunderbolt. Every hair raised, she did not pause to think on its source. Screaming with hate and rage, she unleashed this new energy upon the Cro who was daring to hold her, targeting every vital point within his pathetic body.

He was dead before he hit the ground, his face twisted forever into an expression of horror.

Eyes burning indigo fire, Rebaa snarled down at the dead man until a cry drew her attention back to Nen's plight. Murzuk was still standing over her, the other men approaching. Rebaa's triumph over the Cro had taken but an instant, though forever seemed to have passed in her mind.

Rebaa focused on the rest of the Cro. She could not kill them all from this distance. Her mind raced. The memory of Murzuk charging Nen down like an angry bull tugged at Rebaa's mind, and the solution was quick to follow.

With the newfound power still pulsing ferociously alongside her own, Rebaa gathered her strength and reached out to the energies farther up the hill. They were still there. The oxen. It was a fairly large herd. Rebaa needed only to get them to run. The Cro would not guess the danger until it was too late.

Condensing her will, she stretched forth. The distance would have been too great ordinarily, but the terrible power within responded, dragging energy recklessly from the living earth. Channelling it, Rebaa planted an image into the wary minds of the oxen. A large cave lion was stalking the herd from above...

Thunder rolled through the hills and Rebaa let loose a cry of triumph. The ground quaked beneath her feet as the herd funnelled down into the gully on mighty, unstoppable hooves. The Cro paused in their attack upon Nen, faces lifting towards the source of the disturbance high above. Their uncertainty turned to fear as they spied the clouds of snow cascading down the gully, bearing down upon them.

"Avalanche!" Murzuk bellowed as his men stumbled backwards away from Nen, scrambling in their haste to retreat. In the confusion, Rebaa darted to her friend's side, pulling at her hand.

"Rebaa...?" Nen's eyes fixed in horror upon the approaching cascade.

Rebaa did not waste time on explanations. "Get up!" she cried. "Run! Run!"

Nen struggled to her feet. It was Rebaa's turn to drag her friend behind her, pounding back down the slope towards the only shelter against what she had set into motion. She was aware of the Cro fleeing blindly ahead of her, but she paid them no mind. They would not escape.

The thundering of hooves grew to a deafening pitch as Rebaa reached the cave and pulled Nen into its embrace. As Rebaa panted over her knees, Nen grabbed her spear, readying herself to defend once more, not knowing where the threat might come from. "Rebaa?" she asked again.

But Rebaa had eyes only for Murzuk, glaring down at his fleeing form in fierce triumph as the herd of massive herbivores came crashing down the hillside, breaking all around the cave in a terrifying force.

Even the Cro could not outrun the stampeding oxen, and they knew it. Another bellowed order from Murzuk had them turning and extending their spears in a futile attempt to cleave through the tide. The wall of charging muscle smashed into them, charging them into the ground and trampling them beneath the crushing hooves.

Murzuk was the last to fall. He stood like a rock amidst the thundering herd, flinging his spear this way and that, driving the oxen around him. Rebaa glared down at the man who had violated her mate's body and threatened her unborn baby. A fury like she had never known filled her heart. The strange power crackled in response. Snarling, she unleashed her newfound source of energy once more, uncaring as the Great Spirit shuddered around her at the violation. A huge bull caught her attention, and she reached out to him, filling his mind with her rage, giving it focus.

The Child of the Great Spirit merged with her will and lowered his head with a deafening bellow, bearing down on the Cro leader. Murzuk's spear drove into the bull's shoulder and Rebaa cried out as she felt an echo of the blow in her own body, but it was not enough to stop the mountain of charging muscle. The bull's horns caught Murzuk in the chest in a bone shattering impact. Rebaa revelled in the Cro leader's screams as the ox pounded him into the dirt. His bloody spear with its grisly adornments toppled into the snow.

Rebaa bared her teeth. *That was for you, my love...* She hoped that somewhere Juran's spirit would know that Murzuk was dead by her hand.

The rumble of hooves faded into the distance, and a deathly stillness settled over the crushed bodies lying in the snow. Rebaa gazed upon them without emotion. Never again would these Cro threaten their lives.

The frightening energy that had risen from nowhere drained away and Rebaa sank exhausted to her knees. Her baby rolled over inside her, his mind falling into the stillness of sleep. Rebaa's eyes widened in realisation as a shaking hand flew to her belly. *You!*

Movement on the snow outside snapped her back into focus. A single Cro had escaped the massacre. Rebaa staggered back to her feet. It was the half-handed warrior. He had avoided the oxen by taking shelter behind a large rock. Not completely unscathed, however. His left hand dangled uselessly by his side as he limped to his fallen Chief's side.

Bile rose in Rebaa's throat as she saw the bloody mass that was Murzuk twitch. Somehow, the monster was *still* clinging to life. A mangled hand rose and clutched at the half-hand's furs. The other man bowed his head, cocking his ear over his fallen Chief's mouth. The half-hand stiffened before touching his good hand to his chest, agreeing to whatever Murzuk had said. Then Murzuk's bloody limb fell back and Rebaa let out a breath as she felt the dark flame snuff from existence at last.

The surviving Cro reached out and touched his hand to his dead Chief's face. Rebaa pictured him closing the staring blue eyes. There was a moment's pause before the warrior bent and pulled Murzuk's carved pendant from around his lifeless neck and plucked his fallen spear out of the snow. The half-hand then lifted his face to stare up the slope to where

Rebaa waited.

Rebaa tensed, exhausted beyond thought. She had no heart for another fight, but injured and outnumbered, the Cro warrior wisely stayed where he was. He stood with his gaze locked upon hers before lifting Murzuk's weapon and twisting it in one smooth motion before him. Rebaa recognised it as the Cro salute of respect to a worthy opponent.

She did not honour him with a response.

He did not wait for one. He ran back the way he had come, as fast as his injuries would allow. Rebaa watched him go. Much as she hated it, there was nothing she could do to stop him.

The silence that followed was loaded. Nen was staring down at Murzuk's crushed body, one raised fist still clutching her spear in a white-knuckled grip. Blood trickled down her thick brow. She would have a second scar to match the one that already marred her forehead.

"Relax, Nen," Rebaa soothed in a weary voice. "They're gone now. Dead."

Nen twisted her head, eyes wild. The fist holding the spear trembled. Rebaa moved back inside the cave so she would no longer have to see the mangled bodies outside. She added a few more logs to the dying fire and poked it with a stick to breathe new life into it. It felt odd, returning to the mundane chores after everything that had just happened, but she needed to distract herself from their brush with death and what she had done and experienced. Her hands shook as they went again to her belly. What *was* he?

Nen paced up and down, radiating nervous energy. "Dead. Murzuk. Dead."

"Yes, Nen. He's gone. He can't hurt us now."

With a guttural cry, Nen threw her spear at the wall of the cave. The tip shattered on impact. Rebaa flinched at the outburst. Her friend's temper was frightening. It grated against her own already frayed nerves. She needed to calm Nen down.

"I'm glad my brother taught me that trick when we were children," Rebaa said by way of distraction.

It had the desired effect, and Nen stopped pacing to face her. She still appeared a little wild. Rebaa kept talking in a soothing voice.

"Baarias and I were playing where we shouldn't," Rebaa recounted. "We had ventured to the edge of our forest, which was dangerous. We almost got caught by the Elders who had come to look for us. There was a deer herd browsing nearby. Baarias made them think they were being chased, and they stampeded into the path of the Elders." She cringed at what they could have done. "Luckily no one got hurt and in the distraction we got away unseen." Rebaa's heart ached at the memory. "I miss my brother," she murmured.

Nen crouched beside her. Her body was still as taut as a snare trap, but her eyes became less wild. "When last see?"

Rebaa gave a weary laugh. She was so tired. She was always tired now. She had never realised carrying a child could drain one's energy so. "Many Furies ago now. It's been a long time since I've seen any of them…"

Silence. Instead of calming further, Nen's agitation spiked. Rebaa's eyes darted to the cave entrance in panic, expecting to see an enemy. But Nen was not looking at the cave mouth, she was staring Rebaa full in the face.

"How long wood sprite carry baby?"

"Eight blinks of Ninsiku." Rebaa answered, unnerved by the

sudden, intense scrutiny. "Eight black nights," she elaborated further into the silence, indicating the darkest of nights when Ninsiku's great silver eye was fully closed.

Nen seemed to guess what she meant. Her black eyes bored into Rebaa's as her hands flexed. "Then... baby can not be Dryad."

The blood drained from Rebaa's face as Nen reared up to her full height.

"You carry the Forbidden!"

14

The Truth

Nen was pacing up and down, her stride fierce. Rebaa eyed the entrance to the cave that had become her haven in the worst time of need. Now it was a closing trap from which she needed to escape. She wondered if she fled, Nen would just let her go. She had just saved the Thal woman from the Cro after all.

"I'll leave, Nen," she said in a placating voice, though it sounded more like a plea. "I'll take the curse with me and go back to my People. I never wanted to put you at risk."

Nen stopped pacing and stared at her askance. "You not go! I not let you! Bad. *Bad!*"

"Nen, please!" Rebaa tried to edge towards the opening. "I'm sorry I lied! I'm sorry. Just please let me go!"

Nen shook her head, hollow eyes haunted but determined. "No. Can't let what happened to me happen to you. No. You no go back. Bad."

These words caught Rebaa off guard. "H-happened to you?"

Nen jabbed a finger at one of the pictures on her walls. The picture where a lone figure was being chased by those hurling rocks. "Me," she said. "I birth Forbidden child."

"B-but…" Rebaa stammered, sinking back to the ground, her escape forgotten as her head swam. "How?"

"Cro," Nen spat. "They took everything. My life happy. Daughter of *Sag Du*, Thal chief. People live well. Great Ones plenty. I loved strong man. He promise choose me when kill his first Great One." Nen's eyes filled with pain. "Then Cro come. Their spear better than our. Throw longer, kill lots of Great Ones. None respect. Take what they like.

"Our clan get hungry. Then Cro came for clan, too. Cro marked with bear. They kill father. I tried to stop them. I angry." A mocking smile twisted the wide lips. "Better to have run. I failed. They beat me, then they hold me down." Nen's hands balled into fists. "Many men."

Rebaa's breath hitched as she listened to Nen's words. She had been so lucky to have been captured by Juran. If she had not fallen under his protection, she could have suffered the same fate.

"People saw," Nen continued. "They no help. Alok, my chosen one, turned his back. I dirty now. Our mighty Eron forbid breeding with the other Children. Strongest lore. Forbidden act to breed with those not of People."

Rebaa nodded, her heart rate slowing. Perhaps she wasn't in danger after all. Tentatively, she reached out to lay a comforting hand upon Nen's arm. "Ninmah taught this to my People, too," she said, her voice hoarse. "It is the worst trespass."

Nen put her hand over the top of Rebaa's and squeezed. "Cro no care. They turn backs on gods. I had no People now. Bear Cro took me as slave. Nowhere else to go. Lived to do bidding." She waved a hand towards the mouth of the cave and the bodies that lay outside. "Cruel chief made me his mate. Liked my strong. Made child. I was frightened. Not child I should have. Eron punish me with curse!"

Rebaa blanched, her free hand going to her belly as Nen spoke. *Curse... The child had been a curse.* The memory of the terrifying power burning through her veins rose like bile in her throat.

But Nen's anguished face brightened with a fervent light, surprising her once more. "Then baby born. He beautiful. No curse like People say." She tugged at her red hair. "Like mine."

The words washed over Rebaa like a cool tide. Tears pricked in her eyes as she smiled. "He had hair like yours?"

Nen nodded, eyes shining with wonder for a moment. "I love him." She pointed to her etching of a mother and baby. "He mine."

"What happened?" Rebaa asked, though she knew she probably didn't want to hear the conclusion of this doomed tale. Nen's son obviously wasn't here.

"Clan settled near great forest. South. Many dangerous animals. When boy still young, only seven summers, chief sent on hunting trip. He too young to go!" Nen burst out, anger burning at the memory. "Hunters came back. My boy gone. They say boy mortal wound by big wolves, dragged into forest. Hunters left him." Nen scraped viciously at the ground with her fingers, fury plain on her face.

"He was killed?" Rebaa whispered.

Nen flicked at a loose pebble. "No. Eron sent me miracle. Boy came back. He say he healed by being in forest. By Dryad." She raised her head to gaze softly at Rebaa's stunned face. "When strong enough, he travel home. Clan celebrate long. I not. What if put boy in danger again? I not stand cruel

160

life of Cro anymore. I made weapon in secret." She pointed to her now broken spear. "Carve with Eron's markings of protection. I try escape. I took boy. Stole out at night. I ran into warriors. I kill one and cut face of another but they pull boy from me." She looked forlornly at her empty arms. "I forced leave him. Chased with spears. Broke lore, I tried to escape with chief child. Killed man." Nen drew a long, shuddering breath. "Ran for life. Boy cried but could do nothing. He only child. Murzuk sent hunter after me, but I escape. My baby stay with Cro. I search again after but clan move on. Lost, lost."

The silence that followed was long and uncomfortable. Rebaa could not imagine what Nen had gone through. Something clicked into place then as she recalled Nen's unexpected appearance when she had been caught in the Cro trap and today's inexplicable behaviour in leaving the cave. "Is that why you go out after Cro?" she asked. "You are hoping to see if your son is with them." It was not a question.

Tears were standing in Nen's eyes. "Yes. Every Cro clan who come near, I search. I frightened but I can't help. What if he there? Want to see him grown. Very much."

Rebaa squeezed her friend's arm; any lingering anger she had felt at Nen's earlier actions drained away. She tried not to imagine the horror of having to leave her baby behind in the hands of her enemies. Her free hand curled unconsciously around her belly. She vowed no-one would ever take him from her.

After long moments of silence, Nen continued her tale. "After I forced to leave child and escape, I burn away marks of Cro mate." She rubbed at the ugly scar below her hairline, causing Rebaa to stare at it in a new light. Her hand went to

161

her own marks where they stood in exactly the same position. She felt foolish now for having missed the signs.

"I then search for People." Nen went on, dropping her hand. "Only hope. As woman of my tribe, I not learn how lead hunt. Only follow. Cro women not hunt at all. I need tribe to protect, strong men. I travel long way and found People. I happy see them." Her fists clenched. "They not happy see me. I told them no curse," she patted her belly, "but they chase me with rocks. Chase me far. I have no People now," she said again. "I learn to hunt by self, using Cro way, I learn to survive. But I still alone. Eron curses me for wickedness. For bearing Forbidden."

Rebaa did not know what to say. "I'm so sorry, Nen," she whispered at last. Only the crackle of the fire broke the silence as the shadows flickered upon the walls, making the etchings dance and come to life. Rebaa watched them for a while with her renewed sight.

When Nen could speak again, her gaze was questioning. "You have Cro baby?"

Rebaa closed her eyes in final admittance. "Yes."

Nen's lips pressed into a thin line. "How you survive the curses of Cro? All sprites die when taken from trees. Get sick."

Rebaa shrugged. "My brother was learned in the skill of healing. I was able to counter their curses and survive. I could not just give up. I wanted to see my home again."

"How you escape? You use Dryad magic like now?" Nen gestured towards the outside.

Rebaa shuddered at the reminder of the Cro bodies cooling in the snow not far from where she rested and shook her head. "No, Nen, no magic."

"How?"

Nen had shared her ordeal but Rebaa still did not know

if she had the courage to speak of hers; the terrors that so haunted her dreams. "I didn't escape," she said finally. "The clan chief took me for his mate, too."

Nen's face darkened. "He cruel to you?"

"No. Juran was good to me. He treated me gently." Rebaa's throat closed. As she had feared, the words cracked the surface of her control and the memories she had so carefully buried came seeping to the surface. Memories of warm nights and the feeling of complete and utter safety. "I loved him," she confessed, as her voice trembled. "At first I survived out of a desire to escape. Before I knew it, I was surviving because I wanted to be with *him*." Too much! She straightened her back and fought the memories down. He was not coming back. He had *abandoned* her.

Nen rocked back at the confession. "Love? Then why you leave? Baby not accepted anywhere else."

Rebaa clenched her fists to stop them from trembling. She drew a deep breath. "As the Fury set in, the clan found new territory at the base of those distant mountains to the west on the northern plain," she said. "The ones the Cro call the Mountains of the Nine Gods. There was plenty to hunt through the cold time. The territory would have sustained us. Juran saw it as a blessing."

Her voice grew soft as she got lost in the memories, seeing it all again behind her closed lids. "But the blessing turned out to be nothing more than a curse. Our hunters started disappearing in the woods around the mountains. They would go in to find game and not return. Those few who did return lost their wits, raving that monsters that feasted on the flesh of men haunted the woods." Rebaa opened her eyes to stare starkly at the fire. "Juran did not believe them. He assumed

163

another clan was ambushing his hunters in the forest, and that was something he could not tolerate. With the Furies getting longer and harder, hunting territories are not something to be shared. Juran went into the woods to flush out the enemy." Rebaa picked up a stray twig and threw it sharply into the fire, watching it sizzle and spit. "It was a mistake. The stories were not the ravings of madmen. The clan was destroyed by the enemy that came from the woods."

Nen blanched. "What could kill Cro?"

Rebaa fixed her with a dark gaze. "Creatures from the blackest nightmare, Nen. I cannot speak of them. Not even now, lest I rouse their spirits. I pray to Ninmah that you never see such things."

Nen shivered visibly and busied herself by refuelling the fire, brightening the cave and driving back the sudden chill.

"Your Juran not survive."

Rebaa's eyes burned. "No. He got me away from the killing, hid me in the foothills and told me to go, to get as far away as I could." She could still see his grey eyes as he beseeched her to leave him and run. "He promised he would not leave me. He *promised*. But he betrayed me. He went back to his clan and was slaughtered with them. He left me alone with the curse of his Forbidden child." She realised she was crying now, in grief, in anger. Her carefully built walls were crumbling around her, too weak to contain what was inside.

Nen was thoughtful. "He clan chief?"

Rebaa nodded once through her tears, not trusting her voice as she fought to regain control.

"Then he could not leave clan. Dishonour to soul in Cro lore."

"I don't care about honour!" Rebaa burst out. "I want him

164

with me! Why did he have to go back? Why did he leave me to face this alone?" She swept her arms out to emphasise her pregnant belly.

Nen was silent. After a moment she simply reached out and pulled Rebaa to her, holding her close against the thick brown furs. At first, Rebaa fought to pull away. She could not give in! She had to stay strong! But Nen held her firm, and as the Thal woman stroked her hair, Rebaa could fight no longer. She succumbed to the grief she had been holding so tightly in check and poured out her loss and pain in the comfort and safety of Nen's arms. She did not know if she would ever stop.

"Maybe only way to save you and child," Nen murmured to her. "Maybe had to go so you could live." She continued to stroke Rebaa's dark hair, "Must forgive. He save you. Must find *shalanaki*."

"I don't know if I can," Rebaa choked. "Not yet. Maybe someday I might. If we survive. I-I'm so frightened, Nen. I do not know what he is going to turn out to be." She looked down at the swell below her breasts.

"No fear!" Nen lifted her chin with a finger. "Baby no curse."

Rebaa smiled, but it was without conviction, remembering again the raw power that had come from within her, the sacking of the Great Spirit without a care for the Balance. She shuddered.

"You say must go back to People?" Nen questioned, breaking into her thoughts. "No go. Bad mistake. They hate you. They kill you. Will not accept. I try. Got stoned."

"He left me with no choice, Nen!" Rebaa flared. "I need a People. I have to go back. I have nowhere else to go."

"Do," Nen said, voice firm. She pushed Rebaa away from her and held her out at arm's length. "Can stay. I look after.

We look after. You outcast, I outcast. I hunt, you protect us with knowledge of Great Spirit. *We* take care of baby."

Rebaa blinked as her thoughts buzzed stupidly for a moment. She stared into Nen's determined eyes. The black gaze did not waver, and as her shock subsided, a new hope stirred. She chewed her lip, thinking. If she stayed, she would never see her brother again. She longed to see him. She missed her tribe and her home with all her heart. But Nen was right. They would never accept her back. She had known it from the start. She had only set out to find them because she had been left with no other hope. Now she had another choice. The fear that Nen would kill her if she ever discovered her baby's heritage was no longer valid. Nen had shared in her plight. Indeed, they were outcasts together.

At that precise moment, the baby kicked fervently.

"Ah!" Rebaa protested at the abuse. He was so *strong*.

In a swift motion, Nen placed a warm hand on her belly, feeling the nudges under her large palm. Her dark eyes melted into a loving reverence. "No fear, little *juaan*," she whispered. "I be your *tarhe*." The baby quieted under her touch.

"Tarhe?"

"Protector Mother," Nen answered solemnly. "Sacred vow. You kill Murzuk for me. I pledge my life to baby. Mark of family in Thal tribe."

Fresh tears slid down Rebaa's cheeks but, this time, she did not taste the bitterness of grief. "Oh, Nen."

"Stay?"

Rebaa sobbed as she threw her arms around Nen's neck. "Yes, yes, I'll stay with you. Thank you. Thank you so much."

The carved image of Nen holding her baby stood out brightly on the cave wall before her as she rested her chin on her friend's shoulder. It occurred to Rebaa that she did not know the boy's name. Nen was her family now, and it seemed important to know. "What did you call him, Nen, your boy? What was his name?"

Nen hesitated for a moment, as though deciding how much uttering the name would injure her. She drew a breath and spoke.

"Name him for bear strength. I name him Eldrax."

* * *

15

Rise

Eldrax's red hair flamed in the morning light. The silver face of Nanna had waned to a slit in the night sky since he had returned to the Hunting Bear clan's main camp. Amusing himself with the spoils of Rikal's defeat had done little to bank the flames of his temper. He had taken all the Eagle women that the men had deigned to take prisoner for himself.

Nobody had dared Challenge him for them, not that they were really worth it. None had any desirable features to pass on to future offspring, none were tall or brave, none were strong. He would not have wasted his own time on them had he not needed to slake his frustrations. The men could fight over rights to them when he was done, if they wished.

Rikal's mate had been of value, but he had killed her as soon as he had finished with her. A Thal woman. His hatred had outweighed her uses. Thals were nothing but cowards, worthless except for passing on their strength, and that was of no great consequence. *He* had enough strength to pass on when provided with a worthy Cro female. There would be no place for Thals in the clan he hoped to build when he was Chief. If he needed the fresh blood of another People for his clan, he would seek out the Deni for worthy mates as Murzuk's father had done.

When he was Chief...

He glared bitterly over the top of the shelters and smouldering campfires, back towards the distant mountains to the west. If his... *Chief* had been successful, then Murzuk should soon return with Juran's mate. Eldrax's lips parted. *That* was a female who would be worth his time. The train of thought was distracting and had him swiftly returning to the cowering creature currently occupying his tent.

A soft snowfall had begun when he finally re-emerged. He sniffed the air hopefully. He was hungry. He and the hunters had brought down an adult bull ox the night before. Taking out his frustrations on the Eagle women had grown tiresome, and he had set out with the hunting group in the hopes of a good fight. The sight of the immense bull had made his blood sing. Oxen were difficult and dangerous to hunt. If they banded together as a herd, the fight to separate out a target made for an interesting challenge. But, to Eldrax's disappointment, this great bull had been nursing a festering spear wound to the shoulder. Another hunter had got to it first. The rest of its herd had given up on waiting for it, and it had been disappointingly easy to bring down.

At least the clan would eat well for the next few days. The women had rejoiced at the sight of so much meat. Oxen were a luxury rarely found in this fringe territory. Something must have driven it off its usual migration route.

Eldrax sniffed again. The scent of roasting meat floated to him on the soft breeze. The women had awoken one of the campfires to prepare for an evening feast. Eldrax set out toward the mouthwatering smell, weaving through the erected bone and skin shelters. He took pleasure in seeing women and children scuttling out of his sight as he passed, hoping to escape notice.

"Ooph!"

Eldrax's head snapped around. The sound of spears smashing together and a body hitting the snow drove the hunger from his mind. Some of the men were sparring. He smiled. Time for a *real* diversion. Stepping around a shelter, he came upon the scene he had been hoping for. Tanag was in a mock battle with his brother, Hanak. It was obvious Tanag had just scored a strike and thrown his brother to the ground. Hanak had always been the swiftest hunter, but his brother was the better warrior.

A group of small boys had joined the usual gathering of adolescent females who had crowded around to watch the young hunters spar. The girls' interest was clear on their faces. The boys murmured in admiration of Tanag's skill. All except one. Eldrax recognised the sandy-haired half-breed son of Rikal.

The child could not have been much older than two turns of the seasons, but he was sitting with his arms crossed, raptly watching the two warriors play at combat. As Eldrax came into view, the boy's pale eyes widened in horror.

Eldrax grinned. Here was a boy who would grow knowing his authority. But, instead of fleeing from him as he expected, the infant remained where he was. Fear filled his face, but he refused to give ground to the man who had killed his mother and father before him. Eldrax felt a grudging flicker of respect. He could see why Rannac had kept him. It was time for the boy to witness true skill.

A collection of spears and other weapons were leaning against the nearest shelter. Eldrax selected a spear and whirled it about him, swinging it around his body as he familiarised himself with the weapon's balance. Though only for sparring, spear tips and knives were not blunted. Hunting Bear warriors learned fast or died. He saw Tanag and Hanak pause in their battle to exchange a nervous glance.

Only Rannac would willingly agree to spar with him these days. Eldrax's lips twisted. These softer men had not suffered the upbringing he had endured. He looked into their faces, and beneath the hardened charade of their warriors' eyes, he could see their weakness. They still knew compassion. They still knew love. And that was their downfall. He had stripped such things from his soul long ago. Now he was without mercy, without weakness.

"You." He jabbed a finger toward the two warriors. "Here." He had been awaiting an opportunity to take revenge upon Hanak for days. Now it had arrived. Hanak seemed to guess this, for he hung back behind his brother, his eyes sullen.

"W-which one of us?" Tanag attempted to keep his voice even as his blue eyes flickered to the young women who were still watching. He knew he was about to be beaten and beaten badly.

Eldrax smiled. "Both of you."

His fellow warriors' backs straightened as they regained some of their confidence, misplaced though it was. Eldrax strolled to the centre of the open space and waited as they flanked him, preparing to attack from either side. He slowed his breathing as he adjusted his stance, feeling the ground beneath his feet, the direction of the wind in the air. He did not make any outward sign that he was watching them, but he was listening, attuning himself to his opponents' footfalls, the hitch of their breath, the rustle of their furs as they shifted their weight. He waited.

Hanak was the first to attack. He did so silently and without drama. Rannac had taught them all that it was foolish to announce one's attack with pointless shouting. Eldrax was ready for him, blocking the strike with the haft of his spear. A whistle of the air was his only warning. Tanag had launched himself at his back, spear scything towards him, aiming to pierce his right arm.

Continuing to hold Hanak's weapon at bay, Eldrax shifted his feet and rolled his shoulder back. Tanag's spear brushed harmlessly past the edge of his upper arm. Taking advantage of the other warrior's momentary unbalance, Eldrax drove the butt of his spear into Tanag's ribcage as he stumbled, knocking him to the ground before using the momentum of his twisting motion to swing forward and smash his balled fist into Hanak's nose. Blood spurted as Hanak fell away with a low moan. The whole fight had lasted a mere moment.

Eldrax looked sourly at the two fallen warriors. "The women could have fought better," he muttered as he turned his back on them and began to walk away.

This time Hanak did shout when he attacked. Blood maddened, the young warrior flew at Eldrax, his brother close at his side. Eldrax barely got his spear into position to block the blow that had come for his skull. Hanak had meant it as a killing strike. His eyes sparked. This was more like it!

Heart singing, Eldrax struck and parried, countering the furious blows of his opponents as they came at him from both sides. He bellowed a laugh as Tanag got lucky and separated him from his spear. Weaponless, Eldrax danced between their jabs and strikes, twisting and ducking, often avoiding a blow by a mere breath.

Eventually, he tired of playing with them. Grabbing Tanag's spear as it made another pass, he yanked the other warrior off his feet, flinging him around until he smashed into his brother, sending them both against the unforgiving bone support of a hide shelter.

"Much better." He grinned down at them as they struggled to untangle themselves. The young girls watching upon the periphery now had eyes only for him, watching with a mix of fear and hope. Eldrax assessed them, deciding if any would make a worthy mate to him. A tall, ebony-skinned girl caught his attention. Halima did not lower her handsome face, but held his gaze boldly. *Yes—*

"Eldrax!" a voice shouted across the camp. "Where is the Red Bear?"

The urgency in the tone had Eldrax swiping his fallen spear from the ground. "Tanag, Hanak! Gather the rest of the men!" He did not pause to see if they questioned his orders. He took off in the direction of the call.

A crowd was gathering on the edges of the camp. An elder came hobbling towards him as he neared.

"What is it?" Eldrax's black eyes flickered to the gathering, searching for the threat.

Losing nerve, the elder did not answer. He stepped back and indicated that Eldrax should see for himself. Shoving the man aside with a growl, Eldrax moved towards the disturbance, the spear poised in his hand. The rest of the clan parted as they saw him approach, revealing the source of the commotion.

Rannac was half collapsed upon the ground. His knees had

173

buckled from under him and he was clinging one-handed to a spear braced into the ground to prevent himself from falling entirely. His other arm appeared broken in several places.

Rannac's eyes lifted as Eldrax came to stand before him, and he heaved himself back to his feet, locking his knees as he leaned all the more heavily on the spear.

"Where is the witch?" Eldrax demanded. He scanned the horizon over Rannac's shoulder, but there was no sign of the rest of Murzuk's hunting party.

Rannac pressed cracked lips together before speaking. "We found her in the foothills, your father—" Eldrax's gaze hardened and Rannac quickly corrected himself. The other man knew very well he did not recognise Murzuk as his father. He was his Chief, and that was all he needed to know. "Murzuk ambushed her. She-she wasn't alone, but Murzuk brought down her defence and we captured her."

"So, where is she?" Eldrax was rapidly losing patience.

"She used her witch magic." Rannac's eyes still held vestiges of terror… or was it awe? "Galib was holding her while Murzuk dealt with the other threat, then Galib was dead upon the ground and she was free. She had… no weapons. Eldrax… she is a very dangerous creature."

Eldrax paid him little heed to the stark warning in the other man's eyes. Excitement curled down his spine. The witch was far more powerful than he had suspected. "And?"

"Then she unleashed her full power, bringing a herd of oxen stampeding down the gully straight into us. I—I've never seen anything like it. I was the only one to survive her attack. I return bearing the heavy news that Chief Murzuk, the Great Bear, is dead." Bowing his head, Rannac lifted the spear he carried and swung it round ceremoniously until it rested across his one good palm, presenting it to Eldrax. The carved spearhead of the Hunting Bear chief was tied to the haft. Rannac spoke in a loud, clear voice. "I greet you as our new leader. Chief Eldrax."

Eldrax rocked back on his heels before he mastered himself. He opened his mouth to speak but was cut off by a voice crying out in protest.

"He has not earned the right to be chief!" Hanak called out over the murmurings of the clan. "It is up to the elders to decide now." A few voices raised up in agreement.

Eldrax glared at Hanak, his hand twitching upon his spear. Rannac cut across him.

"But he has earned the right, Hanak. With his last breath, Murzuk blessed Eldrax as his successor. By our lore, he is the new leader of the Hunting Bear clan."

A deathly silence fell. Rannac's face was composed as he spoke, but Eldrax could not control the shock contorting his own features. Murzuk had named *him* as his successor. An array of emotions coiled in his chest, freezing him in place as he stared down at his father's spear resting in Rannac's hand. The decaying finger bones of Juran still dangled from below the tip.

Then the maelstrom of confusion passed, and Eldrax grunted dismissively. Of course Murzuk would have given his blessing to Eldrax's leadership after he was gone. Nobody else was worthy of the title. It did not mean the brute had actually cared for him in any way.

Still, he hesitated to take up the offered spear. "Are you sure?" Eldrax demanded. He had made the mistake of thinking Murzuk dead once, he was not about to be made a fool of again. "Did you look down upon Murzuk's lifeless corpse with your own eyes and make certain that he is gone?"

"I did." Rannac's tone was stiff. "No man could survive such injuries. I took the chief's totem from around his throat myself."

Rannac did not tell blind stories. This time, his father was truly dead. *At last!* The man who had treated him more harshly than he would his worst enemy was gone. Eldrax felt nothing but a fierce, burning pleasure as he reached out and seized the spear from Rannac's hand. The grizzled warrior sank back to his knees before him as Eldrax turned to the waiting clan.

"Chief Murzuk is dead!" He announced. "I hold the totem of Chief and take my rightful position as leader of this clan!" He smiled wickedly as his eyes settled on Hanak. "As my first act, I offer this one chance to any man who thinks me unfit to Challenge me for the honour of leadership. Should he emerge victorious, I will, of course, step aside." His lips twitched.

Hanak glowered, but bowed his head in submission and stepped back. Eldrax revelled in the sight. The wind whistled over the rest of silent camp. No one stepped forward to try to claim the totem and spear from Eldrax, for all knew it would be an act of suicide. Whatever else they might think of him, they knew the Red Bear was the strongest of them all. For better or worse, Murzuk had passed on the right, and now he would lead the clan until his death. One by one, the Hunting Bear clan dropped to its knees. No one spoke or dared to meet Eldrax's inviting gaze lest it be taken in challenge.

Rannac's voice cut through the silence. "Before you stands a new Chief! May his strength lead us true and shelter us from our enemies. Pledge yourselves to his protection from now until the day he can protect us no more!"

There was a rustle of movement as all those gathered drew

blades. The men bared their hunting knives while the women pulled forth the tools they used in their day-to-day chores. One by one the clan approached, sliced the tip of a finger, and reached up to touch the bleeding digit to Eldrax's forehead. The hush was broken only by the cries of children and the wail of babies as their mothers sliced their skin and made the vow for them. Rikal's sandy-haired Thal half-breed had to be forcibly brought forward to touch him.

Eldrax's high forehead dripped red as the last members made their vow. He carried the weight of their blood, their very lives. Every single one of them belonged to Eldrax. At last, after a lifetime of sacrifice and struggle, he stood as the greatest Chief in these god forsaken lands. His fingers trembled as Eldrax untied the spearhead necklace from around Murzuk's weapon and placed it around his own neck, letting the carved totem of the Hunting Bear Clan dangle against his heart.

There was only one thing now that would make his victory complete.

"Where did you find the witch?" he asked Rannac.

The older warrior lifted his head, startled. "My Chief?"

"Speak." The rumble of Eldrax's command brooked no argument.

Rannac hesitated. "East of here, roughly six days' travel as the crow flies. You intend to go back for her?" His dark face was askance.

"There is nothing I desire more, Rannac."

"I caution you to leave her be." Rannac said. "You cannot underestimate this woman. Such a mistake cost Murzuk his life."

"I am not my father!" Murzuk had been nothing but a fool. "I *will* have her. The other clans will see Juran's mate in my grasp and know that I am now the power in these lands. If she is able to bear me witch-children, so much the better. I'll at least have fun trying to find out." He sneered.

"That question has already been answered." There was another momentary pause as Rannac seemed to wrestle with himself. "The witch was… with child. I can only assume Juran is the father of her unborn."

Eldrax had to work to keep the surprise off his face. *So…* Juran had proved it could be done. The witch carried his spawn. It was now clear to him why she had remained in the hills and had not attempted to return to her own People. He gripped his spear while his other hand rubbed restlessly at his chest. He *had* to have her.

"You!" He jabbed a finger at the tribe's crooked old medicine woman as she shuffled away. "See to his injury. I want him fit to travel in two days. You will lead me to her, Rannac. You say she wasn't alone?" His voice turned to a dangerous growl. "Which clan has dared to claim her?"

Rannac shifted more uncomfortably than ever. "She wasn't accompanied by another clan, my Chief. There was only one other with her. I… I almost didn't believe it—"

"In all the gods!" Eldrax's patience shattered. He did not care who the witch had latched on to. They were a dead man walking. "Tell me who has her!"

Rannac lifted his grizzled chin and let the blow land. "Your mother."

* * *

16

Birth

Rebaa's dreams were easier following her outpouring of grief to Nen; her sleep restful. Having shared her story, Rebaa somehow felt lighter. She had taken the first step on her path to recovery. Maybe one day she would indeed be able to make peace with Juran.

In accepting Nen's promise of sanctuary, Rebaa had felt the closest to being complete since the massacre of the Black Wolf. Trembling with relief and gratitude, she had healed Nen's head wound. It had amazed her to find that there was nothing broken. The blow her friend had received would have caved a Cro's skull in. Thal durability had saved her friend's life. Rebaa had been glad of the simple flesh wound, Nen's body proved even less responsive to the energies of the Great Spirit than a Cro's.

When Ninmah had dawned on the morning following Murzuk's attack, Nen and Rebaa had moved the bodies of the Cro men crushed by the stampede. It wasn't pleasant work, and it had taken Nen a great deal of effort to even come near the corpse of her former captor, but they could not leave the bodies in the open to attract unwanted attention. They pulled them into a shallow ravine as far away from the cave as they could get them and then piled rocks on top of the bloody remains. Rebaa had to wash in the stream for a long time after that.

Since then, time had passed by in a contented haze. By day Rebaa helped Nen with the everyday chores of keeping the cave clean and habitable and stocked with anything they may need. Nen repaired her broken spear. Rebaa watched as she bundled bits of tree bark under a pile of ash before setting light to them. It was a complex process, with Nen paying close attention to the temperatures being produced. Her patient dedication paid off and the resulting black, sticky substance fused a freshly knapped spearhead to the haft.

"Did you learn that from the Cro?" Rebaa asked. She had seen the men and women of Juran's clan perform this miracle many times.

Nen's eyes flashed. "Ngathe! Thal discover! Cro steal. Killers and takers!" She spat on the ground.

"I'm sorry." Rebaa was quick to placate.

Rebaa's tuition in the art of hunting small game continued. Her skills improved, though it still felt like a betrayal of everything that the Ninkuraaja stood for when she used her talents to her advantage. She closed her mind against it. She was never going home; she had to forget what she had been. She was an outcast now, without a People.

Nen made Rebaa new, warmer clothes and also wrappings for the baby, ready for when he arrived. To complete her work and using the last of the bearskin, Nen fashioned a warm sling that would enable Rebaa to carry the baby next to her heart while still being able to move unhindered. All this waited in a warm corner of the cave, ready for when it would be called for.

This existence Rebaa had found with Nen might not be what she had imagined her life to be; so far from her People and their forests, living inside a cave with a Thal woman, but she was as happy as she could be. Accepted. She and her unborn. They were safe. She could not ask for more than that, especially when she had not expected to live at all.

But some fears could not be escaped so easily. Now that her chief concern of survival had been removed from her shoulders, the apprehension for what her baby might be had moved to the forefront. Nen's reassurances had not completely set her at ease.

Rebaa had felt no more stirrings of power beside her own since the attack, but she could not forget the wild energy that had rushed through her veins like fire when their lives had been in the balance. The daily tasks with Nen distracted her enough to prevent Rebaa from spiralling into panic, but the nights were a different story. The darkness often found her lying awake in the stillness of the night when all fears seemed to grow greater in the shadows.

Her time was almost upon her. She knew her baby could make his way into the world any day now, and she did not know what to expect. She wanted to turn to someone for wisdom, for reassurance, but in this one respect, she was still completely alone.

Nen might have borne a Forbidden baby, but no one had ever conceived a half Ninkuraaja child before. Rebaa's throat had closed at the thought. Ninmah must have had a reason to forbid the mixing of Ninkuraaja blood with that of other Peoples. Nen was convinced that such a thing was not a curse, but Nen had loved her Forbidden baby as powerfully as any mother. Had that love blinded her? In the shadows of Rebaa's mind, the fear grew.

Rebaa waddled behind Nen in the pale morning light of a new day as they walked to the mountain stream to drink. She had slept poorly and her back was aching. The uncertainty of her baby's belonging in the world was not her only concern. Juran's child was big. Larger than the average Ninkuraaja child, Rebaa would like to guess, and it was putting extra strains upon her small body. Today, the ache was almost unbearable.

She gasped suddenly and had to sit down on a rock as the baby gave a powerful kick. It felt like he was straining, fighting to be free of his bonds. So close. The familiar shiver of apprehension curled down her back. She hoped everything went smoothly with the birth. She had no Ninkuraaja healers, not even old Cro medicine women to help her if things went wrong.

Nen paused when she realised Rebaa was no longer following; her concern evident on her face. Rebaa tried to muster a reassuring smile as she rubbed her sore side. She felt so cumbersome. "It's ok, Nen. He's just kicking like a horse."

"Ah," the shadows in the Thal's eyes eased. She smiled. "Little *juaan*."

"What does that mean?" Rebaa was curious. The word sounded almost Ninkuraaja.

"It mean 'strong one' to my People."

"Strong one," Rebaa repeated, rubbing her belly ruefully. "He certainly is." *In more ways than one...*

"What name him?"

182

The question startled Rebaa. *Name?* She realised she hadn't given the issue any thought. She did not know what name the Black Wolf elders would have bestowed upon Juran's son. A Cro name might no longer be appropriate. "I haven't decided yet."

They drank their fill and made their way back to the cave. The birds were singing in the air as they soared above. Rebaa recognised them all. All except one. There was a distant repeated chirrup that she just couldn't place. Another strange call coming from further away answered it. Rebaa listened intently, but the unfamiliar bird fell silent. She shrugged it off. All manner of creatures were being displaced by the increasing cold and the ever encroaching Fury Wastes. She had better get used to seeing and hearing new things.

By the time they reached the cave, the wind was gathering in power, collecting loose snow on its icy breath and swirling it into their faces. Rebaa shivered. Another storm was coming. Squinting, she saw heavy clouds glowering on the horizon. Nen sniffed the air. "Bad."

Rebaa agreed. She could feel the changes in the air pressure. "We better gather more firewood before it hits. If it lingers, we'll need it." They could not afford to let that fire go out.

Nen pointed further down the slope. "Wood not far. Plenty of branches."

Rebaa pressed her hands into her aching back and groaned. All she wanted was to get back to the cave and gather a nest of furs around her heavy belly, but that would have to wait; continued heat was vital to their survival. "Lead the way," she told Nen.

The wood turned out to be a sparse copse tucked away in a shallow dell. Together, they collected as many fallen twigs and branches as they could carry and climbed back up to the cave to deposit their loads beside their idling fire to dry. Rebaa assessed the wood piles with a sinking heart. It would take several more trips to build up a satisfactory supply.

They were travelling down the slope for a third time when Rebaa heard the strange bird call again. "Do you know what bird that is?" she asked Nen out of mild interest as she struggled down the bank.

Nen listened with an intent frown. "No," she said. "Never heard before."

"Nor have I," Rebaa said. "I wonder—"

All thought of further words scattered as the base of her back contracted in pain.

"Ah!" Rebaa stumbled, catching herself on her hands.

Nen was there in an instant. "What wrong?"

"I don't know," Rebaa panted, wild-eyed. Her dirty hands went to her belly. Fear that was not her own flooded her veins with adrenalin and an echo of the raw energy that she had felt during the Cro attack crackled invisibly across her skin, making her hairs stand on end. *No!* Concentrating hard, she tempered the building power.

She was barely aware of Nen's hands fluttering over her. "Get back home. Get rest."

"Yes," Rebaa agreed, struggling to her feet, only to sink back down when another wave of pain hit home and the sense of panic rolled through her again.

A gush of fluid signalled the breaking of her waters, and it was her own panic Rebaa choked upon this time. She grabbed Nen's arm.

"Nen, he's coming! The baby is coming now!" She wasn't *ready.* She had not yet resolved any of her fears. But nature had no patience for her foolish second thoughts. She had no more time to think, no more time to fear.

"Quick!" Nen stooped and threw Rebaa's arm over her thick shoulders, helping to keep her steady. She half carried Rebaa back up the slope. Her friend was more than a little anxious.

Rebaa's heart was pounding. She had witnessed many births and none of them had looked exactly pleasant. She was more frightened by the coming ordeal than she would admit. She clutched on to Nen with all her strength as the first contraction rippled through her. It seemed to take forever to get back to the cave. Rebaa heard the bird cry again, closer this time. She wished it would shut up. Its strangeness was more an irritation now than a curiosity.

At last they reached the shelter of the cave. Nen piled up some furs and laid Rebaa down upon them. She stoked and refuelled the fire, then looked for other things to fuss with. Failing that, she fidgeted where she stood. "What now?" she asked.

"We just have to wait, I suppose." Rebaa's voice quaked, defying her efforts to keep it steady. "Just talk to me. I'm... scared."

Nen offered her hand as another contraction convulsed through Rebaa's slight frame, tearing a cry from her lips. The pain was moving around to the front. Nen stroked back her hair and murmured comfortingly to her; her voice flowing out in a steady stream. She lapsed into her own tongue for ease, and Rebaa could not understand her words. It did not matter, just the rhythm of the Thal woman's husky voice was enough to soothe her and give her something solid to cling to.

The day grew late. The blizzard swept in, paling its predecessors into insignificance with its ferocity. Rebaa could not see very far out of the cave. The gales of falling snow obscured everything beyond the first few rocks. The bitter wind came rushing through the cave mouth to find them, threatening to extinguish their fire. It bit at Rebaa's fevered brow, and she shivered violently before breaking off into another keening wail of pain, her belly drawing tight. *Would this never end?*

Nen rose and left her side for the first time since the labour had begun. Rebaa reached after her in desperation, not wanting to be left alone. Nen quieted her and then began piling rocks in the cave's entrance. She had a sufficient amount to block the opening. She left holes at the top to permit just enough air flow for the fire. The wind whined through the gaps, furious at being thwarted. They paid it no mind.

Night had fallen when Rebaa's contractions reached fever pitch. She could hardly regain her breath between one and the next. She was screaming, begging for it to end. Nen was beside herself.

"Make it stop!" Rebaa felt sure she was going to die. "Nen, make—" Her pleas were cut off when a familiar howl of challenge split the air outside. Rebaa's blood turned to ice at the sound of it.

That was not the voice of the wind.

Rebaa's wild, rolling eyes turned towards the blocked entrance. "Oh no," she whimpered through her tears and struggles. "No, not now!" Senses heightened in this most vulnerable of moments, Rebaa felt them approach. Every single thought and intent standing out in stark clarity.

"Nen!" she grabbed the Thal woman's arm, fighting through yet another wave of pain. "They're back. The Cro. They've come for us!" She fell back on her elbows, crying out.

Fierce shouts rose above the storm outside, getting closer. More bird calls went up and more answered, swelling in number. Only those calls had never come from any bird. They were hunting calls. Rebaa raged against her own stupidity. The Cro had been watching the entire time. Now they were ready to exact their revenge for the loss of their leader. And they couldn't have timed it more perfectly.

Fighting for concentration, Rebaa searched the energies of the earth outside, hoping for something, anything. There was nothing. All life had gone into hiding to wait out the storm. Maybe that too had been a part of the Cro's design. Rebaa was helpless. Their cunning never ceased to amaze her. Sweat poured from her brow, mixing with bitter tears. She had failed her son. Failed him before he had even taken his first breath.

Nen sat grimly beside her as the shouts intensified. Their enemy knew they were getting close to their target. The Thal woman stared down at Rebaa, convulsing in the throes of childbirth, then turned to the walled entrance, before gazing down at Rebaa again. Rising to her knees, she put her hands on Rebaa's belly. "*Gor cha tarhe, ki juaan*," she murmured.

She stood up, drawing away, her face becoming a fierce mask of cold, hard determination. The look in her eyes sent Rebaa into a panic.

"Nen?" she asked, though she already knew the terrible answer. She had seen that very same look on the day her world had shattered. "Nen. Don't. Stay with me!"

Nen shook her head. "I vow *tarhe*, for little strong one," she said. "If I stay, they find us. I go. Can lead them away. Maybe in snow, can escape. Only hope." She moved to pick up her spear.

"No! Nen!" Rebaa cried, gasping and trying to rise to

prevent her. She fell back when her body would not obey. "Nen! Please. Stay with me! I need you! We just have to stay quiet. Maybe they'll miss us in the storm." She was frantic. She could not lose Nen, too.

Again, Nen shook her head. No more moved by Rebaa's pleas than Juran had been. She was already heading for the cave entrance. "Know where cave is. I have to go. Protect baby." She began pulling rocks away from the blocked entrance, just enough for her to slip out into the fractious, stormy night. "Only one who can."

"No! Nen!" Rebaa shrieked. But Nen had already begun piling the rocks back into place behind her. She met Rebaa's eyes across the space between them before replacing the last. The moment stretched as they stared into each other's faces. One pleading, the other resolute.

"*Shalanaki*, Rebaa," Nen whispered, then the last rock slid into place and she was gone.

"Nooooo!" Rebaa howled in despair. "Nen! Come back!" But she could think no more. The baby began to arrive, and she had to heave with all her might, instinct driving her to do what she must. The pain went on and on. She doubted that if all of her bones had been broken at once, she could have felt this much pain. Through it all, she kept her teeth stubbornly locked together. She would not scream. She would not make it easy for those beasts to find her. The cries outside faded into the distance. Nen was leading them away. *Nen...*

Finally, in blood and fire and the wildness of the night, Rebaa's son was born.

* * *

17

Reckoning

live.

Eldrax stood a little distance away from the rest of his men, brooding into the distance. Since Rannac had told him of the company the witch was now keeping, Eldrax had withdrawn into himself, suffering to talk to no one other than to give commands. Rannac had brought them back to the heart of the now tiresome labyrinth of foothills. He vowed once he had the witch, he would never set foot in this forsaken territory again. He had sent scouts on ahead with Rannac to locate and then report back on the comings and goings of the witch and the Thal woman.

His... mother.

Eldrax tightened his grip on his spear as he struggled to internalise the knowledge. Soon Rannac would report back with the location of his quarry and then... then what would he do? Such cringing hesitation was unfamiliar to him, and he did not like it. His entire life had centred around one thing, the only thing that mattered: becoming the most feared and respected alpha wolf on the plains. He had learned the hard way that being anything lesser left one at risk of being devoured, and Eldrax would not suffer that. When faced with an enemy, he acted quickly and without remorse, thriving on the kill. Now he had ten good fighting men at his command and two insignificant women standing in his way, and he was... afraid.

Eldrax shifted, resisting the urge to pace like a cornered animal in front of his men. He was... *afraid* to see her, afraid that the sight of her would crack his strength and he would fail in his task. Through all the long seasons since his childhood, he had always believed that his cowardly mother was dead. Murzuk had sent Rannac after her to hunt her down and kill her following her betrayal. Eldrax had never known Rannac to fail in obeying his Chief or to bring a hunt to completion.

At first, he had refused to believe that Rannac had been correct in his identification. Even if the older warrior had somehow failed in his task all those seasons ago, Eldrax could not see how a lone, helpless woman could have survived without the protection of a clan. It was impossible and therefore it could not be *her*. Red hair was common among certain populations of Thals.

But the doubt had niggled and gnawed away in his stomach until at last he found he could not continue and see this woman for himself. He had sent Rannac forward instead as a delay, and he hated himself for it.

His desire to possess the witch for his own warred with his need to turn tail and run. It was as though he were that weak, terrified boy again.

Flashes of memory flickered through his mind, strong hands comforting him after he had fallen and cut his knees, a husky voice that sang to drive away his fears in the night, a flash of red against pale skin, a scent that curled on the edges of his senses.

Old wounds tore open, and he bellowed in agony as he launched his spear at the nearest tree. The haft quivered with the force of the impact. The wind whipped at Eldrax's own mane of red hair as he sucked in the cold air through his nose. He felt like he was being ripped apart. It was all Rannac's fault. His anger flared, and he latched on to it. Anger was an emotion that Eldrax could understand. He stoked it into a low simmer until it scalded all other sensations away.

The wind buffeted against him in ever strengthening gusts and moaned through the rocks. He glared at the horizon where dark clouds were gathering. The storm would hit by nightfall. He could see the rest of the men eyeing the growing blackness with mounting apprehension. Eldrax had made them travel light, and such a storm could trap them in these hills without shelter for days. Eldrax ignored them.

Darkness was falling ahead of the encroaching clouds when a whistle went up, announcing Rannac's return. Viciously suppressing the leap of dread in his gut, Eldrax thrilled back.

"Well?" he asked as the scouts appeared.

Rannac scratched at his tightly bound arm. "They are still there, my Chief, both the witch and your mother. They suspect nothing."

Eldrax jerked his chin once in acknowledgment, then beckoned Rannac close; this man who was responsible for his turmoil. "Murzuk ordered you to kill her," Eldrax whispered, the low simmer rising with each word. "You told him she was dead. You told *me* she was dead."

Rannac grew very still beside him. "She… evaded me, my Chief," he said. "But she was alone. I believed the land would claim her as I had not. I did not expect her to survive."

"She evaded you?" Eldrax's voice dripped with scepticism. "You never fail, Rannac. You have never failed to bring down your target. That was why Murzuk valued you so much. How is it you failed with her?"

The older warrior pressed his lips together and did not answer; instead, his eyes flickered to the gathering clouds over Eldrax's shoulder. "A storm is about to hit these hills," he murmured in a low voice. "My Chief, I advise we abandon this hunt and make for lower ground until it passes."

Eldrax silenced him with a cut of his eyes. He rubbed absently at his chest as he brought his face close to Rannac's ear. "I respect you, Rannac," he murmured. "You taught me how to fight. You taught me well. But my respect will not protect you. I am not my father. If you fail me or question my decisions, I will cut out your tongue and cast you from the protection of the clan. Understand?"

Rannac dropped his grey gaze to the ground. "Then what are your orders, my Chief?"

Eldrax looked at the approaching clouds and smiled. He did not see a hindrance there, only an opportunity. Swiftly, he laid his plans; the timing of the storm could not have been more perfect. Murzuk had underestimated the witch, and now he was dead. Eldrax would not make the same mistake.

And the Thal, whoever she was, would not stop him. He forced the weakling doubt from his heart. His mother had abandoned him long ago. If she had lived through all the days of his abuse at the hands of Murzuk, never once trying to save him, then she deserved to die. He yanked his spear from the tree. In his eyes, she was already dead. Nobody would ever stand in the way of what he wanted.

The wind gusted again, tearing at Eldrax's furs and bringing with it the first flakes of snow. More would follow. His resolve hardened like ice, freezing out the last of his hesitation. It was time to claim what was his.

"Move out."

The full force of the storm hit the foothills as Rannac led Eldrax's raiding party forward. The wind's voice had grown to a deafening pitch as it threw blinding sheets of snow and ice into their faces. The men thrilled whistles back and forth to one another to keep from getting separated.

"How much further?" Eldrax shouted to Rannac over the howls of the wind. Ice was forming along the haft of his spear and on the hairs of his furs.

"I'm... not...,... Chief." The wind snatched at Rannac's voice and stole it away. "The storm... every... lost."

One of the other men stumbled and fell to his knees in the snow. Eldrax could not see who it was, but gave them a vicious jab with the butt of his spear, forcing the man back to his feet. His half-Thal blood gave him the advantage in this extreme, but he knew his pure Cro followers were not faring so well. He could not afford for them to perish before he found the witch. He caught Rannac by the back of his furs, spinning him around. "I do not care if the gods themselves brought this storm. Find that—!"

Someone grabbed his arm, cutting him off. Snarling, he turned on Tanag. The other warrior's skin was pale and ice was clinging to the hair on his face, but he did not back down from Eldrax's angry gaze. He pointed silently away into the snow.

Eldrax followed the direction of Tanag's spear. The blizzard obscured his vision to the point of blindness, but in the distance he caught a movement. A dark figure was fleeing as fast as the deepening snow cover would allow.

"They're trying to escape!" Eldrax laughed as he watched the dark silhouette struggling against the wind and the treacherous footing. There at last was his prey, flushed out of hiding or maybe attempting to flee towards it. Whatever their plan, they were *his*. "Hunt them down!"

Eldrax plunged into the storm. The snow was piling higher, dragging at his feet, but he pushed his body on, determined to keep the fleeing figure firmly in his sights. The paths and trails twisted and turned through an increasingly jagged terrain. The hills and cliffs rose higher on all sides. His quarry knew the land well and despite his best effort, the dark silhouette disappeared into the crags, evading them in the storm.

Eldrax growled. *So, you think you're clever, do you?* If they wanted to test his skill as a hunter, then so be it. They were about to lose and lose badly. Eldrax scanned the ground as his men fanned out about him. The falling snow was a hindrance, but not an impossibility. Here and there a scuff mark would catch his eye, a stone knocked out of place. The barest of marks that a lesser hunter might have missed were all plain to Eldrax. He loped along eagerly, nostrils flaring. He could almost smell his prey's fear.

A shallow hollow tucked beneath a rock slide drew Eldrax's eye. Baying, he charged towards it. His prey held nerve only for a moment before they broke cover and ran on into the night. Eldrax boomed a laugh as the chase was rejoined.

His prey darted this way and that, searching for another bolt hole, but Eldrax would not allow it, directing his men to block them at every turn. This was the most diverting hunt he had enjoyed for a long time. He could see his prey was swiftly running out of tricks. And they were growing tired.

The gap closed.

Under a low cliff, the figure ahead finally came within range of Eldrax's spear and he could make out the bulky figure of a Thal. His heart hitched in his chest, causing his fingers to twitch upon his weapon. He ached to strike out, to launch the spear and eliminate the object of his uncertainty before he saw a face. But he could not give in to the temptation. The Thal could be carrying his desired prize, and he could not risk losing the witch. He had pushed his warriors to the limit in his drive to possess her. If he failed to return with her now, it would sow seeds of doubt against his ability to guide the clan.

And that would never do.

It was time to bring this hunt to an end. Whistling a hunting signal, he ordered his men to circle around. They peeled off, loping through the snow, easily overtaking their spent prey, trapping it. The Thal figure slewed to a halt as his men appeared out of the snow filled darkness before her. She turned quickly, looking for an alternative route only to find herself surrounded by silent, spear-bearing shadows on all sides.

Snarling like a cornered spear cat, she brought her own weapon to bear. Rannac was closest, and she struck at him. The seasoned warrior wheeled away from the blow, knocking her spear aside with his own. She recovered and gathered herself to launch another attack.

"You have no hope of escape," Eldrax called over the wind. He had not deigned to speak Thal words since he was a boy and they felt strange upon his lips, the intonations testing his tongue. It mattered not, she understood. At his first word, she

195

ceased in her attack; the hitherto sure hands trembling upon her weapon.

Slowly, the Thal turned and Eldrax felt the world around him stop as black eyes, his own eyes, came to stare him full in the face. More images exploded in his mind, those same eyes gazing at him in adoration when he had lifted his first spear, when he had won his first fight. The protective fire that flared whenever his father approached...

A soft, keening wail went up from the Thal's throat. The spear dropped from her hands. "Eldrax. My Eldrax..."

Eldrax could not move, could not speak. Emotions tore at him from all sides, but in the eye of the storm, his heart was numb. Motionless, he watched his mother take a stumbling step towards him, tears freezing on her pale cheeks as they fell.

"My Eldrax? My baby."

"Mother..." His mind whirled faster as the word slipped from his lips, the memories coming sharp and painfully clear.

Someone was tearing him from the warmth of the powerful arms.

"My baby!"

"Mama!"

Her tortured eyes focused on him once, and then she was fleeing. She did not look back, even as he cried and screamed. "Mama!"

The eye of the storm passed, and Eldrax was at once filled with a terrible fury. She had left him, *abandoned* him, and now here she was, alive and well after all the passing of the seasons, never once having tried to return and save him. His skin crawled as he grew conscious of every one of his scars, every ache of a healed bone. Cold, he straightened to his full height as she halted, hesitating just two short strides from where he stood.

"You are here." Her eyes, so familiar, so hated, raked over him. She appeared afraid that he would disappear in a swirl of snow if she so much as blinked. "Eldrax... My Eldrax."

"Yes." His voice held no more warmth than the fractious air tearing around them. "And here *you* are after all this time, *mother*." Derision dripped from the last word.

Her face contracted at his tone. "My son." A large hand reached forward, trying to bridge the gap between them and convince herself that what she was seeing was not a hallucination. Her lips trembled. "How... how much I have..." She appeared lost for words, dazed. "You must have missed me so." She held out her arms as though expecting him to fall into them.

Eldrax's eyebrows shot up. "Miss you? Why would I miss you, mother? You let me go and fled. You left me behind to the... *mercy* of my father." The terror he had felt in that moment ripped through his chest, as fresh as it had on the night she left him. He closed his eyes, locking the memory of her fleeing form in place to harden the defensive ice around his heart. "You did not even look back as you abandoned me. You did not care about me. You ran as hard as you could to save your own miserable hide."

Horror shot across her face as his words struck like a mortal blow. He took savage pleasure in her pain. "No!" she moaned. "Eldrax. I did not—please. I loved you! My sweet one. I tried to keep you, but I could not fight them. They would have killed me in front of you. Th-that was something I could n-not let you see." Her voice cracked.

"At least it would have proven your love!" Spittle flew from Eldrax's mouth as he rejected her words. "Instead, I was unworthy, too insignificant in your eyes to be worth saving."

His mother's face was carved in the same mask of agony she had worn in his last memory of her. Her hands twisted together in desperation. "No, no. Understand, I had nowhere to go. I-I could barely feed myself. And you were not safe with other Thals."

"Yes, best to leave a Forbidden half-breed where he would not shame you," Eldrax snarled. "Well, here I am, a man grown, a *Chief!* Am I still a shame to you, mother?"

"Please, Eldrax." She stumbled towards him, closing the last of the gap between them. "My Eldrax, please. I loved you more than life itself. You do not know how much I have longed—I'll do anything. Anything. Just... *forgive me."* She reached up and closed her hands around his face, rubbing her thumbs over his cheekbones as her tear-streaked eyes beseeched him.

Eldrax wanted desperately to pull away, to cast her to the ground at his feet, but he found he was once again unable to move. The ice he was fighting to hold around his heart shivered as she touched him, as though her hands held an untold power.

The sensation was not quite how he remembered it. When she had last held him so, his cheeks had been smooth with boyhood. But the warmth of her hands permeated his cold skin, leaching out his anger. *Mother....*

My beautiful Eldrax. How I love you.

Mama.

Here were the hands that had held him as a baby, lifted him when he was small and wiped away his childish tears. Under her touch, he could almost remember the boy he had been. The boy she remembered and loved. Her sweet Eldrax.

Her eyes held nothing but love for him. Eldrax could see it all in the dark depths: the pain of their separation, the relief of their reunion at last, and the desperate longing for his love to be restored. He fought to hold on to his hate, but he could not find it in the swirl of emotion rushing through his heaving chest. Of its own volition, his free hand moved up to clutch at hers as it did in his memory. Fissures appeared in the ice. His eyes drifted closed as he pressed his cheek into the warm touch, her palm both rough and comforting at the same time.

"Mother..."

"Yes. I'm here," she breathed. "I am here now." Weeping softly, she stroked his hair, combing her fingers through the tangled mane. He felt he could live in that moment forever. All the seasons rolled away. The hand still holding his spear loosened. Yes, she was here now. What did anything else matter? He bowed his head upon her shoulder to hide the tears that were coming, his tenuous composure cracking around the edges.

"Chief Eldrax?"

The voice cut in on the moment, and Eldrax blinked. *Chief Eldrax.* The haze of his boyhood memories ebbed away, and he stood once more in the harsh, unforgiving landscape, surrounded by his expectant men. He trembled as conflicting desires warred for dominance in his mind. His mother was with him at last, but there was something else he had come here to find. Something important. He struggled to gather his thoughts.

"The witch... mother, where is the witch?" Eldrax whispered. He fought to keep his focus on what he had come to do as her warm hands continued to play over his face and hair.

"Rebaa?" His words had shaken her back to reality, and her hands paused in their movements. Her gaze flickered warily to Eldrax's waiting men before settling back on his face. The flash of unease melted away as she drank him in. "You wish to know where Rebaa is?"

"Yes. I have come a long way to find her. Please, mother."

She smiled, nodding as she resumed her tender ministrations. She would give him what he desired. She had always sought to make him content. The ice around his heart melted, and he found himself giving her what she wanted in return. "I forgive you, mother," he said as he squeezed her hands. "I forgive you."

A guttural sob tore from her chest as she threw her arms around his neck and cried into his shoulder.

"Just tell me where the witch is, mother." He felt her breath hitch as she hesitated again. "Please, help me, and then we can go home."

At that word, he felt her stiffen in his arms. "Home?"

"Yes. Back to the camp. As soon as we have the witch, you can return home with me."

"Cro camp?" She drew back and once again her gaze travelled over the hard faces watching her in the darkness. He felt her tremble. The indecision on her face cleared, and the expression that remained was not the one he had hoped to see. The motherly indulgence had vanished. "N-no, my Eldrax. I will not go back to the Cro. Nor will Rebaa. Evil men, Eldrax. Cro are evil."

The spell she had woven over him shattered. *Evil? Evil. And yet... you left me with them anyway,* mother.

He allowed her to hold him for a moment longer, letting all that could have been flow through his heart before releasing it for the lie it was. The fierce pain of loss reignited his anger. No true mother would withhold what he wanted. *Lies.* And he had almost succumbed.

"You deny me because you think us to be evil?" His voice was soft.

"Yes, evil men. The Cro are cruel. I cannot go back. I cannot tell you where Rebaa is, for *they* will find her. I vowed *tarhe* for the unborn baby. I protect her."

"You protect *her*?" Fury and betrayal such as he had never known burned through Eldrax's heart. He was shaking with the force of it. Lapsing back into the Cro tongue, he spat. "You guard a spawn not of your blood when you did not bother to protect your own? Evil men? Well, what about me, *mother*? Do you think me evil, too?"

Her face paled at his change in words, and she took a step back from him. "Speak as I taught you," she admonished. "You are not evil. You are not Cro."

"Oh, but I *am* Cro. How could I be anything else? It is what you left me to be." He caught her arms, refusing to let her retreat further from him as he gave her one hard shake. "I am running out of patience, mother. *Where is she?*"

The first flicker of uncertainty travelled through her black eyes as she regarded him. For the first time she was seeing not the boy she had loved, but what she had left him to become.

"No, no." There was denial in her tone. She did not want to believe. She tried to look away, to take another step back, but he dug his fingers into her arms, preventing her from moving. She stilled, but kept her gaze down, avoiding his face, avoiding her crime. "And... if you had the Dryad, what would you do with her?" she whispered.

"I would take her as my own as father took you. She will bear me powerful children and make me the most feared Chief in existence. I will make the gods themselves tremble in their mountains!"

"And what if she doesn't want that, my son?" she asked, still keeping her eyes from his face. "Cruel to make her your mate if she doesn't choose you."

Eldrax barked a laugh. "Cruel? What does that matter? The world is a cruel place and only the strong survive. She will make me strong whether she wishes it or not. Now stop being *weak* and tell me where she is!"

Her eyes were drowning in tears as she finally looked up into his face but, behind the grief, a resolve had been hardening. "You are right, my Eldrax. You are truly Cro now. Like your father." She drew a deep breath as the words spilled out. "My fault. My fault. I made a mistake. Not your fault. My mistake, but I will make it right. I will make it right now. Forgive me, my Eldrax!"

She was so fast, he almost didn't see the knife plunging towards his heart until it was too late. He grabbed her wrist just as the tip buried itself into his furs, stopping it short as it kissed his skin. Shocked, he forced her arm away, twisting her wrist until she dropped the knife. The sound of fissuring stone cracked somewhere overhead, but he ignored it as his vision hazed red.

"Oh, mother," Eldrax whispered in her ear, drawing his own knife. "I do wish you hadn't done that."

* * *

18

Shalanaki

Her baby was born. Exhausted, Rebaa collapsed back, gasping as the sweat dripped from her brow. She was trembling all over, too weak to even raise her head. Then the cries of her newborn reached her ears. Finding a strength she did not know she had, Rebaa pulled herself upright and scooped up her baby from where he lay struggling upon the furs.

She grabbed the sharpened rock that Nen had used for stripping skins. With shaking fingers, she held it in the fire for a few moments, then sliced through the bluish rope that still tied her baby to her. She felt an acute sense of loss as the physical link between them was severed, and it unbalanced her for a moment.

Numb, Rebaa gathered her squalling infant and wrapped him inside her furs next to her breast. With the tears still falling from the trauma of his birth and her fear for Nen, she looked down into his face for the very first time; this being that she had so loved and feared all at the same time.

He was wailing lustily, protesting hard at being brought

into this strange and cold world. The familiar feeling of his distress rolled over her, though it was a different sensation now, separated from her as it was. She held her breath, waiting for that terrifying onslaught of power, but it did not come. She sensed nothing from him, no flicker of energy.

She didn't have time to ponder on it as she studied him from head to toe. She let out a breath when she found he was whole and strong. He showed none of the cursed deformities that had begun to mark so many Ninkuraaja newborns. His piercing wails continued to grow in strength. Rebaa glanced fearfully at the blocked cave entrance. If they heard him, they would come, and they would kill him. Nen's efforts would be for nothing.

"Shh, shh," she put her face close to his, touching at his new and undeveloped mind. "You must be quiet. They must not find us."

And the baby stopped squalling. He opened his eyes and blinked at her. Rebaa gasped. She had never seen anything like them. Green eyes. Forbidden eyes. For a moment they stared at one another, the strange green against the indigo. But... there was no fear.

Gazing down into that serious little face, Rebaa was knocked breathless by a love that transcended everything she had ever felt. She wondered dimly that the ground did not tremble at the strength of it. Nothing else mattered now but him. She would die for him if she had to. Not a monster. Not a curse. Nen had been right. Instinctively, she lifted her head, seeking to share this joyous revelation with her friend.

The impassive walls of the cave were the only thing to meet her glowing eyes, and her breath hitched as she remembered Nen was not there.

The wind lashed against the rocks piled against the cave mouth, sounding eerily like wounded souls moaning through the gaps. Rebaa shuddered and wrapped her arms around her baby, rocking back and forth. She waited for Nen to return. She refused to believe she would not. Nen knew what she was doing. She knew this range better than any Cro. The snow would have hidden her enough to evade their enemies once she had led them away. It must not yet be safe for her to break cover and return. Rebaa repeated this to herself over and over as she continued to hold her son and remain quiet, huddled in the darkness of the night.

The wind eventually blew itself out. Rebaa found the silence it left behind worse than the wailing. She fed her new baby and saw to it that all that had followed him from the birth, including the soiled furs of her birthing nest, were burned, lest they attract predators. She cleaned him and dressed him in the warm coverings Nen had made, all the while hoping to feel at any moment the return of a familiar presence and a soft tread in the snow outside.

It never came.

It was the longest night Rebaa had ever spent. The growing anxiety gripped at her chest like claws, making it hard to breathe. The empty moments slipped by. She knew now that something was wrong. She wanted to go out and find Nen, but she would not take her baby out into danger and the exposure of the night. Still she waited, breathless but with a steadily dying hope.

At last the dawn light reached its fingers through the gaps in the rocks and brushed across Rebaa's drawn, sleepless face. She and her baby were still alone. She could wait no longer. Donning the sling Nen had fashioned out of the bear hide, she tucked her baby into it, making sure he was as protected as possible. She moved stiffly. The birth had taken a severe toll. Blood dripped down her leg, and she knew she was badly torn. She hissed in pain with every motion. It didn't matter. She had to find Nen. Seizing the knife her friend had left for her, she cast quickly about with her higher senses. She felt nothing. No living thing was anywhere near the cave. Rebaa shuddered at the thought. *Nen!* Her heart cried out. *Please don't leave me alone!*

Her hands were trembling as she pushed hard at the rocks blocking the entrance to the cave. She didn't have the patience to take them down one by one. They tumbled outward with a deafening clatter and flump of snow. After so long keeping such careful silence, the sudden din was frightening. Rebaa froze, fully expecting an attack.

Nothing happened, and after a while, Rebaa was able to make herself move again. The cold hit her like a fist, stealing her breath. The landscape tumbling away before her had been transformed by the storm. The wind had swept the snow from the ground and dumped it against the rocks in immense drifts three times her height.

She was alone. Everywhere was stark and empty. Only the tall, dead grasses stirred in the breeze where the wind had swept the snow aside. Drawing a sturdy stick from out of the woodpile, Rebaa used it to brace her aching body as she set out to find what she would.

"Nen!" she called out as often as she dared, listening hard, each time hoping that she would hear a faint answer floating over the deadening snow drifts. "Nen!"

The going was slow. Many of the paths had become impassable, hopelessly choked with mountainous drifts of snow. She trudged for what felt like an eternity, picking her way as best she could, resting often to catch her breath and feed her baby. She was weak. She needed rest, but she could not stop until she found her friend. Nen might have fallen and was injured, unable to walk. She could be trapped somewhere, waiting patiently for Rebaa to come. The image was a torment. She *had* to find her. Whatever awaited, she had to know.

Darkness was once again creeping over the snowy land, chasing away the brief winter day, when Rebaa at last detected the brush of a presence in the near distance. It was a faint energy, flickering like a flame, fighting to stay alight against a relentless wind. Rebaa struggled to increase her pace, bracing herself on her makeshift staff and clutching her baby close with her other arm. He was very quiet.

Scrambling over the rough ground, Rebaa cried out when she spotted something like fire waving gently in the breeze, vivid against the dead grasses and scattered rocks. Everything in the surrounding area was spotted and spattered with deep crimson, appearing black in the looming darkness.

Rebaa's stride faltered. She did not want to witness the scene that awaited her just beyond those rocks. She knew what she would find. She knew it. A cold sweat broke over her flushed skin as she forced herself to move forward.

Rebaa sobbed and fell to her knees beside the body of her friend. Nen was lying partially naked in a pool of blood. The sickly scent filled Rebaa's nostrils. Wounds littered the pale body beneath the torn furs, her fiery hair tangled and matted around her face. Nen's stained spear lay beside her. It was snapped in two. Rebaa noticed several other bodies lying nearby. Nen had killed some of her enemies before they overcame her.

"Nen." Rebaa sobbed, blinded by tears. "Nen." She feared she was too late and Nen had already left her.

But the black eyes opened and Nen's face tipped sideways towards the sound of Rebaa's voice. "Rebaa...?" she slurred.

"Yes, I-I'm here, Nen, I'm here. You're going to be alright, you're s-safe now." She caught hold of one of the thick hands between her own. It was freezing. With trembling fingers, Rebaa did her best to cover her friend with the tattered furs.

"Need to go. Need to run. He looking for you... run..." Nen's voice was barely audible.

Rebaa's hands went around the cold face, bracing it. "Who, Nen? Who is looking?"

"Eldrax... My Eldrax?" Nen's fluttering eyes roved as if she were searching for her long-lost son. Rebaa wasn't sure she was entirely lucid.

"H-he's not here, Nen. It's just me." She cast around the surrounding hills and cliffs with both her eyes and her higher senses, but she and Nen were alone. Her eyes followed a smear of blood leading from Nen to the nearest rock face, which was cracked and tumbled. The freshly fallen boulders blocked off the pathway beyond. Rebaa swallowed down bile as she realised Nen had dragged herself along, perhaps trying to return to the cave, before blood loss and injury finally overcame her and she had collapsed where she lay.

"Was here... tried to s-stop him." The black eyes glimmered. "My Eldrax... My fault."

"Eldrax was here?" Rebaa's heart leaped to her throat. Nen's son, alive? Then outrage burned away her shock. "*He* did this?"

The head between her hands twitched. "He looking for you. Wants badly. My fault. Left him with monster..." Nen's eyes

208

rolled closed. She was drifting.

"No, Nen!" Rebaa shook her face. "Stay with me." Fury was coursing through her veins. What sort of creature could do this to his own mother?

"Baby?" The eyes opened to regard her. Both apprehension and a fervent hope flickered in their fading depths.

"He's here, Nen," Rebaa soothed. "He's here, he wants to meet you, his *tarhe*." She lifted the baby out of his sling and put him near Nen's face so she could see him fully. She was desperate to keep the Thal woman conscious. She needed to stop the blood flow, but the wounds were deep and beyond her skill. She struggled to think of what her brother would do. She would have given anything for Baarias to be near. "He's safe. You saved us."

Nen focused with obvious effort on the baby before her. He stared back solemnly, then reached out with a little fist to tap her cheek. Nen smiled and caught his tiny hand in hers. "Good... Saved little strong one. One thing right."

Rebaa could feel Nen's life energy slipping away. The bright flame was giving up its battle against the relentless wind. "Stay with me, Nen," Rebaa begged. "We need you still."

Nen shook her head once. "No. Weary. I go to Eron now." Tears started in her eyes as she fixed them on Rebaa. "You think he forgive me and permit me into la'Atzu?"

Rebaa's own tears fell on her bruised face. She did not know what la'Atzu was, but she was willing to say anything to ease her friend's pain. "Yes, Nen," she whispered. "He'll forgive you. He'll be proud to have had such a brave child."

Nen brushed at the baby laid close beside her. "Ninmah will forgive you, too." She then grasped Rebaa's arm with surprising strength. "Promise me you look after baby!" She reached for the top half of her broken spear and pushed it into Rebaa's hands. "Let nobody take from you. Teach him good. Keep him safe, even from own People. They seek to kill him. Don't let them."

"Never," Rebaa swore. She scooped her son from where he lay and clutched him to her. She would never let what had happened to Eldrax happen to her son. "No one will ever hurt him. They will have to kill me first!"

A faint smile touched Nen's pale lips and a quiet peace fell over her face. "Good. Do what I could not or live with pain all of life. Protect baby..." Her eyes drifted closed.

"No." Rebaa gripped the slack hand. The flame was now an ember. "Nen." She shook the hand. "Nen?"

"*Shalanaki,* Rebaa." The whisper faded in the breeze.

Rebaa could barely speak the words. "*Shalanaki,* Nen."

And she was gone. The ember smouldered and went out.

Rebaa sat there holding her friend's hand, keeping her company as she passed onto the next journey. Rebaa prayed it would be a happier path than the one Nen had travelled in this most cruel and unforgiving world. Rebaa kept her vigil until darkness fell around them.

"*Shalanaki,* Nen."

19

Decision

Rebaa did not know how long she crouched over Nen's body, wailing her grief to the sky. Unheeding of her torment, Ninmah had disappeared below the horizon, leaving her alone and in darkness.

Alone. She was very much alone now.

Finally, her tears ran out. Her eyes were red and swollen and her throat was raw. There was no more she could do. Nen was gone, brought down by her own son. The cold sucked at her. Stiffly, she rose to her feet. With deadened eyes, she stared down at the lifeless body of the one who had offered hope and acceptance for her and her Forbidden offspring. Both were stolen from her now. All hope was as dead as the cold form lying before her.

Rebaa did not have the strength to move Nen to a better place. Numbly, she gathered rocks and piled them over her friend's body, protecting it from all that would come along. She was tired, in pain, but she did not stop until her task was complete. Her frozen fingers were raw by the time she had finished.

It didn't seem like enough, this faceless grave, to mark the passing of a being like Nen. Casting around, Rebaa picked up a sharp stone and etched on the flat face of the highest rock, copying the marks of protection carved into Nen's spear. As a finishing touch, she drew a twisting symbol, one that matched the purple tattoo between her own brows. She hoped the marks of Eron and the symbol of Ninmah would be enough to keep Nen safe and undisturbed as she slept.

The bodies of the Cro she left to rot without mark and kept her back turned on them disdainfully. Wolves bayed on the darkening horizon. Their cries held a hungry note as the scent of blood drifted to them on the wind. Rebaa smiled grimly. She gazed down at the pile of rocks that marked her dear friend's last resting place. Her face was now dry. She had no more tears. Gracing Nen with one final gesture of farewell, Rebaa picked up both halves of her fallen friend's spear and stumbled away.

The wolves were howling all around her as she made her way back to the cave. She did not hurry. Her face was resolute. She was Ninkuraaja, and she did not fear the wolves. All the Children of the Great Spirit would stay away from her tonight. The familiar cave opened up before her in the slope of the hill. This time, however, it offered no welcome. Exhausted, Rebaa stumbled inside. Holding her baby close, she threw herself down on the furs beside the fire and was sucked into unconsciousness.

When she awoke, it was still dark. The cries of her baby had awoken her. He was hungry. She sat up, groaning at her numerous pains, and fed him. While he suckled greedily, Rebaa tried to avoid looking at all the familiar objects in the cave that had become her home. The piled rocks, the furs, the rock carvings. All served only to remind her of Nen and the life that had now been stolen from her. She picked up the halves of Nen's spear, listlessly pushing them back together and then watching as they tumbled apart, over and over. Broken. Broken.

Broken.

Suddenly she couldn't stand it. She had to fix it. She had to make it right. The fire was smouldering, and she moved on a sudden impulse to rebuild it. Stripping bark from the piled firewood, Rebaa recalled the method of making the binding tar and covered the pieces of silvery bark in ash before burning it. Once the bark had reduced to its bubbling black form, Rebaa dipped the broken ends of the spear into it and fused the jagged edges together. For good measure, she wrapped strips of leftover hide around the join and turned it over and over in the tar to coat it.

The spear was mended. But as the tar slowly set into place, Rebaa realised all she had really fixed was a dead piece of wood. There was no Nen there to congratulate her on her achievement. Her promised haven had not been restored. Everything still lay broken around her, and no amount of tar could ever fix it.

She swallowed back her tears, casting her eyes down at her sleeping baby, letting him ground her. She had to leave. Nen had told her to get far from here. This was no longer the sanctuary that it had once been. Eldrax was still out there somewhere hunting her. She knew it for certain in her bones. The half-handed Cro, the one who had saluted her on the day she killed Murzuk; he knew where to find her.

But where could she run to? Rebaa closed her eyes, confronted with the same dilemma she had faced before she

213

ever met Nen. She had never really escaped her fate. It had simply been waiting for her in the shadows, like one of her nightmares.

She thought again of her own People as she looked down into her son's green eyes. He had woken and was staring trustingly back at her. Rebaa burst into tears. There was no way she could make them believe he was a Ninkuraaja child. If his size did not betray him, his damning eyes certainly would. No Ninkuraa had eyes of that colour. *What will they do to him?* She pressed him to her, burying her face against his neck, despairing and undecided.

She could try to throw herself on the mercy of another Cro clan, one far from this land who had never known Juran or his Black Wolf clan. They *might* accept the little one, but Juran's fearsome reputation had been far reaching. She did not know how far she would have to go to find such a clan, and in these harsh times, they'd as likely kill her as take her in. And the baby... No. She could be less sure of that unpredictable and bloodthirsty race than she could of her own.

Rebaa remembered the power she had felt while he was still inside her and imagined it being twisted into something dark at the hands of one such as Eldrax. She shuddered. She had felt no trace of the power since her son had been born, but that did not mean it was not there. He was a half blood, the first of his kind. The nature of the Gift within him could not be predicted. Only time would tell how it would manifest. Rebaa would need to be on her guard.

At least if she went home, the love of her brother may be enough to protect her. Maybe. It was a faint glimmer in the darkness, and she had to cling to that. There was nothing else.

All that was left to do was to prepare for a long journey.

She was still many rises and falls of Ninmah away from the borders of her old forest home. Despite her apprehension of facing her People again after so long — facing them with the greatest of sins — the part of her soul that still longed to be surrounded by the protective strength of the trees again, grew in strength. In all the time she had spent away, she had never really got used to the feeling of nakedness out on the open plains.

Getting to her feet, Rebaa began to gather what she would need. She picked up one of Nen's leather carriers and slung it around her body, opposite her baby's sling. Moving to the entrance of the cave, she filled the carrier with the hunks of frozen meat Nen had stored outside in the snow. Next, she picked up the pieces of flint needed to spark a fire and stowed them inside her furs, along with a hunting knife and the snare trap Nen had made for her. Rebaa considered the fur blankets lying on the ground. Taking one with her would offer warmth on shelterless nights. Stooping carefully, she lifted an edge. The weight of the thick fur strained her arm as she hauled it up. Rebaa let it drop. It would be too heavy for her to carry under ordinary circumstances. She doubted she could make it two strides from the cave with it now. She would have to do without.

Last of all, she collected Nen's spear. Her beloved friend's final gift. The tar had now hardened, and the haft was whole once more. The weapon would be nothing more than a useless burden in her hands, but the thought of leaving it behind was unbearable. She could at least use it as a brace to lean upon on her journey.

The first streaks of dawn were painting the sky. It was time to leave. Rebaa started forward, then gasped and winced. Her birthing wounds had not yet fully healed. She was not even strong enough to mend herself, let alone travel. It was not a promising start, but to stay here meant certain death. She had to take her chances and hope her body did not fail before her journey was complete. Her baby was depending on her.

That last thought gave her strength and Rebaa stood straight and fierce, setting her will. She glanced around the cave one last time. A picture on the wall caught her eye, and she reached out to trace the etching of a mother and child. It was a gesture of farewell. Blinking against her tears, Rebaa dropped her hand from the stone and strode out into the open air. She did not look back.

The fire smouldered behind her and died.

* * *

20

Trapped

Trapped.

He was trapped in the dark. Trapped with his own thoughts. Eldrax stared at the wall of snow and rock that cut off his escape as he paced the rocky ground. His men worked feverishly, digging at the drift that was burying them.

He could not be still. The maelstrom of emotions raging inside his chest kept him moving, pulling him this way and that. His mother was dead. He had killed her, but not before she had taken him by surprise with her ferocity and strength. Twisting away from his initial attack, his mother had regained her spear.

Half-frozen and blinded by the blizzard, two of his Cro men had fallen to lucky blows before Eldrax's hunting party had overcome her. He had landed the mortal blow himself before ripping her hated spear from her hands and snapping it in two.

All that had been left was to end her miserable life. He had been poised to strike when an ominous cracking of rock and rumble of snow had sounded somewhere above. Rannac and several of the men grabbed him and dragged him away as boulders pounded to the ground around them. They had hauled him, fighting and screaming, across the threshold of a cave. The grumble had become a roar and a mountain's worth of snow and loose rock had collapsed on their heels, blocking the cave entrance and trapping them within.

It had taken a long while for Eldrax's blood rage to drain away enough for his men to risk letting him go, fearing he would turn his spear upon them in his frenzy. His senses returned long enough for him to find that their way out had been cut off. His men had shrunk back into the darkness as his madness descended for a second time. He had attacked the wall of snow and rock in fury and frustration, only stopping when his knife shattered in his bloody hands. Defeated, he ordered his men to search for another way out of the winding cave.

The cragged tunnel had branched several times. Occasionally, the ceiling dropped so low it had barely permitted their passage, forcing them to crawl and squeeze through the damp gaps. As a man of the open plains, Eldrax would rather have faced one of the monsters from the Mountains than compress his bulky frame through those holes, but he had not had a choice. He could not show weakness to the men by letting his fear crush him.

A faint breeze had been their first clue. Eldrax had rushed towards the promised escape, only to find that this new way out had also been blocked with fallen snow and rocks. Eldrax damned the gods for their cursed storm. He had pushed against the rock slide, greedily sucking in the fresh breeze whistling in through the gaps, faced with the same cursed denial to his freedom as he had at the other end of the cave.

But he would *not* go back and face the confines of the tunnels again. They would dig their way out of this avalanche or die of starvation within the earth's tomb.

"Get out of the way!" Unable to stand his thoughts any more, Eldrax shoved one of his tiring men to the side. Grabbing the man's hunting knife, he threw himself at the tightly packed wall of snow, picking away at the icy surface. It was going to take until dawn to claw their way out of this trap. He *needed* to get out. The ghosts were staring at him again. Murzuk stood at his shoulder mocking him, Rikal and his Thal mate glowering at his side. But his mother... his mother stared accusingly from every shadow.

The other men fell away from his frenzied efforts, unnerved by the madness that seemed to have overcome him. Unnerved... and angry. Two of their clan brothers had been killed by the Thal, and now they were trapped in a cave with no food or water.

Eldrax ignored them. It was *worth* it. They did not see it. The possibilities. One day, one day, they would see. But first he needed to get out of this cave! The dying black eyes swam before his vision and he shook his head, snarling at the ghosts as he struck at the snow, chiselling it away piece by piece.

The pink light of dawn greeted Eldrax's blinking eyes when he and his men finally dug their way out of the trap and breathed the fresh air. He had been right. It had taken the entire night to break free. They had emerged into an open expanse of ground. Several trails branched off in different directions, winding away into the surrounding hills.

Eldrax watched as his men leaned upon their spears, their limbs shaking from the effort of shifting the snow and heavy rocks, but he would not allow them rest. He would not lose one more moment. He had to keep moving; he had to keep ahead of the ghosts. First, he needed a starting point. If they set off in search of the witch without a trail, they could search these hills until the Thaw arrived before finding so much as a trace.

"Rannac!" He summoned the older warrior. "Return us to the cave where you first saw the witch and that other woman." He refused to speak her name.

Rannac shook his head. "It is doubtful she would have remained there, my Chief. She knows we are hunting her. She would have been foolish to stay—"

Howling out, Eldrax backhanded him across the face. "She would have been more foolish still to move through that storm! She would have remained there where she felt safe, at least until it passed. If we find that cave, then we will find her or we will find her trail. Either way, she is ours!"

Rannac straightened from the blow and faced him. "I cannot take us back for certain. In chasing the Thal through the storm, we are now far from the path I travelled with your father. I do not recognise this terrain, and many of the trails will now be impassable. Even if I could find the cave again, it will take days."

"Then you had better get started." Eldrax snarled.

"No." A stifled gasp rippled through the other men. Shocked, Eldrax rounded on the older warrior, but Rannac's face was resolute. "I have taught you since you were a boy. You have always been reckless, but now you are slipping into madness." Murmurs of assent broke out, and a few of the other men shifted to stand behind Rannac. "Eldrax, we are weary, we are exposed, and we are now without ration. There is no game left up here. The wisest path would be to follow Utu south to the plains. There we will find game to hunt and can make our way back to the clan. There is *nothing* for us up here."

Eldrax's gaze flickered to the men gathered behind Rannac. Reaching out, he gripped his erstwhile teacher by the shoulder, bringing his mouth close to his ear. "I warned you, Rannac. I warned you about what would happen if you tried to question me again. You should thank the gods that I need you in this moment, for that is all that is preventing me from killing you where you stand." His fingers gripped bone. "I will *not* return to the clan without my prize."

"No rival Chief's mate is worth our lives!" Rannac pulled back.

"She is worth all of your miserable lives! Her *and* the half-breed she carries. You are simply too shortsighted to see it!"

"You don't even know if she is still alive!"

The red mist was descending again. "Are you refusing to obey me, Rannac?"

Rannac swallowed, but held his ground as he lifted his chin. It was the expression he had always worn whenever he had corrected Eldrax as a child. "Yes, Eldrax. I am telling you, you are putting all our lives at risk for one small, sickly woman, one who could prove to be more a liability than an asset. There will be other, more worthy women for you to conquer and to bear you children. I advise you, my Chief, take us home."

"Very well." Eldrax released Rannac's shoulder. He moved as if to turn away, then quick as a spitting snake, he lashed out with his fist, striking for Rannac's jaw.

Had the blow connected, it would have shattered bone. But Rannac had lived a life reliant on his reflexes far longer than Eldrax. Until Eldrax had come into his adulthood, Rannac had been the clan's most formidable fighter. What he lacked in strength, he made up for in speed. He dodged the blow and brought his spear up defensively in his good hand.

"I do not want to fight you, my Chief, only advise you. Your father was a formidable leader, but he always knew when he was beaten and when to preserve his clan. It is something you must learn if you wish to remain Chief for as long as he did."

"My father was a weak fool!" Eldrax swept Murzuk's old spear forward, making a testing strike, which Rannac swept aside. "He let the Black Wolf steal our hunting grounds. He let them claim the prize he risked our hunters to gain. Our clan went hungry for his cowardice, scratching a living off rabbits and stolen game. I will bow down to no one and I will take whatever I want on this land! No one will ever have power over me again!"

Every word was punctuated by a strike at Rannac. He was no longer a boy to be scolded. He was *Chief*. For a short time, Rannac matched his strikes, but the older warrior was no match for Eldrax's strength, and he was still nursing the injuries from the stampede. With one violent strike, Eldrax overcame his one-armed defence, knocking Rannac's spear from his hand. Twisting his own weapon, he drove the butt into Rannac's midsection, forcing the air from his lungs and throwing him to the ground. As Rannac lay in the snow, gasping for breath, Eldrax brought his foot down hard on Rannac's right leg between ankle and knee. The satisfying sound of snapping bone and Rannac's scream of pain ricocheted off the rocky hills.

"If you will not help us, I have no further use for you on this hunt, Rannac," Eldrax said, his voice calm once more as he kicked Rannac's fallen spear far out of reach. "You have my permission to return to the clan... if you are able. If you are there when I return, I will speak no more of this day. If not, I will not suffer to hear your name again. Either way, you will have served your punishment for questioning your Chief."

Eldrax faced the rest of his men. "Do any others among you wish to turn tail and return to the clan like a bunch of meek women?"

Their expressions ranged from horrified to subdued as they glanced at Rannac panting on the ground. All of them took a step back from Eldrax and kept their eyes lowered.

"Good," Eldrax hissed. "We will remain in these hills until we find the witch! No man sleeps until we pick up her trail. Do you understand?"

His men murmured their agreement. Grunting, Eldrax turned away to study his options. A lower path, hemmed in by steep slopes rising on both sides, led away into the mid ranges. Another, more open path looked as though it would lead on up into the summits of the hills. He considered them both; if he chose wrong...

"My... Chief," Rannac rasped from the snow, having the audacity to speak again. Eldrax considered breaking his other leg. "The cave has a rounded mouth and is set into the top of a hill."

Eldrax heaved a tragic sigh. "You should have decided to be more helpful *before* I broke your leg, Rannac." His lips twisted. "Now, is there anything else that you can tell us about this cave that might distinguish it from the hundreds of others that are no doubt scattered throughout these forsaken hills?" Eldrax's voice drawled. "You *have* chosen not to join us after all."

Rannac glowered as he stared up into Eldrax's face. He paused for a long moment, then shook his head. "Simply take the highest ranges. It is the best advice I can give."

Eldrax snorted and turned away. He would search every cave in the mountains if he had to. Utu was rising as Eldrax ordered the rest of his men towards the higher path with a jab of his spear. Juran's finger bones danced on the ends of their cords. He did not look back as they left Rannac to his fate. Predators would finish him before dark.

* * *

21

Ties That Bind

Rebaa's heart felt like it would break into a thousand pieces as she passed down the familiar paths. Nen had taught her every one during their foraging ventures together. Whenever her exhaustion drove her to rest, which was more often than she would like, Rebaa clung to her baby and cried out her grief for all the loss in her life. For Juran, for Nen. Both had died to save her. Both had left her alone.

Only her baby's warmth against her heart gave her the strength to stagger back to her feet each time and keep going.

Stains of blood marked Rebaa's every resting place.

The late afternoon light found her stumbling down the narrow trail hemmed in by the steep hills on either side. This was the very trail that led to the copse where Nen had given Rebaa her first hunting lesson. Her heart gave another sharp pang of pain and regret.

Beside the pain was a growing anxiety. She was moving too slowly. When she had last come here, it had taken less than a morning's travel to reach this point. Now, despite travelling since before dawn, Ninmah was already descending through the sky. The snow had blocked many of the trails, forcing Rebaa to find alternative routes because the usual path had become hopelessly blocked. It had amazed her to find that the trail she currently travelled had remained open. She was thankful for that good fortune, but she knew once she reached the copse, she would leave Nen's territory and enter unfamiliar terrain.

Ninmah was halfway down on her descent when Rebaa staggered against an outcropping of rock. Her baby and the meat she carried were a dead weight on her shoulders. *No. No.* She tried to force herself upright. *You can't rest again. Not yet. Get to the copse. The copse where you caught your first rabbit, then you can rest. Further, just a little further.* This narrow pathway was the perfect place for an ambush.

She had just persuaded her aching limbs to hold her upright when her baby began to cry lustily, fussing in his sling. Rebaa groaned, glaring at him. He had stubbornly slept through her last respite, and now his strident wails told her he would not wait until the next. She had to feed him; his cries were the surest way to attract unwanted attention.

Choosing a position that sheltered her from the icy breeze, Rebaa sank to the ground, resting her aching back against a rock as her son suckled. She winced at the additional pain this caused, though it was a minor discomfort compared to her other injuries. Her eyes drifted closed. If she had to rest now, she would at least allow herself to doze, just for a few moments...

"Hhggrrrmmm."

The inarticulate moan rose from nowhere. Rebaa leapt to her feet, jolting her baby and causing him to cry in protest as she dislodged him from her breast.

"Shhh!" she hissed at him as the sound drifted into stillness.

It had come from close by, and there had been no mistaking the human quality of the voice. Her senses quivered. A lone presence burned just over the rise in front of her. Rebaa's heart leaped to her throat.

It was a Cro presence.

She cursed her foolishness for letting her grief and weariness distract her. She wanted to run like a scared rabbit, but she had to keep her wits if she wanted to survive. Nen would not have panicked, and her friend had taught her much. She pointed the tip of Nen's spear towards the unseen threat and backed away from the trail ahead of her. She scanned her surroundings as she went, searching for another path to take.

There wasn't one. Steep slopes and sheer rock walls still surrounded her on both sides. She should have chosen her way more wisely. The only option was to go back and lose nearly an entire day's travel.

Her knees almost buckled at the thought, but greater was the fear of what lay ahead. The Cro could appear over the rise at any moment and catch her here. Armed though she was, she stood no chance against a Cro fighter.

Rebaa cringing into the nearest outcropping of rock as the moan sounded again. The voice was too close. Even if she turned back now, she would never outrun the Cro. She stretched out her senses again, probing. There was only one. His companions were not in the area. Their absence was unnerving. She would rather have them where she could feel them. The lone Cro's companions could even now be circling around behind her, gaining with every step, leaving this one in place to block her escape. A trap. Desperate, Rebaa looked to the sheer scree slopes once more, irrationally hoping that another path would have somehow materialised before her.

Rebaa weighed her options. Go back, lose a day's travel and possibly collide with the Cro's brothers or go forward and try to evade a single Cro. The single consciousness was hazy, unfocused. Sleeping, perhaps.

She pressed her lips together into a determined line. The strength of her friend's spirit seemed to linger around the wooden haft in her hands, and she gripped on to it. After all she had been through, it irked her to give ground.

With the spear thrust out before her, Rebaa made her decision and crept forward towards the rise ahead. Keeping low, she peered over the summit where the land opened out at last into a branching of ways.

It took a full moment for Rebaa to pick out the object she had been searching for. With his furs covered in snow, she might not have seen the Cro sprawled upon the ground had he not moved, attempting to drag himself forward on his belly. His moan once again drifted over the snow as he did so. The reason for his abandonment became clear. Even from this distance, Rebaa could see that his right lower leg was broken and his left arm tightly bound. She doubted he could even stand right now, much less attack her. He was unarmed. He was no threat.

Nevertheless, it took Rebaa a few more moments to summon the courage to break her cover and move down the path into the view of her enemy. It went against every instinct. She tried to be quiet, hoping to slip by unseen, but the loose stones under the snow shifted traitorously under her feet, crackling loudly in the stillness.

The Cro's head snapped around. His hand flew into the furs at his side, producing a flint knife in the space of a heartbeat, his arm flinging back in the next.

"No!" Rebaa cried. Dropping Nen's spear, she clutched one arm around her baby and thrust her other hand out in an instinctive but futile attempt to block the oncoming weapon.

The bite of the blade never came.

"You shouldn't throw away your only defence like that."

With the blood still pounding in her ears, Rebaa dropped her hand slightly at the sound of the rasping voice. He had rolled up onto a shoulder and grey eyes were peering at her from the midst of the rich brown face, currently twisted against the pain. "Don't worry, girl, I do not kill women."

Rebaa's gut lurched; his eyes... his eyes were the exact same shade as Juran's. It hurt to look at them. Instead, she glanced quickly at his hand. It was now empty; the knife had disappeared back into his furs. She let her own hand fall back to her side.

Then she noticed his other paw. A half-hand.

"You!" Rebaa snatched up Nen's spear and rushed at the downed warrior in a haze of fury. She poised the tip over his chest, fully prepared to plunge it through his miserable heart. "You brought them back! Why couldn't you have just left us alone?" Her baby could feel her emotions burning out of control, and his wails of distress punctuated her every word. "Why?"

The Cro's only reaction was to tilt his face up at her, his gaze calm in the face of her fury. It only stoked her rage. She wanted him to be terrified. She wanted him to beg her for mercy. She wanted to be able to *deny* him.

"Kill me if you wish," he said. "You have the right."

Yes, she had the right. She would kill him and she would enjoy it, she would... Rebaa tightened her grip on Nen's spear, readying herself to bring it down.

Her muscles locked into place. The fury rolled through her, but her arms would not obey. She had never killed in such a way. She snarled in frustration. She should drop the spear, reach down and stop his heart in his chest as she had done to the last Cro; but that would be too much of a mercy and doing so would take energy that she did not have. It was more fitting for this Cro to meet a bloody end on the tip of Nen's spear. It was all the mercy they had granted her friend.

His horribly familiar eyes continued to stare up at her, unwavering in the face of his death. Like a warrior. Like Juran. This must have been how he had died, too. Her vision blurred and for a moment all she could see was her dead mate lying before her.

Crying out in anguish, she swung the spear tip up and away, backpedalling from the wounded Cro. "I can't do it!" No matter how much hatred she held for this man, she could not kill in such a way. It would be a step too far.

"You thought about it too much." The Cro fell back off his shoulder, coming to rest spread eagle on the ground. He closed his abhorrent eyes with a sigh.

"Shut up!" Rebaa spat. "Because of you, my friend is dead. It's all *your* fault." It was all *her* fault. She had let him get away. Rebaa could feel the sobs building in her chest. Her fault.

The dark face became downcast. "It's cruel how fate works, isn't it? I let her escape all those seasons ago, only to be the cause of her death now." He opened his eyes. "Just know that I tried to prevent it. I tried to lead him astray, but your friend chose the wrong moment to break cover. Once she did that, I could do nothing more."

Before Rebaa could respond to that, his gaze came to rest

upon the sling where her baby rested. Instinctively, Rebaa turned her body to shield him. The Cro chuckled at her actions.

"I can see why Juran liked you, to protect his babe so." His amusement turned into a cough. Wincing, he clutched at his chest. Rebaa could detect that two of his ribs were broken. "But there are far more deadly threats than my gaze coming after you, girl. If you wish to keep him safe, you must travel fast. I brought you as much time as I could, but not much."

Confusion muddied Rebaa's thoughts. "You... helped me?"

"Yes. I sent my Chief on the wrong path to find you, but he is cunning and it won't be long before he picks up your trail." He gestured to the spear in Rebaa's hand. "Next time, do not hesitate. It could mean the difference between life and death. Yours and the babe's."

"Why should you care about my life, Cro? You've already sentenced me to almost certain death. Do not pretend to care now!"

"Oh, but I do care." He half smiled and pointed at the sling. "I suppose I cannot help having an interest in his or her fate."

"His," Rebaa blurted before thinking. Her heart raced. *Interest?* Did they guess how dangerous her son might be? "Why would the likes of you have an *interest* in my baby's fate, Cro?"

"You do not know me for who I am, witch. I wasn't always Hunting Bear. I left my birth clan many seasons ago after I made a foolish Challenge to my brother." He waved his crippled hand. "As you no doubt know, Juran was a very formidable warrior."

Rebaa gasped as the world shifted. "You're—?"

"Yes," he answered the question she could not bring herself

to pose. "The babe is of my blood. We are bound. Juran and I may have parted as enemies, but he permitted me to escape with my life. I owe him for that. The Hunting Bear adopted me into their ranks as a skilled fighter and hunter, and I served their old Chief loyally. Murzuk was a hard man, but he protected his clan, he respected lores. His son... his son, he is something else entirely."

"He's a monster," Rebaa whispered. "He-he killed her. His own mother."

The Cro shrugged his good shoulder. "Eldrax is not like ordinary men. Perhaps Murzuk was overly cruel to him, or perhaps there is a reason the gods forbid such half-breeds, I cannot say. But his mind is broken. He has no compassion, no mercy. Not even for his own followers." The Cro's grey eyes focused on Rebaa. "I do not wish to see my brother's babe in his hands—"

A sound of skittering rocks coming from further up the slopes startled him. Rebaa knew it was only the scurrying of a rabbit, but the Cro's eyes were now fearful and filled with urgency. "Go. Now. And go fast. Do not stop until you reach the safety of the shin'ar forests. Eldrax is a monster, but it would take a monster greater than him to follow you there."

Rebaa hesitated, torn. She hated this man for what he had done, and yet this was her beloved Juran's own *brother*, blood to her son, lying abandoned and injured. He had helped them—

"Go!" he shouted at her as loudly as his broken chest would allow. "Do *not* drop that spear again! Never hesitate. Go!"

The bite in his voice shook her back to her senses, and Rebaa spun on her heel. As she did so, she spotted an object in the snow. The Cro's own weapon. She swooped down on it and tossed it toward the fallen warrior before fleeing down the path that would lead to the copse. Somehow she knew he wouldn't turn it upon her, and now he could use it to rise and support his body. She had thrown him the slimmest of lifelines, as he had done for her.

Her debt was repaid.

* * *

22

Discovery

Eldrax remained true to his word. Since dawn, he and his men had navigated the high paths of the foothills, searching every cave in the rocky crags. Often, snow drifts barred the way, forcing them to forge through or else take a different, more treacherous path. Now the day was waning, and they had found no trace of the witch. Like a spirit, she had slipped through his grasp once again.

Eldrax paused and leaned on his spear. It had been two days since he had slept, and the lack of food was telling even through the burning desire that drove him. He considered resting, but each time he did, his mother's black eyes would rise tauntingly before him.

My Eldrax....

He shook his head. *Leave me alone!* He could not rest, he would not give her the satisfaction of sleep. He would not allow her to haunt him in the darkness of his mind. Only when he had the witch could he rest, and he would have defeated his mother's memory. But where was she?

"Look! Down there!"

Eldrax's heart leapt as Naboth, the youngest member of their group, jabbed his spear toward a broad gully far below them. Eldrax whipped his face in the direction Naboth had indicated. Through stinging eyes, he could just make out a dark smear on the landscape at the base of a tree. A low hill rose beside it in the centre of the gully.

His heart sank at once. It was not the witch. The object of Naboth's focus wasn't moving, just a stain on the landscape. But the young hunter's face was alive with need.

"A wolf kill?" Naboth started down the slope into the gully, slipping and sliding as he rushed towards the object he had spied.

"Naboth! Get back here!" Eldrax snapped, but driven by hunger and the possibility of a morsel to eat, the other warrior ignored him. The rest were quick to follow, racing recklessly down the scree hillside, pushing and shoving in an effort to be the first to reach the scraps. Hanak over took the rest, his swift strides eating up the ground. Growling low in his throat, Eldrax had no choice but to follow them. His own stomach snarled at the thought of food, and he quickened his pace, rushing to return to the lead.

Stumbling and skidding, Eldrax finally ground to a halt next to the dark stain. Pebbles and powdered snow swirled about him, carried by the momentum of his long decent. From this vantage point, he could see to the far horizon and the southern plains stretching away below. He scanned the distant rolling expanse, hoping for any sign of a small figure toiling through the snow. Frustration boiled low in his chest when his search came up empty.

"Nothing but bones!" Naboth kicked at the animal remains that he had discovered; they clattered hollowly across the rocks. The sweeping wind had exposed the remains of a bear. A glance confirmed what Naboth had already discovered, to his bitter disappointment, only bones and a few stringy scraps of sinew remained. The dark smear they had seen from the trail far above had been old blood staining the rocks and the ground all around the body.

"You brought us all the way down here for bones, Naboth!" Tanag cried, shoving his clan brother in the chest in an uncharacteristic display of temper. "Now we've got to climb all the way back up to that trail to find this accursed cave!"

Naboth recovered his footing and made to fly at Tanag. "I just want something to *eat*!"

Hanak stepped up to his brother's side, his hand twitching towards his bone knife. "Watch your step, Naboth," he threatened.

"ENOUGH!" Eldrax shoved between his squabbling men. He snatched a bone from the ground. "I'll give you—" His building tirade cut short in his throat. Long, thin gouges marred the bone's smooth surface. No wolf or scavenger made marks like that. These were the marks of man. Or—

"Spread out and search the area!"

Eldrax ran his fingers over the grooves marking the bone in his hand. It could mean nothing. The Eagle clan had been hunting in these hills, but something told him they were not responsible for this kill. The knife cuts were deep, made by a being of great strength. A being stronger than the average Cro man, he guessed.

His heart beat faster as he loped over the ground. Here and there, footprints had been frozen into the soft earth between the stone. Broad footprints, squarer in shape than a Cro. His excitement mounted as he continued to track, the trail rising steadily as it led up the hill set into the centre of the gully.

The cave gaped into the mid-morning light. Eldrax's breath caught. Aside from the location, it was exactly as Rannac had described. Eldrax rushed forward and burst into the entranceway. The dimness pressed in on his eyes, hindering him for a few moments. He blinked rapidly, straining to see into every shadow.

The remains of a fire were piled in the centre of the cave. Tools, cracked bones, and furs littered the hard ground around it. Eldrax took everything in at a glance. But these betraying clues of habitation were not what held him on the threshold and made him stagger. It was the *smell*. The scent of her lingered over everything. His mother had lived in this cave.

A movement caught his eye and suddenly she was there, standing in the shadows, staring out at him as she begged for his forgiveness and love. He cried out, staggering back before his vision adjusted and the illusion melted into nothing more than a large fur hanging from a jutting rock. It twitched in the breeze. He shook his head, cursing himself, and stepped into the cave.

Carved pictures littered the walls. Eldrax followed them around, studying the story of his mother's journey. He came to an abrupt halt before the carving of a mother tenderly cradling her newborn, holding him as though to protect him from the world.

"Ha!" Eldrax struck out at the mocking image, furiously scoring through the lying depiction again and again with his flint knife until nothing remained.

"Eldrax?" Tanag was standing in the cave entrance, spear held ready, as his eyes darted. "I heard you shout, my Chief."

"This is the place we have been looking for, Tanag." Eldrax

threw his now blunted knife to the ground. "That fool Rannac sent us too high into the hills. The witch is gone. Summon the men."

Tanag disappeared without another word, and Eldrax squatted down before the skeleton of the fire, holding his palm over it. He could still detect the faintest trace of warmth. *So close.* She had been here as recently as dawn. He shifted his attention to the ground. Now that his eyes had fully adjusted to the dimness, he noticed spots of something dark leaving a trail along the stone and packed earth. He recognised the source of the stains immediately. Blood. Someone had left a spattered trail of blood.

There was only one streak. Whoever had left it had departed from the cave and not returned. He did not remember his mother carrying an injury when he had ambushed her in the storm, and she had certainly not returned to leave such a trail. None other than the witch herself had left this.

The stench of the cave was becoming unbearable. The spirit of his mother watched him from every corner. Skin crawling, Eldrax hastily followed the blood trail outside. A few more strides and he found the very thing that had been denied to him since the day his hunt had started. Tracks. Tanag returned with the rest of the men and they gathered behind him, awaiting his next direction.

He pointed to the diminutive footprints dotting the snow ahead of him and their accompanying trail of red. "The hunt is rejoined. She is *mine.*"

* * *

23

Capture

Rebaa had left Juran's brother behind, but she could not keep up the quickened pace for long. The snow was still deep in many places, and Rebaa found herself wading through drifts that were waist high when no alternative presented itself. She could feel Ninmah's faint warmth on her back like a supporting hand as Her last rays painted the snow with a reddish gold.

Rebaa prayed for the golden face to continue to guide her on her journey. She was nearing the very edges of Nen's range now. It wouldn't be long until she reached the copse. Before then, she must be sure to take the correct fork in the trail. She remembered Nen's warning of the higher cliff path. The copse lay along the lower trail. She shifted the bearskin sling on her aching shoulder. "You are getting heavy," she muttered to her baby as he dozed within its confines.

Hunger gnawed at her belly. She promised herself that once she reached the copse, she would rest for a short while and try to cook some of the bear meat she carried. The densely packed trees would shield her from the sight of the hunting

Cro.

Juran's brother's voice still rang in her head, warning her not to stop until she reached her home, but she could not run forever on thin air. She hoped the false trail the warrior had sent his Chief on would keep Eldrax at bay long enough to allow her to escape.

She should have known such a wish could never be fulfilled.

The shadows of the evening had barely begun to lengthen when Rebaa's senses quivered once more. Something was coming, teasing the edges of her awareness but steadily gaining.

Eldrax had picked up her trail.

The strength went out of her limbs, leaving her numb. It was too soon; she did not have enough of a start. Juran was gone. Nen was gone. There was nobody else left to sacrifice themselves for her. She thought of all the bolt holes Nen had shown her on their travels; none would be sufficient to hide her.

Flight instinct drowned out any other thought, and she bolted, running for her life. She had to stay ahead. It was the only hope. She reached the fork in the trail and raced down the lower path. Her burdens sucked at her, the bag of bear meat beat hard against her damaged leg. Removing the knife and her snare, she flung the bag from her shoulders and away into the snow. It had been slowing her down, and it was no use to her if she was captured. She would find more meat. Eased of the weight, she ran faster.

The copse wasn't far now. She could see the dark shadow of the wood ahead. *Trees. The trees.* They would make her safe. Gasping, Rebaa plunged on.

Her lungs were burning when the copse reached out to

surround her at last. Embraced by the trees, the panic receded enough to allow her mind to function. She slowed to a halt, coming to rest at the centre of the grove.

She had been foolish to run. Running was not how she was going to survive. The Cro had her trail and they would follow it like wolves until they had her. This was the game that Cro played best. This copse was the best concealment she had, but it was nothing if her trail led them right to her. She glanced down at her damning footprints leading right up to where she stood.

Eldrax was smart. She had to be smarter. If she could obliterate her true trail and leave a false one along a different path before doubling back...

It was a chance, a fleeting hope, but there was very little time. The presences of the Cro were a dim flicker on the edges of her awareness, but they were getting stronger all the time. She would need all the speed she could muster to run back along the path, hiding her footprints as she went, and then leave a false trail for them to follow. If she were to have a chance at travelling that fast, it would mean...

Rebaa sucked in a sharp breath as she looked down at her son. It would mean she had to leave him behind, concealing him in the copse until she returned. She baulked violently at the thought, but she didn't have time to think of a better way. If she stayed and did nothing, then they were lost. She *had* to do this to save them both.

She cast around and spied a hollow at the base of a large tree. Dashing towards it, she lifted the bear sling from around her neck, falling to her knees at the tree's roots. Numb to what she was doing, she tucked her baby inside. He fussed restlessly, feeling the physical separation as keenly as she did, letting out soft, muffled cries.

Rebaa covered her mouth with a shaking hand to stifle her own whimpers. "Shhh! Shhh!" she soothed, reaching out to him with a hand, letting her energy flow through the contact. "I-I'll be back," she croaked. "I will not leave you." Now she knew what Juran had gone through in their last moments together. She gritted her teeth. Unlike Juran, she *would* come back. "Stay quiet until mama returns."

He regarded her solemnly, his green eyes holding an awareness beyond that of an ordinary newborn. She knew he understood her.

"I love you. More than anything!"

She tore herself away, running back for the edge of the trees with only Nen's spear for company as the tears blinded her. Every instinct she possessed pulled her back towards the tree where her baby lay alone, but she could not obey. She dared not look back. If she saw him there, abandoned, her resolve would crack.

Reaching the tree line, she hesitated, peering out onto the open trail beyond. It was empty. Pulling a branch from the nearest tree, she ran back up the path, digging and swiping the snow behind her, displacing the glistening folds over her damning footprints. Her arms were aching by the time she made it back to the fork in the path. Her true direction was concealed. Now to lay the false trail. There was only one other route to take from here: the path under the cliff face.

An idea formed before Rebaa was even conscious of it. If they believed she had travelled that way...

His mind is broken. He has no compassion, no mercy. Not even for his own people.

Juran's brother's words floated through her thoughts. Was

Eldrax's mind broken enough to take such a risk? A grim smile played out on Rebaa's face. The man had killed his own mother. She was willing to chance he was capable of doing anything to get what he wanted. The plan hardened in her mind, and she bared her teeth.

The energies of the approaching Cro were now an unbearable burn against her consciousness, getting ever closer. She ached to get back to the safety of the copse. Back to her baby. His absence against her heart was like a physical pain.

I'll be back. I'm coming back! She promised both herself and her son.

Stealing her exhausted body, Rebaa pushed herself to her limit. Dropping the branch for now, she flew up the higher fork in the path. Ahead and swiftly looming larger was the thin trail clinging precariously between the steep wall of rock above and the sharp plunge into the ravine below.

The pathway was worse than she remembered. The storm had eroded the already cracked rocks. At the centre of the path, the rock had detached completely from the hillside and a substantial gap had appeared in the path, the two halves bridged only by one long, crumbling pinnacle, jutting up from the abyss like a giant stepping stone.

The snow along the trail had been swept into random patterns and Rebaa was careful to place every foot fall so it could be seen clearly in the drifts. She was conscious of the shifting rocks beneath, fully aware that one wrong step could plunge her to her death below.

Panting from the exertion, Rebaa reached the point where the path had crumbled and fallen away into the darkness below. To move forward from this point would mean a sickening leap over empty air onto the precarious pinnacle rising from the centre of the void. It would then take a second leap to reach the safety of the path beyond and away.

Rebaa eyed the pinnacle. One would have to be a fool to make that leap. She only hoped that Eldrax would believe she had been desperate enough to risk it and, Ninmah willing, follow to his own demise. Here was where her false trail needed to end.

Time crawled over her skin as she turned and picked her way back down the trail, avoiding the snow this time and keeping her feet on the scattering of hard, bare rocks. If she left so much as a toe print, a Cro tracker would deduce the truth and all her efforts would have been for nothing.

Their ever nearing presences pulsed fear through her veins. She had to fight the urge to break into a reckless run, abandoning all caution in her need to beat them to the split in the path and disappear before they saw her. It seemed to take forever to make it back down the trail, but at last, the fork in the path appeared around the bend ahead of her.

A little further, just a little further.

But, even as Rebaa comforted herself with the thought, she was forced to come to a halt. She had run out of rocks. An expanse of snow lay between her and her destination. Her concealing branch lay far out of her reach.

The whispers of distant hunting howls carried to her on the breeze. Her fresh tracks were betraying her proximity to her trailing enemies. Panic threatened to overwhelm her, but she fought it back, thinking hard. Her fingers cracked against Nen's spear as she gripped it for support.

The spear. Seized by a sudden inspiration, Rebaa took one quick step back and then threw herself forward into a leap. Holding the spear in both hands, she brought the butt down into the ground, using it to vault clean over the expanse of snow. Landing neatly beside her branch, she let out the breath she had been holding in one silent rush. It had worked!

She risked a glance in the direction she knew the Cro to be approaching from. The way was still empty. She had time to make it to the fork and away before they came into sight.

I'm coming! She thought at her waiting baby. Her need to return overwhelmed all else. Keeping low, Rebaa rushed for the fork in the trail and made to continue her flight down the lower path, obliterating her footprints with the branch as she went.

Elation at her success and the longing for her baby blinded her to the ambush that awaited. Two tall figures materialised out of the snow ahead of her, cutting off her escape.

Crying out, Rebaa almost fell in the effort it took to halt her momentum.

She stared up into their dark, grinning faces and knew they had been waiting for her. After all her efforts, she had been the one to be outsmarted. She backpedalled as they started up the trail towards her. They were unhurried, assured that she could not get away. Their predatory eyes glittered.

No, no! Rebaa whipped around and fled, zigzagging this way and that, searching for an escape route, for a way around them.

Before she knew it, she was back at the fork. She kept her senses upon the two Cro, waiting for any signal that they were about to pounce and bring the hunt to an end. She was unnerved by their lack of activity. They could have caught her, but they seemed content to watch her run like a scared gazelle.

The reason for their inaction soon became clear. Coming

down the trail from the other direction, the rest of the Cro pack had caught up. She watched their dark figures racing against the snow. A familiar red flame flickered at the centre. Eldrax was at their head.

She was caught between the oncoming party and the two beasts who had herded her into this trap. Her fist tightened around her friend's spear as her chest constricted.

There was nowhere for her to go. Nowhere except—

Triumphant howls sounded as the main hunting party saw her cornered before them, and Rebaa's feet were moving before she could think, plunging on up the only trail left open to her. Part of her mind was aware that she was exchanging one trap for another, but flight instinct had her in its grasp as she ran heedlessly up the path leading to the cliff face. All that mattered was being able to remain free and run for just a little longer.

One small whisper of self-preservation broke through the overwhelming need to keep running, and Rebaa paused on the threshold of the cliff path. One thoughtless step and the ground would give way and plunge her to her death.

"Finally!" a deep voice called out from behind her. "Juran's prize!"

Rebaa turned to face Nen's son for the first time. He was standing fifty strides away from her, his men blocking the only safe escape route back down the fork in the trail. Familiar black eyes glinted at her across the space separating them in a sick parody of Nen's own. The sight ripped through her. Instead of seeing warmth and compassion in the dark depths, Rebaa saw only malice, cruelty, and not a little madness. How Nen must have suffered in her last moments when she had seen what had become of her beloved son. Agonised tears leaked down Rebaa's cheeks as she thought of her own son, abandoned and defenceless, in the copse. She had failed him. She had failed Nen.

"Come to me, witch!"

Rebaa flinched away, raising Nen's spear as she took a step backwards onto the crumbling rock. Fury thrilled through her as she gazed into the burning black eyes of her saviour's murderer. Grinning at her defiance, Eldrax took a step nearer, unperturbed by the threat of Nen's spear. Her hands trembled. Rebaa glanced over at the abyss yawning beside her and took a bold step towards it. "Come any closer and I'll jump," she threatened. "I swear on all the gods."

Eldrax halted. She had him. If he moved to take her, then he risked losing her altogether, and she knew that would be the last thing he desired.

"I don't think you want to do that."

"There are some fates worse than death, Eldrax!"

Eldrax didn't appear to hear her. "A living witch." He drank in every part of her. "How? How did you accomplish such a feat, Juran? Every one of them withers. Every one. What was your secret? How did you make her live long enough...?"

Rebaa wasn't sure if he was even talking to her anymore. "He captured something you will never understand or possess." She answered and poised herself all the more precariously upon the edge. "Now let me *go*."

Eldrax's eyes snapped back into focus and he smiled. There was no warmth in the expression. It was the grimace of a predator. "It is no matter, for I have captured something *he* will never possess. Would you abandon your baby so willingly?" His soft yet deadly tone carried to her on the breeze. "Aren't mothers supposed to want to survive anything to save their young?"

Rebaa stopped breathing. How did he know about her son? Nen would never have— "I don't know what you're talking about." She tried to keep her tone even, but the panicked edge betrayed her.

The cold smile stretched into a grin. Pursing his lips, Eldrax let out a low whistle. The ranks of Cro men parted, and the last man in the group made his way towards his Chief. In his arms was a bear skin bundle.

A keening cry shivered in the air, and it took a moment before Rebaa realised the sound was coming from her own throat.

"Just look at what my men found in the woods." Eldrax took Rebaa's baby from the hunter and cradled him in mock tenderness within his own massive arms. Rebaa could only stare in horror, her cries coming in whimpering gasps as she beheld what she had tried so hard to prevent. "So…" the red-haired beast drawled. "*This* is the babe my mother cared about more fiercely than her own blood?" Madness flared the cold, dark gaze and the hand that supported her son's head squeezed. The bundle let out a thin wail.

"Please. D-don't." Rebaa was numb to everything but the cruel visage before her. Eldrax would crush her baby's skull and not so much as blink.

But the deadly grip relaxed and the flash of insanity melted away, replaced by a detached regard. "Such pretty green eyes," Eldrax crooned, speaking only to her son now as he stared down into the bearskin. "What a loss it would be if something had to happen to you because of *her*." He flicked his gaze towards where Rebaa stood. "Unfortunately, you'll find mothers can be fickle creatures, little one." He sighed. "I should know. My mother put her own selfish desires above mine. Why don't we find out if yours is any better!" And he swung his arm out, dangling Rebaa's son over the abyss.

"No!" Nen's spear clattered forgotten to the ground and rolled away behind her. All her senses were on fire. She could *feel* everything. There was a roaring in her ears, pulsing, powerful, uncontrolled. But the energy was not her own. The waves she could feel came in time with her son's screams of distress. The strength of it took her breath away as it had when it had come from inside her own body. It was coming from *him.*

Eldrax's body throbbed in the light of the Great Spirit. Such was the power radiating from her son, it would only take a thought to cease that pulse of life forever. Her enemy was oblivious to the deadly threat he held so casually in his hand. But the energy was uncontrolled, undirected. Nebulous. Her son was yet a baby, his thoughts unformed, and she was no longer connected to him, unable to direct the sheer force he was wielding. She wasn't sure she wanted to. Birds shrieked overhead, spooked by the unnatural disturbance.

"Come to me, witch!" She heard Eldrax's demand, as though from a great distance. "Obey me and I might yet let your son live."

The wild energy of the Great Spirit pounded around her as Rebaa took a helpless step forward. She had no choice but to go to him. She was under no illusion that Eldrax would kill her baby if she did not do as he asked. She did not have the power to stop him. Keeping her eyes fixed on the gloating black depths, she continued to move down the path back towards her enemy.

Her knees almost buckled as she came to stand before Eldrax

and spoke the words. "I give myself to you, dread Chief. You have me. Now please, give me my son!"

Elation burned over the pale face and the arm holding her baby aloft twitched. Rebaa held out her own in a silent plea.

"You should have jumped when you had the chance." The madness flared. "Now that I have you, I have no further need for *this*. The creature that my mother loved so much more than I."

And he opened his fist.

"Nooo!"

Rebaa threw herself from the path as her son fell away and plunged into the darkness below.

24

Defeat

Rebaa snatched her infant from the air and twisted around. Throwing out her free arm, she searched for a handhold, anything to break her fall as the wind seared past her ears. For one sickening moment, her fingers found only empty air. Then her arm wrenched in her shoulder as her fingers caught a protruding rock in the cliff face.

Gritting her teeth as the rock cut into her fingers, she slung the bearskin holding her precious bundle back around her shoulders and took hold of the rock face with both hands, easing the strain on her supporting arm.

For a few moments, all she could do was hang there as her mind caught up with the shock of what she had done. Listening to the echoes of angry shouts floating down to her from above, Rebaa tried to master her ragged breathing as it rasped in her ears. Once she could persuade her frozen muscles to respond, she glanced down at her baby. He blinked back at her, his green eyes wide with fright. The unfocused power swirled about them.

"Shhh, shhh! I've got you. I won't let go. I won't let us go."

251

His eyes calmed, and the wild energy drained away as though it had never been. It was mystifying, but she had no time to think. They were dangling from a cliff with the Cro waiting just above. She could not see them, and they could not see her from this vantage point.

She hoped they would believe that she had fallen to her death and give up the hunt. But they did not leave the trail. They remained, arguing and howling at one another. Rebaa could not wait for them to move to a safe distance. Her arms might give out before they did.

Rebaa considered her options. She could not go up, nor could she move to the left, back towards the opening of the cliff trail and escape. The rock was too sheer that way. The only way to move was sideways towards the crumbling rupture in the path away to her right.

The hand and foot holds barely merited the name, but Rebaa was Ninkuraaja and influence over the Great Spirit was not her only skill. She had spent her early life in the treetops of her forest home. She might have lived with the ground-dwelling Cro for many seasons, but her muscles remembered and instilled in her a sense of calm.

Branches were one thing, however, unforgiving rock was quite another. It bit and cut at her fingers. Every hold along the treacherous cliff shifted, threatening to give out under her weight. *Please...* she begged to nothing in particular as she tested each foothold.

Slowly, carefully, Rebaa made her way along the side of the cliff, away from the fractious Cro above, but the rocks continued to deteriorate until at last she could go no further. A landslide had created a great flat expanse that even her clever fingers could not exploit. Her only choice now was to go up and return to the trail.

The rock splintered and cracked as she clambered upwards. *Please,* she thought over and over until at last she pulled herself up and back on to the narrow pathway.

She did not have time to feel the relief of solid ground beneath her body. Before she could regain her breath, she was rolling to her feet, ready to meet the disbelieving black gaze of Eldrax as he witnessed her reappearance from the abyss.

They had returned to the very positions they had held when their confrontation had begun. Only now he had no hold over her. She locked her arms around her baby and backed away, further widening the distance between them. Nen's spear lay where she had dropped it, and she snatched it from the ground. The feel of the wood under her hand was like the touch of an old friend.

"How...?" Eldrax's voice strangled as he took a step after her. But Rebaa would not let herself get within reach of him again. She turned and ran, pounding along the crumbling trail towards the break in the path. The open air beckoned upon her right and she clung to the hillside, leaping from one solid surface to another. She didn't know what she was doing. Pure instinct guided her.

"No!" Eldrax bellowed.

The rocks groaned and cracked in protest at her careless haste. The mountain of snow and rock above grumbled in response. At any moment, the balance would tip and all would come crashing down. The gap in the path opened out ahead of her. To escape, she would have to make the leap onto the finger rock jutting from the abyss; the leap she had thought no one foolish enough to make.

The spear burned in her hand, and Rebaa ran at the gap without breaking stride. Jamming the butt hard into the ground at the last moment, she vaulted across the space, flying through the air until she landed catlike upon the precarious pinnacle of rock.

She felt the surface sway and shift as she landed, and the mountain moaned. She froze in a crouch, afraid to move so much as a finger. Sucking darkness yawned about her on all sides. For the first time in her life, Rebaa felt dizzy at height. The recent memory of falling without knowing if she would ever stop herself rushed through her mind.

Eldrax had come to a halt at the edge of the crumbling cliff trail. His eyes were almost beyond reason as he glared at her. The other men looked apprehensive as they studied the path ahead of them. She would like to bet that they were more uncomfortable with the height than she was. One of them muttered to their leader, and the growing insanity in the black eyes sparked. "She is mine!" Rebaa heard him scream. "No other Chief will have such a prize as that!"

Rebaa snarled. She was nobody's prize. "Then come and get me!" she challenged before she could stop herself. "I am right here! Claim me if you wish!"

Eldrax gathered himself, but one of his men caught his arm. "No, my Chief!" Eldrax shook him off, almost tumbling his own clan member into the ravine below.

Rebaa was thinking fast. Part of her idea in laying her false trail along this path had been to goad Eldrax into making a wrong move. She had never dreamed that she herself would be here as bait for that moment. Now that she was, she had to push him.

Eldrax was unsound of mind. He only needed the slightest

nudge, and Rebaa was prepared to give it. She laughed in their faces. "Is the great Chief too *afraid* to come and claim his prize?" She sniffed in disdain. "Perhaps some other Chief will be more worthy of me."

The veneer of reason that had all but held him in check left Eldrax's face. With a roar of anger, he ran out onto the crumbling path towards Rebaa. The rocks fell away behind him as his greater weight crumbled them to dust.

He only just kept ahead of the tumbling stones until at last he stood just on the other side of the abyss from where Rebaa crouched on her pinnacle of rock. He had destroyed his own way back, and now there was only one way forward — for both of them. Rebaa felt the rock wobble again as she shifted her feet. *Please,* she thought, *please hold just a little longer!* She faced Eldrax across the dark chasm.

"You have led me on a good hunt, witch," Eldrax acknowledged with a mocking dip of his head. "I am amazed you made it this far. You're stronger than you look."

"It was only because of your mother's strength that I still live," Rebaa said.

"Do not speak of her! She is dead, she who was too weak to protect her own son. At least in the end she was able to provide me with one gift. I thank you, mother!" He cried out to the emptiness as though he thought Nen herself was watching.

Rebaa's heart contracted as tears spilled down her cheeks. "She was not weak. She loved you, Eldrax. All she ever wanted was to see you again. Out of love for her, I give you one last warning. Leave me be."

Eldrax's face was a distorted mask, showing him for the deranged creature he was. "I do not care what she wanted, *witch*! You and your child are mine!"

No, we are not. Rebaa gathered herself. "I will never be yours, you *monster*! And neither will he! I am going home!"

"No!" Eldrax leaped across the gap, but Rebaa had already gone. She threw herself from her precarious perch, feeling his fingers brush her back even as she cleared the last of the distance and onto the safety of the solid path beyond. She heard a grunt behind her as Eldrax landed heavily on the pinnacle of stone where she had just stood. She turned back in time to stare into his crazed black eyes before the rock gave way beneath his feet, unable to hold his weight.

His face was frozen in horror at the realisation of his mistake. Scrambling, he tried to jump to safety as Rebaa had done, but it was too late. With a roar that drowned out his scream, the rocky hillside above gave way, avalanching down into the ravine and sweeping Eldrax along with it in an unstoppable force. Rebaa and the rest of the Cro could only watch as it carried him into the abyss in a whirl of furs, red hair and tumbling rocks.

The roaring went on and on, and when it finally stopped, there was no sign of Nen's son. Rebaa sank to her knees as the adrenaline drained from her body, leaving her shaking. Her thoughts buzzed. Distantly, she knew she should feel avenged, relieved, but, oddly; she felt empty. There was no pleasure in her victory.

"I'm sorry, Nen," she whispered. "I had no choice."

Howls of rage shook her from her daze and drew her eyes across the now impassible ravine. The remaining Cro were screaming and brandishing their spears at her in fury for the loss of their leader. Rebaa's victory further soured in her mouth as she read the dark promise in their furious eyes.

This was not over.

The surviving Cro were now out for revenge, and nothing drove them more fiercely than the need to settle a blood debt. It would take them days to find another way around, however. She had gained her much needed head start and she could not waste it. Rebaa forced herself back to her feet and ran on down the path.

25

The Will To Survive

The following days blurred together in a never ending torture. Exhaustion, hunger, fear, cold, pain. That was all there was. Still, Rebaa kept going. She must travel south and not stop until she had reached the forests of her ancestors. She had to get there. She had to. The entire time she remained alert for signs of pursuit as the rocky foothills around her gave way at last to the open reaches of the southern plains.

But now that she was free of the foothills, she felt more vulnerable than ever. Fear of the remaining Cro rejoining the chase drove her by day; by night it was the elements as she tried desperately to strike a fire for warmth, but failed each time. She had never truly mastered the skill, and the fuel she gathered was always wet with snow. She had no means to dry it, and no shelter from the relentless winds that sabotaged her every attempt.

The snow thinned the further south she travelled, but the conditions became no less fierce. Rebaa stumbled through the nights, fearful to sleep lest she succumb to the elements and never wake up again. She tried her best to ignore the stain of blood that continued to mark her every resting place.

She starved. She had dropped her supply of bear meat in her attempt to outrun the Cro. The bite of its absence was now painful. Her baby had a voracious appetite, and he sapped what little strength she had left. She had to eat, otherwise she would not be able to feed him.

The snare trap Nen had so carefully trained her to use became her only lifeline. She was not always successful, but she caught enough small game to keep her upright. Without a fire, Rebaa could not cook the meat and she became so desperate that she skinned and ate her catches raw, fighting down her revulsion so as not to bring the nourishment back up again. Survival was all that mattered. If she died, her baby died.

Days could go by before her next catch. Rebaa attempted to carry meat with her but, warmed by her body heat, anything she tried to save quickly turned bad and started to smell. She had no means to cure her scraps for leaner times.

She continued to walk, the blood of her wounds dripping a crimson trail behind her. Carrion birds wheeled overhead. Rebaa hissed her defiance to their watchful waiting and struggled on.

Birds, however, were not the worst creatures to stalk these lands. She was many rises and falls of Ninmah into her journey across the plains when Rebaa finally detected the distant presence that told her something far more deadly had begun to haunt her footsteps.

The Cro had picked up her trail.

What hope she had left fled. She was dying; she was still far from home, and now they had found her. The knowledge crushed her. If she had ever needed a miracle, it was now. Rebaa leaned heavily on Nen's spear and turned her face to the sky. Ninmah was hidden behind the roving clouds. "Please," she whispered to the unseen face. "I know I have done wrong. I know I have shamed and betrayed you in the most terrible way, but please let me save my baby. He is innocent. He does not know. Give me strength, most sacred Ninmah. Let me reach my People before my enemies catch me."

Ninmah did not answer. Rebaa lowered her eyes to her baby's face. He seemed to know that his mother was in trouble. Reaching out with one little curled hand, he patted her cheek. His green eyes were very determined.

Rebaa laughed and sobbed at the same time. "You think we can make it?" she asked. The green eyes held steady. Rebaa nodded. He, at least, had not abandoned her. "Alright then, we'll make it together. You and me, little strong one. Let's go home!"

Rebaa pushed herself upright, wove a little on her feet as the world swam before her eyes, then she found her balance and plunged on into the frost-hardened landscape. She quickened her pace, keeping her mind's eye on the energies flickering like wildfire behind her. She had to stay ahead. But even with her increased pace, she knew they were gaining. She could not keep this up for long.

Finally, when Rebaa believed she could not force her body to take one more step, Ninmah rose on yet another day to reveal a dark line along the horizon. It blurred like a mirage in Rebaa's vision as she crested a low rise in the land.

The giant forests of her birth place stood before her at last.

Tears sprang to her eyes. "We did it!" she rasped at her sleeping baby as he dozed next to her heart. "We made it!"

Overcome, Rebaa stumbled forward towards the dark line. Joy drove out all her sorrows and lent her a last trickle of strength. She was home at last.

A faint shout behind her made her spin around with a cry on her lips. She fought to focus her failing eyes as she stared back in the direction she had come. She could just make out five figures standing on the crests of the hills behind. They had closed the distance without her notice.

Rebaa snarled at the tall, lithe forms silhouetted on the horizon. Even after all she had gone through, even as she stood upon the borders of her home, they would not let her rest. They would pursue her until the very last step. She knew they could see her now. Rebaa could see them and she was in the open on white, frosty ground, standing out like a black ox in the middle of a plain.

She turned back to stare at the distant border of the great forest. She was closer to the tree line than the Cro were to her. They would have to travel twice the distance to catch her. If she could get into the trees, she knew she would be safe. Five Cro would not dare follow her into Ninkuraaja territory. As Juran's brother had said, it would take greater monsters than them to enter the forest.

The world narrowed down to this one breathless moment as Rebaa assessed her chances. She was closer to her goal, but she knew the Cro could travel twice as fast as she could. They also had the advantage of not currently dying on their feet. This would be an even race.

Rebaa's mouth set into a grim line. She had not survived all that she had just to fall now! Facing her pursuers up on the hills, she cried out her defiance once more. She was going home! Gathering her most precious bundle to her, Rebaa turned and ran for her life.

The chase was joined. Hunting cries sounded behind as the Cro threw themselves after her in pursuit.

Rebaa sprinted across the expanse between her and the protection of the trees. Her breath soon came in short, laboured gasps. Her legs burned. The old injury from the bear caused her to limp. Her baby became a rock weight in her arms. Already she was slowing. Still she ran, the tree line growing larger and larger with each ragged step. Her heart pounded in her chest.

The eager voices grew louder behind. They were gaining, gaining. She felt their murderous energy bearing down upon her.

Go, go! She chanted to herself. *Run! Not far now!*

She was almost there, only fifty strides away. She was stumbling now, utterly spent. She did not know what strength kept her on her legs. She pushed herself on. Nearly there.

A whooping cry and the sound of rushing feet behind her told her she was too late. She was not close enough. One of them was faster than the rest, and he was right behind her. She felt him reaching out in triumph, his fingers about to brush her back and bring their chase to its violent end.

Rebaa acted. Screaming with rage, she wheeled around, acutely aware of the spear she somehow still clutched in her hand. *Never hesitate...* She stopped and braced herself, holding the point of the spear out and up, its butt against the hard ground.

The startled Cro did not have time to halt his momentum. He drove himself upon the sharpened tip that waited for him, his weight thrusting him forward, deeper and deeper until it pierced his heart. Wide blue eyes stared in shock at Rebaa as he coughed up blood, gurgling wordlessly. The life drained from his face, and he tumbled to the ground, dead.

Rebaa stood for a moment, frozen with revulsion and disbelief at what she had done, before shouts of fury from the dead Cro's companions shook her back to reality.

"Hanak! No!"

Rebaa gave Nen's spear a tug, but she could not dislodge it from the Cro's twitching body. Her heart cried as she was forced to abandon it. It was not worth her life. She spun and fled for the trees, leaping at last through the protective line just as a poorly aimed spear seared past her ear and bounced off an unyielding trunk.

Rebaa continued to run until she was a safe distance into the woods, and adrenalin could take her no further. She stumbled to a halt and leaned heavily against a tree, listening to the curses and shouts of frustration behind her. They were murderous, angry, but no sounds of pursuit reached her pounding ears. She had been right. The Cro would not dare violate these borders.

She had made it. She had... The pounding in her ears became a roar. The world turned and Rebaa stumbled, clutching at the tree as her heart beat unsteadily in her chest. That last effort had been too much for her failing body. The trees blurred before her eyes.

She shook her head to clear it of the growing darkness. She could not die now! Her baby still needed her! It was not safe. But the darkness did not heed her will, and it continued to grow. Boneless, Rebaa slid down against the roots of the tree. She was losing the battle. Wrapping her arms around her baby, she held him tight. She would not let him go. He was the last thing she thought of before endless darkness enveloped her.

26

Promise

"… what happened to her?"

Voices. The voices were coming from all around. She had no sense of her body apart from the weight against her chest. She did not know where she was or what was happening, but knew she must hold on to that weight. It was important.

"… don't know. The wolves dragged her in…"

"What is she dressed in?" came another disgusted voice. "She wears the garb of accursed flesh-eating ground-dwellers!"

The words sounded strange to her ears. It took a long moment for her to realise the reason. She had not heard this tongue spoken outside of her own thoughts in…

"She's nearly dead," a familiar voice spoke near to her head, shaking with suppressed emotion. She felt fingers brushing her temples. "She's barely there. Let me look at her!"

Baarias? She wanted to speak, but she could not gain the control needed. She drifted again. The scent of winter trees, earth and leaf mould was strong in her nostrils. She clung to that sense. The scent of home.

"What's that she's holding?" came yet another voice.

"It's a baby," somebody else said.

"But it doesn't feel right. What *is* it?" The tone became fearful, filled with dread and hardening certainty. "Baarias, move out of the way!"

Someone pulled at the weight she held so firmly in her unfeeling arms. It began to cry. That roused her, and she felt a little of her physical awareness return. Pain washed over her.

"It's a monster!" Somebody exclaimed. "Get it away from her. Look at its eyes! In the name of Ninmah, I will end this curse!"

Someone tried to drag the warm weight in her arms away from her. It cried louder in distress. They were hurting it! Full awareness rushed back to Rebaa like a bolt of lightning.

"No!" She pulled her baby back and threw herself over the top of him. "Get away from him!" Her words were Cro out of habit, but her meaning was clear.

Her vision swirled. She saw a leaf-clad figure before her, a large rock raised between his hands.

"Get away!" She curled her body around her baby. If they wanted him, they would have to go through her!

Angry muttering broke out as Rebaa fought to stay awake, braced over her newborn. She could feel his strange, wild power building. She had to stop it, to hide it from them. She had to stay awake. His very life hung in the balance.

"Unnatural."

"Accursed!"

"Forbidden."

"Forbidden!"

The words buzzed like angry bees from all around her, and she was in the midst of the nest. Emotions were fanning quickly into a fierce, unstoppable wildfire.

"We cannot allow it to exist. It will bring an end to us all!" Their combined determination set on one terrible course of action. "It must die."

Rebaa began to cry. "Baarias!" She called for her brother, unfocused eyes searching for support. "Help me. Don't let them!" But he did not step forward. He did not come to her aid. The anger continued to grow. Her sobs grew desperate. All this way, all that suffering and she had still lost. Her one hope evaporated into nothingness. She had underestimated the power of Ninmah's teachings. No one was going to defend her. Not even her brother. She had made the wrong choice and broken her promise to Nen. She could not keep her baby safe. Her eyes screwed shut, tightening her arms. She would at least hold on as long as she could...

"Get away from that girl!" A voice cracked out over the din. "Let me through!" It was a female voice, and it rang with a terrifying authority. Rebaa felt a power moving toward her, such as she had not felt in a long time. She had forgotten. She heard the crackling of leaves as many feet shuffled backwards, then thin, cool fingers were brushing her brow.

"Easy, young one." The voice said. "You are safe now."

Safe? How could she be safe? She was never safe. Rebaa blinked up into the face so close beside hers. It was an ancient visage, deeply lined and framed with long, silvery-white hair. A face filled with endless wisdom and violet eyes that burned with the energy of the Great Spirit himself.

"Sefaan," she rasped in recognition. Her tribe's Kamaali. A Seeress of the Spirit. The sacred Guide to her People.

"Sefaan!" another female voice snapped. "She cannot stay here. Not if she refuses to give up that thing. It condemns us all in the eyes of Ninmah. It is Forbidden!"

Sefaan stood straight and faced the speaker. "Very well, Aardn," she spoke. "If you insist. But know that if you cast this girl from our trees, I will accompany her."

Gasps of shock rippled around the tribe. Rebaa saw the pale red-gold faces and varying shades of indigo eyes fill with doubt and fear. They shifted uncertainly. The choice Sefaan had faced them with was unthinkable. Keep the abomination or risk losing the voice of the Great Spirit for their tribe.

"We cannot keep it, Sefaan," Aardn's voice held a desperate edge. "It is a monster! It puts everybody at risk. There is a reason such things are Forbidden!"

Sefaan regarded her steadily. "It is only a baby for now, Aardn. You must indeed have grown weak in your old age to fear an infant." Her words struck at the Elder's pride. "A child cannot hurt us. We will watch him closely. Once he is old enough to survive on his own, you may send him on his way. Until then, he must stay with Rebaa under her protection. And mine." She added as an after threat. The silence was deafening. Not even the birds dared to speak.

Rebaa could not believe what she was hearing. She trembled all over; the world swirling dangerously. She could not hold herself together any longer.

"Baarias!" Sefaan snapped at her brother. "Don't just stand there. Heal her. She is dying!"

A soft tread. Then Rebaa felt hands against her head and tears dripping on her face as her brother's energy flowed into her. She latched on to it greedily as she felt him work. His skill in the healing art was unsurpassed, and it seemed to have only grown stronger in her absence. Her pain eased almost immediately. She drifted in and out of consciousness, never

267

letting go of her baby until she heard Baarias whisper in a broken voice. "She will live now. Her wounds are healed, but she needs food and much rest."

"Good," Sefaan murmured, then her voice rose to address the rest of the tribe. "To cast this child from our borders now would be a grave mistake. He must live among us until he is ready to fend for himself. Swear to me you will honour my word," the Kamaali pressed. "No one will attempt to harm this girl or her offspring. Not until the time comes for him to leave." The silence stretched. "Swear it!" Sefaan's power radiated out, lashing at them.

It was Aardn who finally spoke for the tribe, voice heavy with unwilling defeat. "It seems you have left us with little choice, Sefaan. We swear."

Rebaa blinked her eyes open, and this time her vision was clear. She was in the very heart of her old home. The mighty *eshaara* trees, the standing spirits of Kamaalis long past, rose all around, protective and watchful, leaves whispering the secrets of the ages just as she remembered.

Standing before the trees, the entire tribe surrounded her, dressed in the draping leaf-leather of green, gold and red. She grew very conscious of the tattered wolf and bear furs still hanging from her shoulders. Her Peoples' fine faces were filled with unease or downright revulsion. They backed away as she sat up. Even her brother. She caught sight of another familiar face. Jaai. She and Jaai had been best friends as children. Rebaa looked to her with hope, but fear had cooled Jaai's warm gaze and she turned her beautiful face away, tears glistening in her dark purple eyes. Saddened, Rebaa staggered to her feet and nearly fell. She might be healed, but she was still dangerously weak.

Sefaan reached out to steady her. "Get her some food," she commanded.

Nobody moved. Sefaan glared around at them all.

"No, Sefaan." This time Aardn's voice was firm. "You may have forced us to keep her here, but we will not help her or look after her. We will not anger Ninmah by aiding what she Herself forbade at the beginning of time. The Holy Creator is already leaving our People. I will not risk provoking Her further. Mark my words, you have brought a curse down upon us this day. I will never forget it." She stared around the group, her eyes lingering on Baarias' tortured face. "Listen, all, I speak as your Elder. No one is to help the heretic or her Forbidden offspring. She must live on the fringes, unseen and ignored, unless one wishes to evoke the wroth of Ninmah Herself."

The tribe shrank further away from Rebaa and Sefaan, who still stood by her side. Rebaa gazed around at them. They who had once been her friends and family. Baarias had his eyes fixed upon the baby in her arms. He might as well have been staring at a venomous snake; his scarred features agonised. Rebaa's face closed against him. Fine. She would do without him. As long as they let her keep her baby and stay under the protection of the trees, that was all that mattered. She had learned how to fend for herself.

Sefaan snorted. "I guarantee Ninmah has more important things on Her mind, Aardn. So be it," she said, and pulled Rebaa away from the wall of prejudiced eyes. "Come, child."

Rebaa stumbled after the Kamaali woman as she led her through the massive *eshaara* trees her People called home. They came to a halt at the roots of one of the last red-gold sentinels at the very edge of the mighty grove.

269

"She will look after you," Sefaan said, staring up at the tree. Rebaa studied the *eshaara*. Unkempt and deserted, it was unoccupied and out of the way. Perfect. This would be hers. This would be where she raised her strange child by herself without the help of her tribe.

"Here," Sefaan said. The ancient woman held out a large root. Rebaa took it hungrily. A gora root. Her least favourite as a child. Now her mouth watered at the sight of it. No more meat, she realised in relief.

"I'll make you some clothes," the Kamaali continued, eyeing Rebaa's grisly attire with thinly veiled contempt. "There's no need for you to stand out any more than you need to."

"Thank you," Rebaa whispered, finally slipping back into her native tongue. She caught Sefaan's hand. "Thank you for saving our lives." She would be forever in the Kamaali's debt. But she would not get too close. Never again. She would put no one else at risk for her mistakes. She must walk this forbidden path on her own now. She had survived. That was all that mattered. She looked down at her baby and smiled as all else fell away. He blinked at her adoringly, unaware of the commotion he had caused.

"The Great Spirit commanded." Sefaan said by way of explanation. "Though his purpose remains a mystery to me. I will leave you alone now." The Kamaali turned away. "Rest. They will not touch you. I have their promise. Just promise me you will stay out of their way. Do nothing to provoke them. Especially Aardn."

Rebaa dipped her head in thanks once again. She started for the tree, holding her baby to her.

"Oh!" Sefaan called, turning back one last time. A smile played around the corners of her depthless eyes. "What are you going to name him?"

Rebaa blinked. In all that had happened since his birth, she realised she was no closer to deciding upon a name than she had been when Nen had first asked. It was time he had one. Peering down into his bright green eyes, she felt the strength of his spirit, powerful even now. *Little strong one,* Nen's voice floated through her memory. She could almost see her friend there, black gaze warm and comforting, nodding her approval. She smiled gently.

Rebaa's eyes were enigmatic as they met Sefaan's. Wordlessly, she turned away and climbed up the abandoned tree that was to be her home from now on. She paused long enough to call back over her shoulder to the ancient one waiting below.

"His name is Juaan," she said, and disappeared inside the living walls.

27

An Ending

Eight *years later...*

"Juaan, come here."

Her son shifted on the far side of the tree where he sat looking out over the darkening forest beyond. She knew he did not want to come to her. He did not want to face what was about to happen. Rebaa could hear her own voice, how it rasped like dry leaves inside her throat. For eight long turning of the seasons, she had done all she could, but now sickness had come to claim her and she had no more left to give. It wouldn't be long now. Tonight, it would be tonight.

"Juaan," she struggled to get the words out, the effort almost too much.

He came, moving cautiously through the shadows, his gangling frame bowed. He knelt at her side, his green eyes filled with untold pain and unshed tears.

Rebaa's failing heart fluttered as tears started in her eyes. Her precious son. She had given so much, fought for so long, and here he stood, a beautiful young man. She reached out and touched his cheek. Who was going to look after him now? She was going to leave him unprotected, at the mercy of her tribe. She couldn't give in to the darkness that pulled at her knowing that. She fought against it.

The deathbed promise she had given on the day of his birth still resounded in her head as if it were yesterday. *Protect baby...*

I tried, Nen! She cried silently to the long absent presence. *I've done all I can...* How could she protect her son now? He had only lived through eight Furies. He was not old enough to fend for himself in the world beyond the trees. She had prepared for that day, but she had not planned on it being this one. Not so soon.

She looked up into his steady gaze. So like his father... His father, who had always been so strong. A warrior without peer. She felt a stirring of hope. Perhaps his son *could* survive the impossible. She had to believe it, for there was no hope that the Elders would allow Juaan to remain under the protection of the trees once she was gone.

With a shaking hand, Rebaa reached under the leaves and pulled forth the object she had kept hidden for so long. Nen's spear. She ignored her son as he pulled back in surprise, savouring the texture of the wood under her fingers, worn smooth by the most mighty and yet the gentlest of hands. A sad smile tugged at her pale lips. This weapon had saved its creator's life once. It had saved *her* life, and now she hoped its protection would extend to her son.

When she had returned to her tribe all those Furies ago, she had been forced to leave the spear embedded in the belly of her enemy out on the plain. But the idea of abandoning it there, this last connection to her old life, had been too much of a torment and when she had regained enough strength, she had crept out of the shelter of the trees to retrieve it. As Juaan had grown, she had kept it hidden, knowing that one day he would need it. She hoped that wherever Nen was, she could see what she was about to do. She had a feeling Nen would be pleased.

"Here." She held the weapon out to her son. He flinched away, his eyes widening with a blank terror she could not understand as they flickered over her shoulder into the shadows behind. The Great Spirit whispered about them. "Do not worry," she soothed. As the seasons had passed, she had grown successful in keeping his frightening power buried and hidden. "It won't hurt you. It is here to protect you."

The swirls of energy faded away as the panic receded from his eyes. He paused, mastering his fear, and then reached out to take the long spear in his hands. He ran his fingers over it, studying it solemnly. "What are these markings?"

Rebaa struggled to keep her eyes open. Her breath rattled in her chest. Not long now. "It-it was made by your *tarhe*. Those are Thal symbols of protection."

"Thal? *tarhe*?" Juaan tore his attention away from the weapon in his hand, face full of questions.

"Your protector mother, you will not remember her."

"My protector mother?" His confusion deepened.

Nen. The past swirled suddenly before Rebaa's eyes, loosed by the name she had not spoken for so long. "I was alone, so alone. Monsters in the mountains... killed your father." She cried out softly as the old fear and pain seared through her chest. "I never imagined such monsters—"

"Shhh, shhh." She heard Juaan's voice as though at a distance. "There are no monsters, mama."

Her head shook back and forth, trying to clear the vision that she did not wish to relive. "They ate the fallen. Destroyed the clan. Your father... Left so alone. The world is not kind to one who travels alone. And then... then..." Rebaa smiled as a shaft of light broke through the darkness of her mind. Nen. The name still had the power to sting her heart, even after all this time. The words tumbled forth. "She loved you even before you were born and vowed to be your *tarhe,* to protect you with her own life."

"Loved me?" Juaan blinked in disbelief. "*Who* loved me, mama?"

Rebaa's lips pressed together as his words shook her from her memories. Her son was so accustomed to living with the fear and hate of the People who surrounded him, he struggled to believe that anyone besides her could look at him with anything other than disgust. The thought grieved her deeply. He deserved so much more. He deserved somebody to love him with all of their soul.

"She loved you." Rebaa swore. "She knew even before she saw you, you were going to be special. She lost her own baby, you see. He too was Forbidden, and they took him from her." She let her eyes drift closed. "I can still remember the exact shade of her hair... red... so red... Take the spear of your *tarhe,* Juaan. The weapon that was made by her hand will keep you safe."

Juaan was looking at the weapon again and a strange light came into his eyes, a far cry from the fear of before. He hefted it in his hands as though his body were responding to some previously unknown instinct. He swung the spear in an arc, then struck a strong pose, the deadly tip braced out before him as if facing down an enemy.

Rebaa's throat closed. "So like your father…" With shaking hands, she withdrew another object from the concealment of her bedding. The leaf leather pouch was soft against her fingers as she spilled the spearhead on its leather thong into her waiting palm. The spearhead Juran had given her, the symbol of his leadership and power. The wolf carving was still stained dark by his blood. "This was his," she said, offering it to Juaan. "He wanted you to have it. Your father was a great and fair Chief to his clan. He hoped you would grow to be the same. He gave his life so that you might live."

She put the spearhead back into the leather pouch and pulled Juaan to her, tying it firmly onto the thong that held the leaves around his waist. "Keep it with you and remember. Remember the people who have loved you and sacrificed themselves for you. *Live*, do you hear me, and know that you were loved. You must survive no matter what. For me. Do you understand?" The darkness was calling. Fear thrilled through her limbs. She wasn't ready.

"Yes, mama." Juaan's tears were dripping down his face now. "I-I promise."

Rebaa's heart struggled against the wasting that was claiming her life. He was so *young*. The spear that he held towered over him, his hand barely fitting around the haft. Too soon. She needed more time! He needed more time before he faced the wilderness alone. There would be no one to protect him.

She pulled her son to her and held him close. Her heart fluttered unevenly in her chest. Her vision hazed. *Too soon.*

"Rebaa," a soft voice called from far below at the base of the tree.

Rebaa flinched and beckoned for Juaan to return the spear to her. "It must stay hidden until you need it," she hissed, and buried it in the leaves once more.

"Rebaa." It was Sefaan calling. Moments later, the Kamaali's face appeared in the entranceway to her home. Her face was sombre. She could feel it, too; the end was close. The ancient face took in Juaan as he stood protectively at Rebaa's side. "You have grown, boy," the Kamaali whispered. "But not enough, I fear. Not enough."

Rebaa closed her eyes as the Kamaali's words sealed his doom.

"Jaai," the cracked voice beckoned. "Come here. You do no good lurking outside."

Jaai? Rebaa's eyes blinked open, and she fought to focus her eyes. Jaai was here? Her friend climbed reluctantly into her tree, and Rebaa felt Juaan stiffen at once. Even her old childhood friend could not look upon her son without mistrust, and Juaan knew it. He usually did his best to hide his loathing of Rebaa's kin from her, but he could not contain himself this time. Despite her best efforts to hold on to him, Juaan broke away from her with a low hiss and disappeared out of the tree.

No! She wanted to cry. *Come back.* There was so little time left. So little time... Rebaa's eyes drifted shut.

Now Juaan had gone, Jaai was at her side in an instant. "Rebaa?" Her friend's voice shook. "Please hang on, perhaps Baarias..."

Sefaan grunted.

Rebaa's icy hands sought Jaai's and pressed them weakly. "He wouldn't come, Jaai... and it is too late now..." *Please leave me so that I can be with my son...*

"No." Came the vehement denial.

"Jaai." Sefaan's voice was sharp. "It is too late. Only you can help Rebaa now. You must give her what she needs. Time is running out. She must hear it to know peace."

"Anything." Jaai sniffed through her tears. "What do you need? Please tell me what I can do."

"You must promise that you will take care of Juaan until he can fend for himself."

Rebaa's eyes shot open as Jaai gave an audible gasp and pulled away from her grip.

"No!"

"Jaai…" Rebaa croaked.

"No, that is impossible. You cannot ask that of me!" Jaai was beside herself. "I'll do anything, anything else, but he is *Forbidden*! Ninmah will curse my family. How can you ask this of me?"

Each word was a blow to Rebaa's heart. She groaned.

"Because it is right," Sefaan said. "He is just a boy."

Jaai was shaking her head back and forth. Such was the enormity of what Sefaan was asking.

"Jaai," Rebaa reached for her, reached for the only hope that was being offered, "Jaai please, I love him, h-he w-will die if there is nobody to keep him. The Elders will cast him out. W-what would you do if-if it was… Nyriaana…"

Jaai's expression constricted at the mention of her tiny daughter, "Nyriaana…"

"Jaai," Sefaan pressed. "As your Kamaali, I am guiding you in this. You must protect the boy now, for all our sakes. For Rebaa."

Jaai dropped her head into her hands. "No. I can't, I can't. I can't put my family at risk. My little Nyriaana…"

Sefaan gave a strange little laugh. "Nyriaana won't mind, I can assure you. Their meeting has been ordained by the Great

Spirit for a long time now, perhaps from the first day that Ninmah created our race. It is meant to *be*."

Jaai barked a short, incredulous laugh. "The Great Spirit wants my daughter to meet this monster? You can't mean that, Sefaan."

Rebaa could see that the Kamaali had reached the end of her patience. With an impatient growl, Sefaan stepped forward and placed her hand on Jaai's head. Jaai moved to pull away, but then the power of the Great Spirit was all around them. Rebaa felt it prickle against her skin as Jaai's face grew blank; seeing things that were yet far away.

"*Oh!*" her friend gasped as the vision the Kamaali was showing her saturated her mind. "Oh."

"Now you see." Sefaan withdrew her hand, allowing Jaai to come back to herself.

The younger woman crumpled as tears spilled from her eyes. "Yes."

"Will you swear to take care of him?" Sefaan pressed.

Jaai's lips trembled, her eyes bright with dread.

Rebaa reached out to her. "Jaai." Her voice was now no more than a breath.

Jaai came to her side.

"Jaai... please... he is just a boy... I need to know that someone w-will care for him... as one would care for your daughter."

Jaai dropped her head with a helpless sob, ghosts of the vision still lurking in her eyes. "But my Nyriaana, my poor little Nyriaana..."

"Jaai," Sefaan's voice was soft but firm.

"Yes," Jaai spoke, defeated. "I promise. I promise before the Great Spirit and Ninmah that I will take care of this... boy as my own. No matter how I feel, I cannot fight what is right. I promise you, Rebaa, I will keep him safe until he is ready."

And Rebaa breathed a deep sigh, a great, invisible weight lifting from her chest. "Thank you..." Her vision hazed away again. "Thank you..."

She did not hear Jaai leave; she was only just aware of Sefaan's hand on her brow. "Go in peace, Daughter of Ninmah, beloved of the Great Spirit. Your task is done, and you have done well. Be at peace."

And then the Kamaali was gone.

Alone in the darkness, Rebaa rested, counting her breaths. She could feel herself slipping, but for the first time in a long time, her heart was light.

There was a soft rustle beside her, and then her son was there. He had come back just in time. With the last of her strength, she reached out and pulled him to her. She wanted him to be the last thing she saw.

"Mama?"

"It is alright, my precious one. You are safe now... I have made you safe..."

"Mama, don't go." His voice was filled with panic.

Rebaa could barely make him out. "Do not be a-afraid. Remember... remember everything I have told you... everything you p-promised. Y-you must live."

He nodded, clutching at her.

The darkness was rushing up fast now, but this time she felt no fear. She did not fight. Her son would be safe, and her task was complete. Peace was hers at last.

"Remember..."

"Mama?"

Juaan's voice was the last thing she heard as she let go completely and walked willingly into the Great Spirit's embrace. Juran was waiting, and Rebaa was finally home.

"Mama."

* * *

Epilogue

His mother was dead. The knowledge of that crushed Juaan's heart in an unforgiving fist. He collapsed to his knees on the ground at the base of the crumbling tree where he had lived with his mother for eight Furies. They had already taken her emaciated body away to Cast it to the river. They could not afford to attract sickness.

He had not been permitted to attend. He was an outcast. Forbidden. An object to be feared and mistrusted. He did not belong. Juaan gasped, clutching at his chest as another wave of grief and despair tore at him. His mother was the only one who had ever looked upon him without fear or contempt. She had been the very centre of his belonging. Now she was gone, and he did not belong anywhere anymore. The ties that had bound him had been severed, and he was adrift. Lost. A Forbidden child amidst those who would prefer to see him dead.

They were the reason his mother was dead. They had not helped her. They had abandoned her. Anger burned hot beside his grief. He felt the uncontrollable energy building up inside him, such as he'd never felt it before. His fists clenched. Was this what it was supposed to feel like? Ninmah's Gift? He had always struggled to call upon it before, and his mother had always discouraged it. He had seen the fear in her eyes, and that had been something he could not stand. He could not bear for her to be frightened of him, too. And so it had become a habit to bury the whisperings within, to bury them deep. He bared his teeth, uncaring, as he gathered the energy to him now.

"Juaan?" A tentative voice called.

He snarled. It was not the voice he wanted to hear. His mother was dead, and it was all because of them. All because of their hatred. It was *their* fault. All *his* fault for existing! It was everybody's fault! The world was a cruel, awful place.

With a cry, he lashed out with the energy that had been gathering within him. It exploded forth like an unstoppable gale, powerful and completely uncontrolled. A wave of pure destruction. Trees creaked and the younger ones shrivelled, leaving a ring of blackened foliage and barren ground around him. A great commotion broke out as birds took to the air, shrieking in alarm. Somewhere in the distance, the wolves howled, made uneasy by the disruption he had caused. Spent, Juaan finally broke down and cried.

"Juaan?" Now the voice was wary, afraid.

He turned to glare at the speaker. What did they want now? Had they come to throw him to the elements? To strip him of what little protection they had offered?

It was Jaai who stood there. She waited just a few strides away. Her weight shifted in a way that told him she was deliberating whether to flee from him—the abomination.

He snorted and turned his reddened eyes away from her. Let her run. Of all the tribe, Jaai had been the most supportive of his mother. She had helped as much as the Elders' constraints had allowed her. She had avoided him as much as she could, of course, but she had been sympathetic to Rebaa's plight.

A fresh sob shook Juaan's body. Maybe if he just knelt here

283

long enough, the Great Spirit would come and take him, too, and reunite him with his mother. Dimly, he was aware of a soft gasp and he realised Jaai was still standing there. Pity had overcome her fear. She had been reading his emotions. He did not think anyone had ever done so before.

"You are just a boy, aren't you?" she whispered.

Juaan did not really know how to respond to that. All the fight had gone out of him. Her eyes softened for a moment, then hardened with determination. It seemed to Juaan that Jaai had come to a decision. She stepped forward, cringing into the ring of destruction he had caused, and stretched out her hand. Instinctively, Juaan flinched away.

"Don't be afraid, young one. I won't hurt you. I made a promise to your mother. I am going to take care of you now."

Her words broadsided him. His thoughts buzzed without focus as Jaai's hand closed around his arm and pulled him to his feet. Young as he was, he was already as tall as Jaai. Juaan did not miss the flash of unease that crept back into the Ninkuraa woman's eyes.

"Ninmah, forgive me." He heard her murmur to herself. The determined set of her mouth did not waver, however, and she continued to pull him through the massive trees without hesitation.

"Jaai!" a male voice snapped from nearby. "What are you doing with that? Get away from it."

Juaan supposed he should feel angry or hurt by the words, but he felt nothing. He did not care. He was beyond feeling now. Beside him, Jaai sighed in resignation, but straightened her back, preparing to face her mate.

"We have got to take care of him now, Talaan."

Silence. Talaan stood as though waiting for his Joined One

to admit her poor joke and reveal her true purpose. She did not. Jaai's firm gaze did not so much as flicker.

"Have you lost your senses?" Talaan recovered enough to speak. Juaan could feel his outrage as it rolled out in waves. "He is Forbidden! His existence goes against the very will of Ninmah. Would you so curse our family?"

"He is just a boy, Talaan," Jaai replied. "I do not wish to anger the blessed Ninmah, but I made a promise. Sefaan herself said we must care for him as our own. She told me it was essential and sent me to Rebaa before the Great Spirit took her." Jaai tightened her hold on Juaan's arm. "I will *not* go against the wisdom of the Last Kamaali. She who is destined to be the saviour of our People. We must care for this boy. We have no choice. May Ninmah forgive us."

Talaan's lips thinned in anger and his fists clenched, but he could not challenge her words. It was forbidden to go against the will of a Kamaali. He was caught between the two greatest edicts of his People. "This is madness! I will have no part of it!"

Jaai shrugged. "That is your choice, Talaan. It is I who am bound, not you." With that, she released Juaan's arm and bounded into the nearest *eshaara* tree. Juaan stood, swaying on his feet. He avoided making eye contact with the raging Talaan, who was pacing defensively before his home. He did not want to anger Jaai's mate further by sullying him with his accursed gaze.

After a few interminable moments, Jaai returned, climbing back down the great tree. She was carrying something. Talaan's rage spiked to a new level, and he moved to block her with angry protest. One glare from Jaai stopped him in his tracks. The force of her will unassailable. "It is meant to be, Talaan. Do not interfere." Then, muttering a quick prayer, she placed the bundle that she carried on the ground between herself and Juaan.

Juaan blinked in mild surprise. The bundle was an infant. All wrapped up in cotton moss and leaves, she protested as her mother placed her on the ground. Her rumpled face was disapproving. She obviously hadn't been ready to be roused from her nap. The light hurt her sleepy eyes. They were the deepest indigo.

"Nyri," Jaai spoke. "I want you to meet Juaan."

All sleepy protest fled. Juaan felt a strange thrill as the little girl met his gaze for a brief instant before ducking her head. He watched as she pushed herself clumsily onto her still unsure feet and tottered away to hide behind her mother's legs.

It surprised Juaan to feel a fresh stab of pain in his heart. He had thought he was beyond all feeling. So what if the child was afraid of him? Everybody was afraid of him. He should be used to it by now. And yet he felt this infant's rejection keenly. His eyes fixed upon that little girl as they had not focused upon anything or anyone since his mother's spirit had left him.

"Nyri," Jaai spoke to her. "Juaan lost his mama last night. He is going to be a part of our family now. We have got to look after him because no one else will."

Talaan snorted, and the girl looked to her father. A confused little frown wrinkled her tattooed red-gold brow. She did not respond to her mother's words.

"Nyri?" Jaai questioned. "Nyri." She gave her daughter a nudge with her heel. "Nyriaana!"

The words struck a chord in Juaan and before he even knew

why he did it, he rhymed: "Nyri, Nyri, Nyriaana."

She giggled. The sound was like the soft bubbling of a brook. Indigo eyes peered out at him. She crawled from behind her mother's legs to get a better look. Her gaze missed nothing, and Juaan realised just how strange he must appear to her. He felt like hiding himself away before the inevitable happened. He was tired of everyone's fear and mistrust. He wanted his mother. He wanted to be wrapped in her unconditional love. His grief rose, threatening to cripple him. But as he stared with increasingly blurring vision into the face of this child, he saw no fear there, merely innocent curiosity.

Her eyes widened in consternation at the sight of his tears. With a determined frown, the little girl pushed herself up onto her unsteady legs. This time she came tottering towards him. Juaan was so stunned by this that he did not think to move out of her reach. By the time he recovered his wits, it was too late. She had him. Tiny arms reached around his legs and tightened in an embrace, seeking to comfort him.

"Hello, Juaan," she said in a halting little voice. "Don' cry. I be your friend. Make it better?"

Juaan's voice choked off in a strangled sob. The little girl's arms only tightened further. She could not know that they had reached right in to his soul and wrapped irrevocably around his heart. Binding him to her forever.

He sighed helplessly. "Hello, Nyri, Nyri, Nyriaana."

* * *

BOOK 2: Find out what fate holds in store for Juaan and Nyriaana...

Daughter of Ninmah, Book 2 of the ANCESTORS SAGA is available on Amazon: getbook.at/daughter-of-ninmah

YOUR EXCLUSIVE FREE BOOK IS WAITING...
Download your exclusive free copy of *Forbidden Son* and discover the beginnings of Juaan and Nyriaana's relationship: loriholmes.com/forbidden-son

About the Author

Growing up in England and having had a misspent youth devouring everything science fiction and fantasy, Lori enjoys reading and writing books that draw a reader into new and undiscovered worlds with characters that are hard to part with long after the journey comes to an end.

Lori's debut novel, The Forbidden, begins the epic journey into the Ancestors Saga, combining history, mystery and legend to retell a lost chapter in humanity's dark and distant past.

When not lost in the world of The Ancestors Saga, Lori enjoys spending time with her family (2 twin boys, 2 whippets and her husband - it's a busy house!) usually outdoors walking and exploring the great British countryside.

Find out more at www.loriholmes.com

You can connect with me on:

- https://www.loriholmes.com
- https://www.facebook.com/loriholmesauthor
- https://www.amazon.com/-/e/B06XBFF5RR
- https://www.bookbub.com/profile/lori-holmes

Subscribe to my newsletter:

- https://loriholmes.com/forbidden-son

Also by Lori Holmes

The Ancestors Saga

Book 1: The Forbidden
Book 2: Daughter of Ninmah
Companion Novel To Book 2: Captive
Book 3: Enemy Tribe
Book 4: The Last Kamaali
Companion Novel To The Ancestors Saga: Raknari

Made in the USA
Monee, IL
04 August 2021

74895582R00177